LAST ONE STANDING

MACAYLA DAWN

To those who feel unseen,
and the ones who stand up for them.

A NOTE FROM THE AUTHOR

Before you read, I'd love to share with you my heart behind *LAST ONE STANDING*.

The characters in this book have traumatic, heavy backstories. As you'll find, there's a reason for that. But I also wanted to share with you why I wrote these characters this way.

First, this book serves as a reminder that everyone is going through something. Everyone. Including me, including you. We all have baggage and stories some of us would rather forget. Kindness is the greatest gift we can give to those around us.

Second, people will take advantage of those in the midst of hard times. I hope this book encourages you to fight for those the world has forgotten about, and gives you hope that things will get better.

Nothing traumatic is seen firsthand on-page, and I had sensitivity readers comb through my pages and give me their thoughts. That being said, I understand if this is not the book for you. Above all else, take care of yourself.

All my love,

Macayla

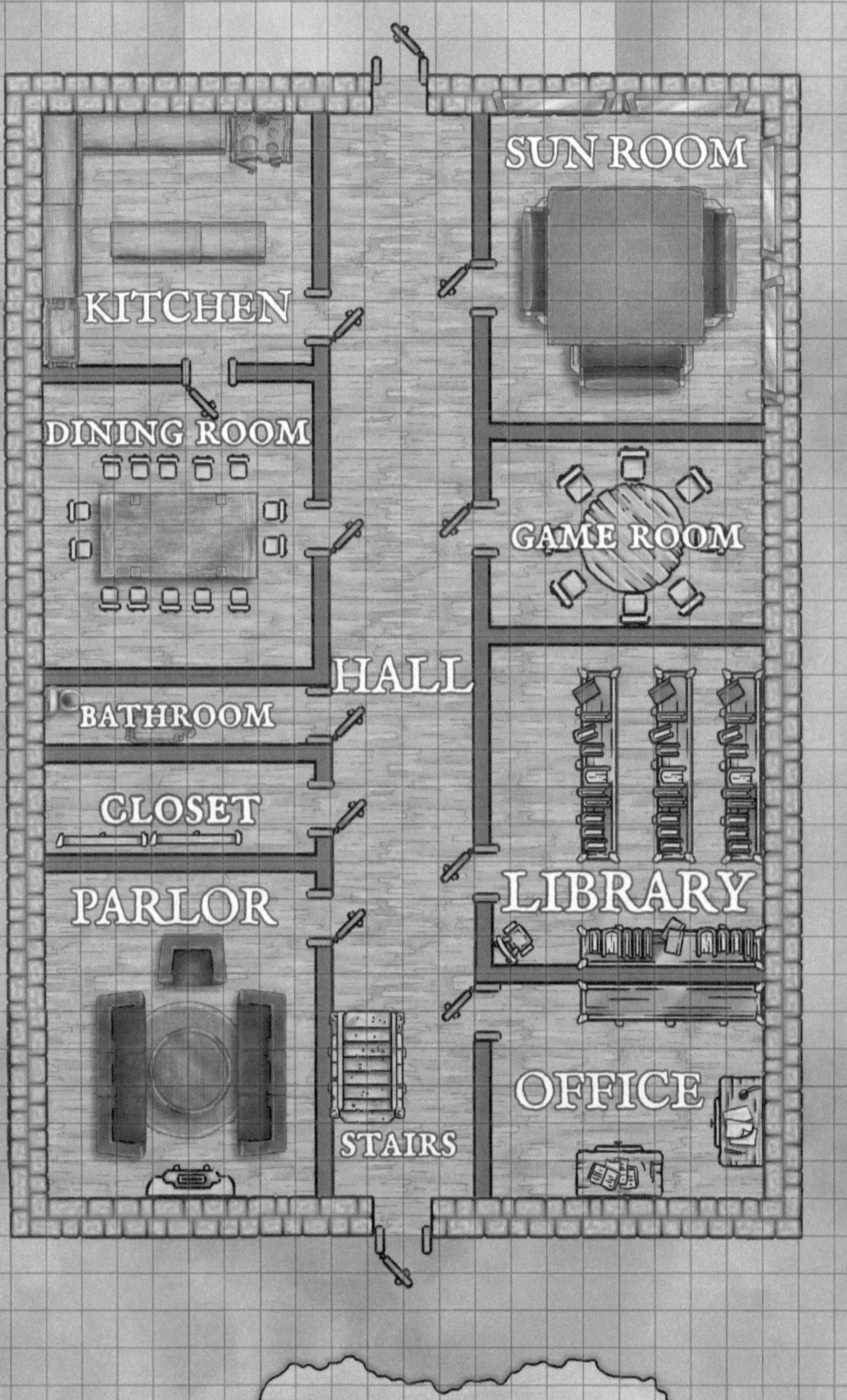

KITCHEN
DINING ROOM
BATHROOM
CLOSET
PARLOR
HALL
STAIRS
SUN ROOM
GAME ROOM
LIBRARY
OFFICE

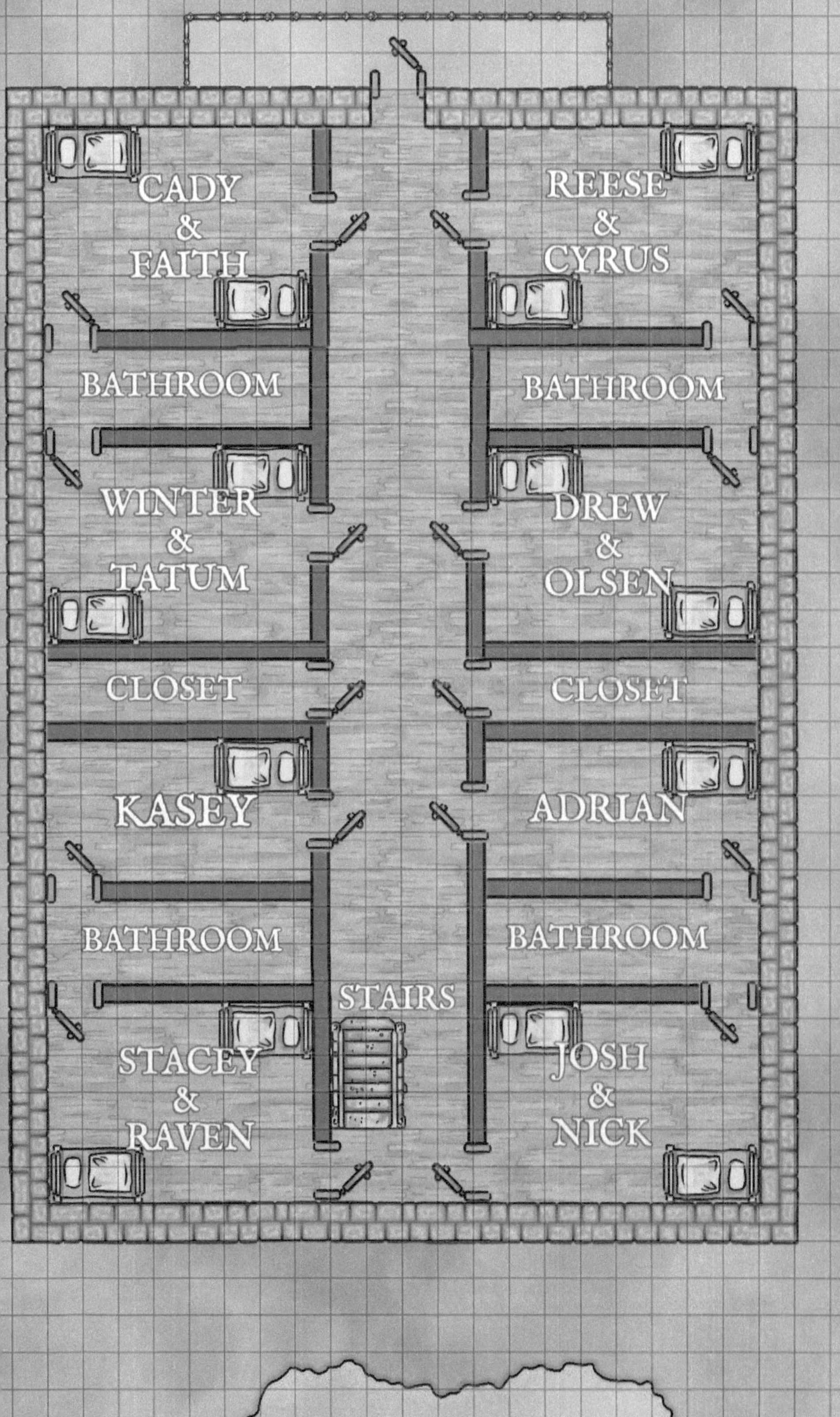

CADY
&
FAITH
BATHROOM
WINTER
&
TATUM
CLOSET
KASEY
BATHROOM
STACEY
&
RAVEN
REESE
&
CYRUS
BATHROOM
DREW
&
OLSEN
CLOSET
ADRIAN
BATHROOM
STAIRS
JOSH
&
NICK

DAY ONE

ONE

Cold, dark shadows reach for me from the corners of an unfamiliar room.

I clutch my pulsing temples as I struggle to sit up from where I'm sprawled. My stomach threatens to spill itself onto the dark, antique wooden floors. There's a sliver of light peeking in through blackout curtains pulled shut around the few windows.

I squint my eyes to survey my surroundings. A… parlor, of sorts? I lean back, brushing against the feeling of velvet. It's soft, but slightly worn. I reach a hand up on the sofa, and dust flies off at my touch, dancing in the slim beams like ash.

Coughing, I pull myself up, dizzy now that I'm on my feet. My sweaty palms wipe against rough fabric. I tilt my head to the right as I look down at my shoes. The last thing I remember… Was it going to bed? Glimpses of my evening routine and my powder blue bedspread flash behind my eyes. I didn't go to bed with tennis shoes on, right?

And I *definitely* did not go to bed in *jeans*.

My eyes start adjusting to the lack of light, and I can see the room a bit better. It's nowhere I recognize, but it feels like something you'd see in a museum. A dusty brick fireplace stands across from me unlit. There are portraits lining the walls in gold frames, fourteen in total. I look closer, wondering if I might recognize a face to see whose house this is…

My blood turns to ice in my veins.

A portrait of sapphire eyes and unruly blonde hair stares back at me.

My face. *I'm* in this photograph. It's one I recognize, a picture one of my friends took of me that I posted halfheartedly on social media.

I think I'm going to be sick.

I look around for something to throw up in—a plant, or a basket, or something. *Anything.*

As I stumble around holding my stomach, swallowing down the never-ending nausea, a groan comes from an onyx-coated corner.

My kidnapper?

I quickly suck in air through my teeth, eyes wild as I look around for a weapon.

Not even a fire stoker remains. I creep slowly toward the unconscious person, ready to dart at a moment's notice. Maybe I can knock them out again—I can't remember anything, but surely I'm the reason they're lying on the floor right now—and run out the door to look for help.

A boy sits up, clutching his head as I did, blinking slowly. I brace myself to throw a kick at his head, but something stops me. He looks… confused. Just as he opens his mouth to say something, a quick cry comes from behind him. A girl is curled on the floor with her knees drawn to her chest, mumbling something under her breath.

My chest rises and falls in quick succession as I take a few steps back. Who are these people? Is this a college party drink-spiking situation gone wrong?

Slowly, shadows I deemed harmless all begin to stir. A few

others stumble in from the hall adjacent until there are four-teen of us in the parlor.

The same number as there are portraits.

I survey the others, marking six as girls and seven as boys. It's too dark to see specifics of their appearances, but we all seem to be around the same age.

A shiver runs up my spine as I remember our predicament.

Why am I stuck in an unfamiliar room full of strangers?

Could I be dreaming? That must be it. I shut my eyes tight, expecting that when I open them again, I'll be back in my dorm room. I pinch my pale arm, just below my white t-shirt sleeve, and open my eyes again.

Brown eyes stare back.

I take a step back, nervous at the proximity at which he stands. My throat tightens.

"Who are you?" the boy asks.

"Uh…" I mutter.

He huffs, moving on.

Okay, then.

"Where—" a girl close to me starts, then stops. Her voice is hoarse. "Where *are* we?"

Everyone is fully awake now, up and moving. Some of them have wandered toward the portraits, and shock coats their tones.

"I don't know," a boy answers from near the windows. He's trying to pull the curtains back, but they're stuck in place. "I don't even know what time it is. I can't find my phone."

It's as if we all remember our devices at the same time. There's a flurry of motion as we pat our pockets and go back to look where we woke up.

Nothing.

"Does anyone have a watch?" someone from across the room asks.

I check my own wrist as everyone else does, even though I've never even *owned* a watch. Watching heads shake, I take an unsteady breath. I open my mouth to say something, but before I can, someone yells from behind me.

TWO

A guy has another by the shirt collar, holding him up against the wall. "You think this is funny?"

The smaller guy is smiling from where he hangs, even so, he hesitates. "Life's too short not to laugh when you're stressed. Wouldn't you agree, Goliath?"

The bully growls, and we all stifle our own giggles. He *does* kind of look like Goliath, in a big ogre way. His arms are bigger than my head, and he has to have at least a foot of height over most of us.

Goliath notices our reactions, and his grip loosens a bit. He drops our resident comedian, who nearly collapses as his knees buckle on impact.

"Not my name," Goliath mumbles under his breath. When he sees us still watching, his tone turns angry. "Well? Anyone have any clue why we're here?"

"The last thing I remember is being at a party," a girl offers. "And these were *not* the clothes I was wearing."

It's then that I look around and notice we're all wearing versions of the same thing. Blue jeans, white t-shirt, and black tennis shoes. I shudder. Who dressed us?

More importantly, who *undressed* us?

Another boy runs his fingers through his messy hair. "I think I was at work last I remember."

"I was going to bed," I chime in.

Everyone chips in their last memory, but it's at one girl's voice that a boy cries out in shock. "Cady?"

The girl, tall and lean with short honey hair, screams. "Reese!"

They run to each other, embracing tightly. When they pull back, tears running down their cheeks, Reese looks at the group.

"So? You gonna tell us what just happened?" another boy asks in a rude tone. I don't blame him. On my current list of 'weird things that have happened today', that's number two on it.

"She's here. My twin sister," Reese states, a bit out of breath. I peer at them. Now that I'm looking at them both side-by-side, the likeness is uncanny. "But that doesn't matter. Why are we *both* here? Why are we *all* here?"

Another girl's voice, soft but firm, interrupts the sudden chatter. "We need to stay calm," she says. Her voice has a strange tone to it, like she's used to being in control. "Panicking isn't going to help anything. We should check the rest of the house."

Cady yells back. "Yeah! Maybe there's a way out!"

Goliath groans, rolling his eyes. "We don't even know where we are. We could be in Africa for all we know."

"Should we really split up?" I ask, ignoring the negativity. But really, he's right. We have no idea what state or country we're in. There could be murderers in the house waiting for us to fall into their trap. My stomach is in knots. "I'm not one to watch horror movies, but isn't that what they always say not to do?"

The girl standing next to me scoffs. "If someone's going to die, better you than me."

Someone clasps me on the shoulder. "I'll go with you."

I turn at the familiar voice, and abruptly stop in my tracks when my eyes meet his. "No. What are—"

He shakes his head at me, ever-so-slightly, lips shut tight.

I freeze, the nausea in my stomach revolting tenfold. I look around, panicking, hoping for a way out of this partnership, but it looks like everyone else has already paired up. Reese and Cady especially are clinging to each other like their lives depend on it. I shake off my partner's hand urgently, angry at his touch.

I will do what I must. But I'm not going to like it.

As we make our way out of the parlor, I avoid eye contact, shoving my questions and concerns down deep within me. There's no time to think about the implications of this. The only thing that matters right now is getting out of here.

And never seeing *him* ever again.

We step into the shadowed hall hesitantly, wooden floors creaking under our every step. It stretches, dim and narrow, lined with peeling maroon wallpaper. My adrenaline starts to wear off, and my brain begins to shut down with fatigue.

I follow my brunette partner to the left, letting him lead the way. A sudden noise makes me jump—a faint scraping sound coming from somewhere in front of us.

"It's just a door. Someone is probably exploring another room," he says. It doesn't make me feel any better. *Him* being here certainly doesn't make me feel better.

There's a staircase next to us, and a group of six makes their way up it, clutching the railing. My partner and I go to the end of the hall, where a wooden door stands slightly bent on its hinges on the right. The smell of cleaner hangs pungently in the air, covering up the distinct smell of something musty. Almost like this house stood unused for a while...

Until recently.

I slip into the dark room behind my partner, standing just at the threshold of the open door. My hands survey the wall, finding and flicking a light switch to 'on', not expecting anything to happen but silently hoping something does.

I cannot be in a dark room alone with him again.

Just as he turns back to look at me, mouth open and ready to speak, the overhead light blinks on. I squint, adjusting to the yellow glow coming from the ceiling, a breath of relief escaping my lungs.

The floors are pristine, and grand windows overtake the wall across from where we are. There are no curtains on these windows—they're far too tall to cover. It's definitely night, but there's no way of knowing what time exactly. There's a grand chandelier hanging from the ornate ceiling, glistening in the golden glow.

I swing the door wide open, letting the light sweep out into the hall. My partner takes a step to join me as I side-step couches, heading for the windows and wondering if I'll be able to see anything. I give him a warning look, one that says, 'Do anything, and I'll make sure there are witnesses.' I might have been too scared five years ago to speak up, but I've grown since then.

I've spoken up since then.

He ducks his head, but not before pouting. "Darling, come on," he whines.

Clearly, my look wasn't enough to shut him up.

I hold my hand up, creating a space between us, but as I open my mouth to respond—to tell him to *never call me that again*—the light flickers.

Looking up, I watch as the electronic candles adorning the chandelier start to dim. I hold my breath, waiting, not daring to take another step.

The light goes out completely, casting us into sudden darkness.

I leave nothing to chance, sprinting the entire way back to the parlor.

THREE

I heave, sucking in as much stale air as I can muster. My partner tries to place a comforting hand on my back, but I move away, not even trying to hide the disgust on my face.

How dare he try to touch me after everything he did?

Another thought itches the back of my brain, but I'm scared to bring it to life. Still, it slips through the cracks.

Someone knows.

And if our captor—whoever they are—knows about our past… What else could they know?

I bury my secrets down deep within me, locking them up behind familiar bars. I don't have the time or the energy to go down that trail right now. My focus has to be on getting out of here. And once I'm out, life can go back to the way it was.

My stomach churns, and I run to the corner of the room, unable to hold back any longer. I retch until nothing else will come up, my body shaking when I finally stand back up. I wish I had something to rinse the horrid taste out of my mouth.

The other groups come back in waves as we wait for them, voices overlapping as everyone says what they found. The locked front door did not budge, and no window opened. We never got around to checking the back door, but my guess is that it was locked too. One boy found a grandfather clock in the hall and said it's just before midnight.

The kitchen appeared completely stocked, a trio explained, which terrifies me. That means that whoever put us here plans on keeping us for longer than just the night. Apart from the parlor, there's an office, sunroom, library, dining room, kitchen, and game room all on the first floor of the house.

I leave the group's mumblings to go survey the portraits again, brain distracted. How did I miss his picture the first time around? I must have been too shell-shocked to see my own that I didn't see it. And now I'm trapped in a house with *him*.

But why? How?

I drown out the voices, closing my eyes and focusing on my breathing. It's then that I notice someone else breathing rapidly from the floor nearby. A boy sits cross-legged, arms clutched around his middle, clearly trying to keep from rocking back and forth.

Kneeling, I try to keep my tone soft as I speak. "Hey, you okay?"

It takes him a second to peel his eyes off the floorboards in front of him, but when he does, he stills a bit.

"Sorry," his voice shakes. "I'm not good with being locked in."

"Claustrophobic?" I ask.

"Sure… something like that." He forces a small smile. "I'm Drew."

"Winter," I respond. "Can I sit with you?"

He nods, scooting over a little.

"I'm trying to be calm," I admit, sighing. "If I don't stay calm, I won't make it out of here. That's what I'm telling myself."

"It feels like I'm being punished." He takes a deep breath. "Where do you live?"

"Utah. Don't you?"

Drew shakes his head. "Colorado. Seems like everyone's from a different state." He points to Goliath, then to our funny guy. "I was in their group when we all split. Nick from Indiana. Adrian from New York."

My spine straightens. "I assumed we were all from Utah, which hopefully meant we were still *in* Utah. I never considered we might be from different places."

"Makes you wonder how whoever is behind this pulled that off, doesn't it?"

I shudder. "Why are we here? How did they find us? Where are we?" I cringe at myself. My default is to ask questions—it's the journalism major in me. But I try my best not to subject others to the endless questions sounding off in my head.

He looks down, golden brown hair falling over his forehead. "Questions we're all thinking. I wish I knew."

My eyes wander, now watching the group argue, all of them bringing up different ideas about how we could escape when we know there's probably no way out. It feels like a waiting game—that we are at the mercy of our kidnapper.

Someone laughs then, a brittle sound, and it turns into a desperate cry. "I don't want to be here!"

I turn toward the sound, watching Reese comfort his sister. They may not see it this way, but they're lucky to have each other through this. A familiar face, someone they can trust. Nevertheless, it brings me to the question of *why*.

Voices quiet as we all run out of ideas and things to say to each other. Soon enough, almost everyone resigns themselves to a spot on the floor. Maybe to process, maybe to plan. Either way, the only sounds we hear are the wind whooshing around the house's exterior and muffled sobs.

That, and the grandfather clock striking midnight.

Dong.

Dong.

Dong.

The heavy toll echoes until I count twelve. It's a new day, though I don't even know what day it is. My last memory… Was that a Saturday?

Then, just as my eyes start to drift shut without me thinking twice about it, a sound interrupts my weariness. The crackling of an intercom buzzes from somewhere above us. Our heads whip up in tandem, and our muscles freeze. Even Cady, still crying, quiets.

The speaker comes to life. "Hello, my houseguests. You may be wondering what you've gotten yourselves into."

I look wide-eyed around the room, everyone's fear permeating the still air.

The gravelly voice continues. "One of you knows exactly why you're here. Find them, and you *might* survive. Fail, and you'll forsake your life. One of you will die twenty-four hours from now, and we won't stop taking lives until one of you is the last one standing."

The intercom clicks off with a sharp, metallic pop, leaving behind a heavy silence.

I'm not the first one to start screaming.

DAY TWO

FOUR

Panic spreads fast—like a wildfire in dry air. Someone shrieks from behind me, the sound piercing my ears. Voices pile up over each other.

"This has got to be a prank, right?"

"I just want my mom!"

"I'm not supposed to be here."

"I've never done anything wrong ever! In my life!"

Heads tilt at that last sentence as we look curiously at the girl. Her tan face blushes as she shrinks back into herself, embarrassed. "Okay, maybe I have. But probably not anything as bad as *you* all."

Nick scoffs. "So whose fault is it then that we're all here? Who's gonna fess up?" He scans the room. No one moves a muscle—no one dares to breathe. "Huh? You gonna make me beat it out of you?"

I step forward, hands up in surrender. "Hang on, there's no need for that. This is probably just a big… misunderstanding."

A girl with a black pixie cut laughs dryly. "Yeah, potential murder is *so* chill."

One boy rushes toward the wooden front doors, throwing

his weight against them again and again. We follow him, slightly hopeful, and a few others join in. Still, the doors don't budge.

"I don't want to be locked in!" he screams. He's banging his clenched fists against the door now, punching it with no restraint. Blood blooms across his knuckles, but the door doesn't even shake. I yell at him to stop, trying to grab his shoulder to pull him back, but it's no use.

Eventually, he yells out in anguish when we hear a *crack*. He pulls his arm back, clutching his wrist against his chest.

"You probably broke it," one girl says, reaching out to touch it. "I'm Faith—I'm studying to be a nurse. I'll see if I can find something to wrap it in. There was a closet over here…" Trailing off, she disappears into the shadowed corridor.

The intercom crackles again momentarily, just enough that it sounds like someone started to say something, but then decided not to.

"They're probably watching us," Drew whispers from over my shoulder, voice strangled. I jump, startled. His chest is rising and falling in quick succession. I look up at the ceiling, spotting small red lights in the dark corners—a sure sign cameras are on and recording.

"Hey! We know you can hear us! Let us out!" another boy yells. He must be from the south—his accent is *strong*.

Soon enough, everyone is yelling at our mysterious captor, begging and pleading for their lives and freedom. My pulse is so loud I can barely hear myself think. It's as if I'm stuck in place, somewhere between frozen and floating.

The voice from the intercom rings out over and over in my head:

One of you knows exactly why you're here. Find them, and you might survive. Fail, and you'll forsake your life. One of you will die twenty-four hours from now, and we won't stop taking lives until one of you is the last one standing.

Someone will die.

Tonight. Maybe even every night we are stuck in this place.

No one is safe.

Shivers run up my spine.

I could die.

"I can't—" Drew's voice says behind me, breathy and mumbled.

I turn and see him falling to the floor, head lolled. His breathing is jagged and quick.

Without thinking, in the middle of all the chaos, I drop beside him.

"Hey, you're okay. Breathe. You're hyperventilating," I murmur.

"I can't—can't do this again," he whispers through gritted teeth.

Again?

I tuck that away in a folder called 'Questions to ask later'. "Follow my breathing. In for four, out for four. Ready? In." I breathe deep, exaggerating the motion so he starts to do it too. About halfway through, he catches on. "Good. Now out."

I exhale loudly through my mouth. He follows suit, regaining a steady breath after a few rounds.

"Better?" I ask. His skin looks so pale. Maybe I should see if Faith can check on him…

"I'm fine," he responds. "For now, anyway. Thank you."

I nod, and it's as if time resumes. People are still screaming, crying, and running amok, but I can tell we're all losing steam.

Eventually, the girl who took charge earlier regains control. Her hair is tied back in a small, slick bun at her nape, making her look older than the rest of us. "Alright, everybody shut up!" I stifle a giggle. So much for being calm and controlled. She's banging a wooden spoon against a stove pot.

"We need to think logically. Yelling isn't going to get us anywhere."

"Logically?" Nick snaps. "We've been brought here to die, and you want to talk about *logic*?"

"No one's actually going to kill us, right?"

"You don't know that."

"Neither do you."

"I'm doing the best with the information I've got!"

Again, voices overlap. I look around, exasperated. I don't know what I feel exactly, only that I am *tired*.

And then, just like that, the energy shifts.

"Uh, guys? Which group found the bedrooms?" Adrian asks.

A few people tentatively raise their hands.

"Did you all just miss the name tags on the wall, or are those new?"

Everyone rushes up, ready to investigate, but I pause to help Drew up off the floor. He tries to wave me off, but eventually he gives in. Once he's mobile, we head upstairs and file down the hall behind everyone else, my nerves prickling. I'm half-expecting someone to jump out and kill me on the spot, even though the voice said we have twenty-four hours. Someone flicks the light switch, and so far, it's staying on.

Five doors line the hallway on either side, plus one glass door at the very end of the hall.

But whether this was a new addition or a missed detail, fourteen brass name tags are hanging on the walls just outside the doors.

And my name is going to be on one of them. And this feeling inside of me… It's like someone is *watching* me.

We wander, all of us looking for our own nameplate. We've all come to stand in pairs in front of our designated bedrooms. My soon-to-be roommate is a girl named Tatum. The girls stand on one side of the hall, with the boys opposite us.

To my right, two people stand at their doors alone. Adrian is left without a roommate, as is our self-appointed leader. I shudder, thanking our captor that they didn't place *me* in my own room. Even though I have my own room at home, I don't think I could handle it here. The fear, the silence… it would be too much.

I turn back toward my door, running my finger across my nameplate. It's cool to the touch, and so shiny that I leave a fingerprint behind.

"How do they know us?" I whisper.

Tatum responds, a Midwest accent poking through. "Beats me."

Drew stands across the hall with his roommate, a frail-looking boy named Olsen.

Olsen coughs dryly, pulling me out of my mind. "Dusty—up—here."

I survey the group. There are so many of us, all with different backgrounds and stories. Is it possible we are all connected somehow?

But why? For what reason?

Our leader speaks up from my right. "I think we should try to get a few hours of sleep. We'll be able to think better once we're more rested."

"I don't want to sleep with a stranger in my room," Nick whines. It looks like he's roommates with *him*. Good. They deserve each other.

"Then sleep downstairs by yourself for all I care. Personally, I'm going to bed. Goodnight."

And with that, she opens her door and shuts herself inside.

One by one, most of the group retire to their bedrooms. Sure enough, Nick huffs and enters his room, slamming the door behind him in his roommate's face. I'm so tired and delusional that I nearly *laugh*. He shoots me a glare, and I give him a mocking look. I won't be letting him off the hook, even under these extreme circumstances. I'm over his anger.

Tatum is already inside when I join her. There's not much in here—two identical beds, nightstands with lamps, and one big closet. I peer through the hangers, finding more white shirts and jeans. My exact size, and Tatum's.

Too many questions, not enough answers.

Only twenty-four hours to find out *why*. And try to escape.

I sit on the navy comforter to take off my shoes. The sheets smell and feel fresh, like they were washed hours prior.

Again, I'm reminded of my circumstances, and I push back the tears brimming in my eyelids.

After lying down and turning off our lamps, I hear Tatum quietly sobbing in the dark. I wish I could join her, but if I start crying now, I won't be able to stop. There's no way for me to comfort her. We're all stuck in the same nightmare. Plus, I don't know anything about her yet—where she's from, how old she is, if there's anyone back home she's missing.

I twist a piece of my hair around my finger. Tomorrow—or, today?—I'll start asking those questions.

For now, I need to rest.

FIVE

The scent of bacon wafts up toward me from downstairs. I blink the exhaustion from my eyes, taking a moment to remember where I am. I stretch as I sit up, finding Tatum's ruffled bed empty. Neither of us got any sleep, both tossing and turning all night long.

I shuffle across the wooden floor in my day-old clothes to use the restroom.

Our room is joined with Cady and Faith's, with a shared bathroom in the middle. We discovered early this morning, after Cady nearly peed her bed by accident, where the restrooms were located. She caused such a commotion that, had we been asleep, it would have woken us up.

The light is blinding as I walk inside, reaching toward the large cabinet that looms against the only empty wall. There are toiletry necessities fully stocked inside, including wooden toothbrushes with our names on them.

Whoever it is behind this thought of everything.

I run through the motions, throwing my hair in a ponytail and washing my face with the sink water. As I brush my teeth, I try to force my brain to think, plot, question, plan, *anything*, but it refuses.

My stomach growls as I rinse my mouth. I feel less over-whelmingly nauseous this morning, even though I didn't sleep at all. I bet some food would help my brainpower. I can't remember the last meal I had…

A glimpse of a memory rushes through my brain, like rain dripping down a car window. Me with my Communications study group, laughing over ice cream sundaes and homework.

Was that last night? I remember not feeling great once we got back into the dorms, so I went to bed earlier than normal instead of staying up to talk with my friends.

I shake off the confusion fogging up my brain as I change clothes and head downstairs. Maybe someone else has discovered something and will share with the group.

Or maybe the person who knows why we're all here will give us some clues, apologize, and help us leave.

"Wouldn't that be nice?" I grumble to myself. As I pass the grandfather clock in the hall, I make sure to take note of the time.

Just after 9:00 a.m. Fifteen hours until the first death.

Suddenly, I'm not hungry anymore.

Bacon, eggs, toast, and fruit line the dining room table as I enter. Thirteen faces stare back at me, and I take an empty seat at the long table next to Tatum. It looks like I'm not the only one who doesn't have much of an appetite, but everyone is forcing themselves to eat at least a little something, anyway.

"Finally! You're up. Good to know you can sleep through a crisis," Nick starts, chewing with his mouth full. "Reese had the grand idea that we should share names and 'get to know each other'." He quotes the last phrase with his fork, sarcasm dripping at the seams. Really, it's not a terrible idea. The more we know about each other, the better we will see connections and probabilities.

Reese blushes, coming from the kitchen to add more eggs to the serving bowl. "I just figured, knowing each other might matter. And help us figure this out."

"I mean, do you really believe the person who knows why we're here is going to tell us? Obviously, they're not on our side," pixie cut snarks.

"It's better than waiting around to see if someone is actually going to die or not!" Cady cuts in.

Tatum exhales next to me, whispering her words. "I'd rather keep trying to leave."

Still, she doesn't move. And as I take a bite of bacon, I realize that all of us could just leave right now and go to our rooms. We could cry, hide out, beg the hidden voice for mercy. But we don't. We stay.

Which means that even though we're all scared, we're in this together.

"My name is Winter," I call out over the bickering. Someone has to start, and it might as well be me. For once, everyone quiets. "I live in Utah. I'm nineteen. And… I don't know what else is important to say. The last thing I remember is being in my dorm room."

It's silent at first. I think I've said just enough that they'll remember those few details about me, but not too much that I'll stick out. It's important to go first. I'm hoping that no one will be bold enough to ask me questions just yet.

Questions I don't have the answers to, and questions I prefer not to answer.

"I'm Drew," my new friend says from the other side of the table. He looks better today—more color in his face. I give him a quick, reassuring smile. He nods at me. "I'm from Colorado, and I'm also nineteen. I'm hoping to become a doctor, but I don't know what I want to specialize in yet. Maybe pediatrics."

"I only just started schooling to be a nurse," Faith says, fidgeting with her fingernails. "This is my first year at the University of South Carolina."

Down the line, everyone goes. Reese and Cady are both freshmen at a state university in Ohio.

"I want to be a chef," Reese admits. "But my parents wanted me to have a 'normal college experience'."

"Breakfast is great, I guess," Nick mumbles through bites of toast. How is he still eating?

"And dad is a professor there," Cady adds, ignoring him. "We get free tuition."

"What are you going to school for, Cady?" Adrian asks.

She ducks her head. "I just want to be a librarian."

"Have you *seen* the size of the library across the hall? It's huge!" Tatum exclaims.

For a minute, we sit up excitedly, Cady especially. Then, it's as if a bucket of cold water is thrown on our heads.

And the room is quiet once more.

I look down at my plate, my heart sinking into my stomach. What will sharing our names and where we're from really do for us? It's not going to save us. It's not going to give us the answers we're looking for.

"I guess I can go next," *he* says, voice like nails on a chalkboard to my ears after so long without hearing it. My body tenses, spine rigid. "My name's Josh."

"Okay," a blonde with circle-rim glasses says, drawing out the end of the word. "Where are you from, Josh?"

He looks right at me then, blue eyes full of something I can't read. Not anymore.

Arizona, I think. Arizona, where we grew up together. Arizona, where I called home until earlier this year.

Shaking his head, he finally answers. "Arizona."

I'm ready to question him, but I don't want to draw attention to the fact that we know each other.

And because of that fact, Josh just became suspect number one on my list.

"He snores. Like, *so* loud. Sounded like there was a dinosaur in our room," Nick says. He pretends to think for a second. "I have a great idea. Josh, you should room with Adrian."

"Why, so you can have a room to yourself?" Adrian deadpans.

Nick shrugs, leaning back in his wooden chair. "I don't mind taking one for the team."

Josh rolls his eyes. I chide myself for looking at his reaction; for even looking his way at all.

"I'm Kasey," our courageous leader calls out, smiling. "I'm about to graduate with my Bachelor's Degree in human resource management."

She sounds like she's from a northern state, and her tone is very composed. Her brunette bob swishes when she talks.

Another southern accent emerges from the group. The blonde from earlier. "My name is Stacey. Honestly, I just want to go home."

"Obviously, we *all* do, Goldie," pixie cut scoffs.

"Your turn," Kasey cuts in. "Tell us about yourself."

"Name's Raven. Someone," she waves her hands around toward the ceiling, "Decided that happy-go-lucky and I needed to share a room. And let me tell y'all. She. Did. Not. Shut. Up. All. Night. Long."

Stacey frowns. "I talk when I'm nervous. You didn't *have* to listen."

"How could I not? Our beds are ten feet apart!"

Kasey holds up a hand, and they quiet their bickering. "We still haven't gotten through everyone. Who's left?"

Tatum raises her hand, as does Drew's roommate and another boy with shaved dark hair.

Kasey motions for one of them to go, and both the boys look at my roommate.

She wraps a strand of pink hair around her fingers. "Um, I'm Tatum. And I like to bake. Especially when I'm stressed. Mostly when I'm stressed."

"What are you gonna be making later then, sugar? I've got an idea." Nick leans back in his chair, two legs off the floor. He eyes Tatum with a stupid smirk on his face.

She looks like she's going to be sick. I wish she would be—I wish she'd throw up all over his shoes.

For a split second, we look around awkwardly, waiting for someone to step forward and say something. But it's clear we're all still learning our group dynamics.

Even then, one minute, Nick is lounging. The next, he's flat on his back on the ground, chair sprawled next to him.

"Hey!" he shouts, propping himself up. "Who did that?"

All of us stifle a giggle as the boy with the shaved head winks at us. "My name's Cyrus, and I'm a pilot. I try to stay very calm in chaotic situations, but I'll be honest. This one is throwing me for a bit of a loop."

Drew's roommate raises his hand. "Olsen. And yeah, I'm super spooked. Honestly, I don't know how to tell you guys this, but…" he looks to Drew for support, who nods. It's good to see that some of us have already taken steps to get to know the other people we're stuck in this house with. Olsen takes a deep breath. "I was diagnosed with Leukemia yesterday. Like, literally yesterday. Last thing I remember is lying in a hospital bed."

We all sit stunned, my jaw dropped. *What?*

"We've got to get you out of here," Tatum urges.

"I mean, what are we supposed to do? Obviously whoever brought us here knows. And they don't care," Drew adds.

"Why are we here?" Cady cries. Reese leans over to hug his sister.

"All I've learned in the last thirty minutes is that I'm going to outlive all of you," Nick states, now back in his chair.

"You think this is a joke?" Raven slaps her hand on the table.

"It's a trap. And I'm just stating the facts."

Before arguing can ensue again, crying starts.

Faith presses her fists into her eyes. She's shaking, rivers of tears running down her cheeks.

Stacey reaches over to put a hand on her shoulder.

"Olsen's going to be okay, Faith. Maybe some of your nursing training can help!"

Faith shakes her head, throwing Stacey's hand off. "It's me," she says, voice barely a whisper. "I think I know why we're here."

SIX

There was a story a few months ago about a sailor who went missing at sea for five years. He was out fishing on a Tuesday evening when he felt an overwhelming peace coming from the wind and waves.

In a post-rescue interview, he deemed himself the most scared he'd ever been. "The wind quieted. The waves stopped rolling. And it was at that moment that I knew there was a terrible storm coming. I pulled in my gear, went to start my boat. And there was nothing. I tried and tried as the sky got darker, but it was no use."

He sat as the storm grew to be the biggest one he'd ever seen. The wind and waves tossed his boat with unmatched fervor. By the time the rain stopped, he was cold and hypothermic and had no clue where he had ended up.

This moment—the one right after Faith's confession—feels just like that.

Everyone freezes. She looks up, mascara smudged, eyes wide and undoubtedly panicked. "I think I know."

"Why are we here, then?" Cyrus asks, tone harsh.

A thousand things rush through my head at once as I look

around at everyone's reactions, but one thought stands out louder than the rest.

Could it really be that easy?

"I don't know. It's just… I've been here before," Faith sniffles. "I recognize this house."

"What?" Tatum exclaims, exasperated.

"I stayed here with my extended family for Christmas last year. It's an Airbnb."

Voices overlap. Nick gets up and walks over to Faith's chair, leaning it back. She squeals, shrinking down from his aggressive manner.

"Where are we then?" He spits in her face. Whether accidental or not, it's still gross.

She gulps. "North Carolina. Highlands, I think. I don't remember exactly."

"Okay," I start, trying to keep my tone calm. North Carolina. It's far from home, but at least it's a start. At least we are still in the United States. "But how does knowing that help us?"

Faith starts crying again. "I don't know! But it has to mean something that I recognize where we are, right? Right?"

Nick rolls his eyes, taking his hand off her chair so it lands with a *thud*. "It's the only lead we've got. I say we tell the Voice that we've caught our perpetrator and they need to let us out right now."

"No way it's going to be that easy," Reese says.

"Doesn't hurt to try," Stacey responds. "Hey! Voice!"

We all start shouting, hoping this time for attention rather than silence. I know they can see us. I know they're listening to our conversations.

Finally, an unseen speaker somewhere in the ceiling crackles. "Hello, houseguests. How was breakfast?"

We look down at our half-eaten plates of food, my stomach suddenly nauseous. I try to focus on the voice to see if it's familiar, but nothing clicks. The tone is warbly, as if they're using some sort of bad PA system, or a voice-changing device.

"We have information!" Kasey yells. "She knows why we're here. Let us out!"

"Hmm," the Voice hums. "Perhaps. But knowing is only the beginning."

We look at each other, all standing up and wide-eyed. What does that mean?

"There's a time for jokes," Adrian calls. "And this isn't it."

"It's a good thing the comedic character never dies. Isn't that right, Adrian?"

A shiver runs down my spine. The Voice knows our names. Of course they do. Our pictures are hanging on the walls. We were chosen for a reason. We are here for a reason.

We just don't know what that is yet.

"I think it's time for our first game."

I gasp as the lights go out. In the pitch black, I feel for my chair in front of me, wanting something steady to hold on to. The wooden material feels sturdy underneath my fingertips. Someone grabs my shoulder, clutching tightly. I look to my right, relieved that it's just Tatum. If it had been Josh, I would have thrown hands faster than he could blink.

"Leave your dishes where they are. The game room is now open."

A light flicks on in the hall, beckoning us to follow. We shuffle our way out of the dark room and into the corridor, following Josh and Kasey across the walkway and into the lantern-lit game room.

"Sit," the voice calls out as we enter. Each of us takes a seat at a large, empty wooden table.

"Here's how our time together will go: Every day, you will join me for a game where truths will be revealed. Each evening, you will vote for the person you believe poses the greatest risk to the group. You will have the afternoons to discuss."

Sweat beads on my forehead. I wasn't expecting all of this to be so… *intricate.*

"The person voted the most will be put up as a sacrifice. The rest of you will return to your rooms for the night. Each morning, the games will continue until only one of you is left."

Tatum grabs hold of my hand, and we squeeze each other's fingers tightly. No one speaks. No one dares to breathe.

"So the question is, houseguests, how far are you willing to go to be the last one standing?"

SEVEN

"What's this game, then?" Raven calls out. "If we only have the afternoon to discuss, hurry up so we can start talking."

She's bold. For now, I like that. It could end up being a liability in the future, though. I tuck that away in my mind, ready to reopen that box when I see fit.

The Voice tsks at her over the intercom. "So pushy, so insistent. I see you, Raven. You know why you're here."

My head whips in her direction, and her pale skin is white as a ghost.

"Now," Voice says. I have no time to process what just happened. "Split into two teams of seven."

As if on impact, we all distance ourselves from Raven and Faith, the only two who are deemed suspicious as of now. Faith for being in the house before, and Raven for the Voice's snide comment.

"I'll lead a team," Josh states, his voice a fork scraping across a plate to my ears. I cringe without meaning to, somehow almost forgetting that he's in the room with me.

"I can take one too," Nick adds.

"If a boy gets to be a captain, then a girl should be the other captain," Raven spits. Her arms are crossed, and something within me says that she's overcompensating for what the Voice said. I wonder, is she hoping we'll all forget about the tidbit of information they shared? I doubt we will. Not when our lives are on the line.

"Fine," Nick grumbles.

"I can do it," Cady volunteers nervously. She looks around the table, eyeing the rest of the girls. None of us offers ourselves as captain instead, content in letting that burden fall on her shoulders. We have no idea what this game entails, nor what's truly at stake.

"Should we just… pick? Like, dodgeball team style?" Kasey asks.

Josh and Cady look at each other, nodding, and I watch him quickly look her up and down with interest. Disgust boils up in my throat. She's four years younger than he is. But I guess I shouldn't be surprised—he's always gone for younger girls.

"Ladies first," he bows at her, gesturing with his hand that the floor is hers. We all get up from where we sit at the rounded table, the two captains splitting so they're on opposite sides of the room.

"Reese," Cady picks.

"Surprise, surprise," Tatum grumbles. It's then that I realize we're still holding hands, so I give her palm a quick squeeze and let go, wiping my sweat on my jeans.

Josh surveys the room, but pauses when he makes eye contact with me. I look down, picking at my fingernails.

Please don't pick me. Please don't pick me. Please don't pick me.

"Winter," he states.

I fight the urge to collapse on the floor in a heap, walking over to where he is. It's at that moment that I wish anyone—*anyone*—would have volunteered as captain instead. I wouldn't be surprised if he only offered himself so that he could do this to me.

He gives me a smirk, fully *knowing* what he did. And yet, he chose to do it anyway. It appears that in the two years we haven't been in contact, he hasn't changed a bit.

Cady and Reese consult each other. "Cyrus."

Josh doesn't look at me before he says quickly, "Nick."

Great.

They give each other a fist bump as Nick joins our team, and I can't help but roll my eyes. What a pair these two are. Thorns in my side already.

Back and forth they go until our teams of seven are complete. Cady's team is composed of Reese, Cyrus, Stacey, Tatum, Adrian, and Faith. Josh picked me, Nick, Drew, Kasey, Olsen, and Raven.

It's no surprise that Faith and Raven were picked last. I think I can assume everyone has similar thoughts to me at this point—that they are viewed as the least trustworthy until we know.

The Voice tells us to sit at the table so they can go over the rules of the game. I wait until Josh sits first so he can't follow me, and then head to a seat closer to where Cady is. His frustration radiates toward me, but I brush it off. I'm across from Tatum, and she gives me a raised eyebrow, as if noticing my discomfort. One day in, and somehow, I already feel comfort in having her as my roommate and hopeful friend.

She could be dangerous, a voice inside my head whispers. *You can't trust any of these people.*

I flinch in response. Drew clears his throat to my right, as if hearing my train of thought. I look at him, giving him a nervous smile.

He opens his mouth to say something, leaning into my space, but the Voice cuts him off.

"Houseguests, this is a simple game of rock, paper, scissors. One by one, you will compete against someone from the opposite team. You get one chance to beat your opponent. If you win, your team receives a point. If you lose, you must give up one secret to everyone."

Gasps are heard around the room, and I feel Raven go rigid beside me.

"Just one moment, I haven't gotten to the best part," the Voice continues. "It is from the losing team that you will decide who will be your first sacrifice tonight."

You could hear a pin drop. Just like that, battle lines are drawn. It's officially *us* against *them*.

"You may begin. And don't forget: I'm watching."

With that, the intercom system clicks off. Absent-mindedly, I look for this room's cameras. They're harder to see with the lights on, but they're there. I can just tell.

"Team captains should go first," Cyrus says. "We can just go in line with who was picked. There's no reason for us to prolong the inevitable."

"Okay," Josh sighs. He gets up from his chair, the feet of it scraping across the wooden floors as he meets Cady. The wall behind them lights up with a digital scoreboard.

They hold out their hands, stating that we will all go at the word 'shoot'.

Cady and Josh face off, and the air in the room is utterly still as they begin.

"Rock," Josh starts. "Paper, Scissors, shoot."

They throw out their symbols, and we all lean in, eager to see who will get the first point.

Cady holds up scissors, and Josh throws his triumphant rock-fist in the air. Our team cheers, Nick clapping Josh on the back as he returns to his seat.

I watch as a tear slides down Cady's cheek, and Reese gives her a quick hug as she sits back down. "It's okay," he murmurs. "There's still six rounds left."

Ding. The scoreboard pings as the number one emerges underneath Josh's name.

I flick my ponytail over my shoulder as I get up to face Reese.

"Not so fast," the Voice interjects. I didn't even notice the speakers turn on, ready to get my turn over with. "As the losing person, Cadence owes us a secret."

EIGHT

I suck in a quick breath of air, holding it for a moment as realization dawns on our faces. I forgot about this part of the equation.

She looks at Reese, hesitating. "My mother was murdered."

My eyes widen, looking back and forth between the twins. I was not expecting something as big as that.

She's lying, my inner voice calls out. *She wants pity.*

I shake it off, getting up to meet Reese. I look intently at his face, searching for any sign that he has malicious intent or that he was surprised at Cady's confession. I don't see anything but sadness in his eyes.

And maybe a shred of guilt.

For a moment, I consider going rock, wondering if he might choose Cady's scissors unintentionally. But then I think he might see that coming. I don't *know* these people yet. They could be much smarter than I give them credit for.

I go with paper instead, and he beats me with scissors. My heart sinks. I'm not ready to tell my truths to this group. The other team cheers as I return, embarrassed, back to my seat.

Maybe I can sit down without them noticing I didn't share anything, and we can just move on…

Before I can finish that train of thought, the room quiets, all eyes waiting expectantly for me to share my secret.

I mull over my options in my head. If I think too long, they'll assume I'm lying. But would it be a bad thing? To lie? And yet… something within me says to tell a truth, no matter how small. I want to be seen as trustworthy so that I might gain information that will help us get out of here.

And so I can make it another day.

"I'm studying to become a news reporter," I admit. I keep my gaze forward, looking toward the opposite wall. Specifically refraining from looking toward Josh to see what his reaction is. The Voice never said it had to be a big secret.

I hold my tongue, not willing to give more details than needed. I don't want to tell them the reason *why* I chose reporting. And if this sliver of information tells them that I pay very close attention to words spoken and body language, *good*.

Ding. The scoreboard now reads one to one.

Cyrus and Nick face off next. At 'shoot', Cyrus holds up paper. Nick holds up a single finger.

"It's dynamite," he barks. "Trumps everything. You lose!"

Before anyone can argue, the intercom crackles to life. "Point, Cadence's team. There is no room here for cheating."

Our team groans, obviously displeased at Nick's attempt to be funny.

He plops back into his seat, complaining. "I play football," he blurts. I look around the room, catching the disappointment on some people's faces. It wasn't a game-changing secret, but it does tell me something.

First, he's an athlete. He plays at the collegiate level. He's most likely good at playing the game.

Second, my best guess is that his answer is a cover-up to keep us from looking deeper. Perhaps he thinks we'll assume he's just a dumb, rude college football player. But nothing—and no one—is ever as it seems.

Ding. Two to one.

Stacey and Drew are next, and I root silently for Drew. Not just because he's on my team and we need to even the score, but also because there's something about him—like Tatum—that makes me think I can trust him more than the others. Maybe it was the breakdown yesterday, or the small conversations we had.

Or maybe my gut is completely wrong.

Stacey holds up paper, and Drew presents his scissors. I feel immediate relief. Part of me didn't *want* to hear whatever secret Drew might have admitted to the group. If he has secrets to be shared, I want them to only be offered to *me*. As allies.

Ding. Tied back up, two to two.

"My glasses are fake," Stacey admits, tossing her blonde hair over her shoulder. Interesting style choice. You couldn't pay me to wear glasses just for fun. My little sister needs glasses to read, and they give her a headache.

Tatum and Kasey face off in their round, with Tatum winning with rock. She looks *incredibly* relieved to have won. Could it be that her secret is big enough to get her voted out? I sigh. Only time will tell.

"I already have a guess as to who did this to us," Kasey smirks. We wait for her to offer more, but that's all she gives us. Whether that was an intentional thing she did simply to shake us, or she's throwing out a lie as a way to lead us off her trail, I would guess that it's going to work.

But if it was a lie… I think the Voice would interject. I get the sense that they want their game to be played exactly how they want it to.

Ding. Back and forth we go, three to two.

Olsen tries to stand up to meet Adrian, but he's having trouble getting on his feet. Adrian walks over to him instead, letting him stay sitting. That small act of kindness warms my heart. We might be enemies at this current moment, and we might all be confused and scared out of our minds, but simple acts of humanity still exist. They go, Olsen tying up the game with scissors.

"I have fake teeth," Adrian says. He takes his hand and pulls out a retainer-like wire, bringing his two front teeth with it. Giggling a bit, he shows them to the group, like show-and-tell. Then, he pops it back in his mouth and goes to sit back down.

Ding. Three to three. Only one round left.

Raven and Faith get up, Faith shrinking back from Raven's towering figure. Raven leans in, a malicious grin on her face, as she whispers something in Faith's ear. Her face goes pale, eyebrows raised in surprise. Faith whispers something back, and all we can do is watch in anticipation of what might happen.

They hold out their hands.

Rock.

My chest tightens, making my breath feel shallow.

Paper.

A trickle of sweat runs down my forehead and into my eye.

Scissors.

I grab hold of Drew's arm without thinking, clutching it so tightly my nails are sure to leave marks.

Shoot.

NINE

Raven holds up rock proudly. Faith weakly presents scissors, not making eye contact with any of us.

Josh and Nick jump up, hooting and hollering, just as the scoreboard finalizes the game's score.

Ding. Four to three. Josh's team wins.

I collapse back into my chair, both relieved and full of fear for what is to come. Sure, it's not my team's fate on the chopping block tonight. But what about tomorrow? And the night after that?

When will this end? How are we ever going to get out of here?

Drew gives my shoulder a quick squeeze as he gets up, following the rest of our team to one side of the room while we await more instruction.

"Faith still has to give a secret," Raven shouts above the commotion, arms crossed as she leans back against the wall. Geez, read the room.

Cady's team looks like they are all one second away from throwing up, Faith most of all. She hesitates, but still we wait. For minutes, it feels like we stand by for her to offer up whatever secret she might be holding onto within.

I can't imagine she has much else to tell that might have to do with this game. She already offered information freely this morning when she told us she's been here before.

"I'm on academic suspension because I couldn't keep my grades up in my first college semester," she says, eyes downcast. Something pings in the back of my brain. That feels way too easy, especially for someone who wants to be a nurse.

Before anyone can respond, the sound of clapping comes from speakers above us. "Well done, Houseguests. Please go back to your seats. We aren't done yet."

Someone's stomach growls as we sit, and as if on cue, the grandfather clock in the hallway chimes. Noon, already? Time doesn't exist here in the inner workings of this nightmare.

Raven pulls out her chair to my left, and I lean over to her, hoping she'll see me as a friend. "What did you say to Faith?"

She just glares at me, daggers in her eyes. "Why would I tell you?"

Taken aback, I just nod, accepting that she will not be someone I get information from.

For now, anyway.

"Josh, Winter, Nick, Drew, Kasey, Olsen, and Raven. Congratulations, you have won our first game, and therefore, you have survived to live another day."

Nick cheers obnoxiously again, as if he wasn't one of the points we lost. Idiot.

"Cadence, Reese, Cyrus, Stacey, Tatum, Adrian, and Faith. For one of you, this is where your time here comes to an end. A permanent one, might I add." The Voice laughs into the microphone, like our lives are just a joke to them. "Houseguests, here is how this will work. Tonight, dinner will be at 6:00 p.m., and I will call on you soon after. It will be at that time that *all* of you will vote for someone from Cadence's group. The person with the most votes will receive... special one-on-one time with me, you might say."

I shudder, mind racing with endless possibilities of what something like that could mean.

"Your vote will change everything. One of you will die tonight."

Eyes glance around the room, full of fear and resolve.

"Go. Eat, talk, make decisions. It won't be long before you hear from me again."

The intercom stops crackling, and the room seems to shrink in on itself. There is no way to escape, no true way to get out of here other than to play the game our captor has set for us.

A thought hits me with clarity. One of us *knows* why we are here. They *want* us to be stuck here. They *want* our lives on the line.

And it's not just that they know something we don't. It's that they think, for whatever reason, every person in this room deserves this.

They think I deserve this. Which means, in some way or some form, they *know* something.

And that changes *everything*.

We aren't fully strangers anymore. That much is true. But we're also suspects—every last one of us.

And victims. Victims of crimes we did not commit.

And victims of crimes we did.

TEN

Deli sandwiches don't taste as good when you're twelve hours away from death.

There is a divide now within our group of fourteen—*us* and *them*. What's not clear, though, is who will take the first step in initiating discussions regarding tonight's… circumstances.

Nervous anxiety permeates the dining room where we eat. Eyes glance back and forth, watching side conversations and body language. Faith can't stop sobbing. Cady's team's fate is held in our hands, and I've never felt less prepared for anything in my life. I'm not usually one to follow, but if someone wanted to rally the troops and tell us all who to vote for tonight, I might listen.

Reese won't stop pacing back and forth between the kitchen and the long dining table, offering sides, sandwich toppings, and more meat to anyone whose plate looks a little empty. I can't help but grow a little frustrated. His stress is stressing *me* out. And I'm supposed to feel safe tonight!

I lean over to talk to Olsen, maybe get a feel for where his head is at, when Faith clears her throat. "I know my confession earlier might mean that I'm the obvious vote tonight. But I wanted to give my reasons for why you shouldn't pick me."

A knife scrapes against a plate in a *screech*. "You basically placed yourself upon a silver platter that read 'pick me'," Raven deadpans. "You can't take it back now just because it's actually happening."

Faith pouts. "That was before I knew I would *die* tonight!"

Arguing once again ensues, and I can't help but wish for some peace and quiet. Drew catches my eye from across the table. Even though he's safe tonight too, he keeps rubbing his chest like he can't breathe.

I tilt my head at him, taking a deep breath in hopes that he will follow suit. My plan works, and I watch his chest rise and fall more slowly than it has been. He nods at me, and I make a mental note to try to talk to him privately later. If the Voice is making us play their games, I'll need allies. People I can trust to help me make it to the end. And Tatum and Drew are at the top of my list. Olsen too, as long as Drew thinks he's a safe person.

But Tatum could die tonight, and that would ruin my plans. Wincing, I push that thought deep, deep, deep down within me. I can't let that happen. I can't be thinking like that. Right now, my life isn't on the line. Therefore, I need to be someone who can protect those who are.

"I've seen stuff like this on reality shows before," Adrian quips. "No one ever kills the funny guy. The Voice even said it himself. So I'm safe."

"You can't dub yourself as the funny guy," Stacey remarks. "Literally no one here has said that you're funny."

"Yet," he responds, mouth quirked. He has a goofy smile, one side coming up higher than the other, so it always looks like he's smirking.

Stacey rolls her eyes, mumbling under her breath. It's like she doesn't know how to stop talking.

"I think everyone from Cady's team should make their

case as to why we shouldn't vote for them. That can help us make level-headed decisions," Kasey says.

Something shatters on the ground by the adjoining kitchen door. "Nothing about this is level-headed! You're crazy. You can't keep bringing logic into this!" Reese shouts. Apparently, he's reached his breaking point.

"I only want everyone to feel like they have a voice. A chance. If you could plead your case to a jury, and that plea meant the difference between life or death, wouldn't you take it?"

He grumbles, plopping down in an empty seat. "I'm just… so tired."

We all nod along, agreeing with him. We've been here for less than twenty-four hours, and yet, our whole lives have changed. One of us sitting at this table won't be here tomorrow.

Faith stands, straightening her spine in an attempt to demand attention from the room. "I know I told you all I've been here before. And that's true. But that piece of information helped us realize that we are still in the United States, with some of us not being all that far from home. I remembered something from my trip that could help us get out of here, and if you vote for me to die tonight, you'll never know what it is."

Alright, the threats have started. I like it.

Raven scoffs. "So what, are we just supposed to never vote you out? Because if you won't tell us how we can get out of here *now*, what's stopping you from withholding that information forever?"

"Yeah," Cyrus adds. "Why not get us all out before someone's head is chopped?"

Faith hesitates, her voice pitching. "I promise to tell you tomorrow?"

Nick laughs dryly. "Hilarious. Shut up, Faith."

She sits defeated, clearly thinking that plan was going to work.

"This is like that dumb board game," Adrian mumbles. "Mustard in the living room with the candlestick."

I tilt my head at him, waiting to see if that's all he has to say.

Shoving her plate to the side, Cady shifts in her seat. "Please don't vote for Reese or me. Our mother was murdered just a few years ago—we can't go through that again with each other."

She starts crying, and Reese places a hand around her shoulders. I don't like the guilt trip. It almost makes me want to vote her out *more*, just to see what would happen.

"I'm almost tempted to vote for Cady just so we don't have to hear her whine anymore," Raven mumbles. Tatum squeaks a laugh.

"So if we can't vote for Faith because she 'knows something'," Josh quotes. "And we can't vote for Reese or Cady because they're already 'traumatized', who's left? Stacey, Tatum, Adrian, Cyrus? You guys have anything to say?"

I'd be happy to vote for Josh tonight. It's too bad we were on the same team.

You already have blood on your hands. Do you really crave the feeling of more? My inner voice all but screams at me. I fight the urge to gag and place my palms underneath me so that I can't look at them. Now is not the time to spiral.

"Uh, I still believe there's a way out of here. And I bet I could find it if you choose to let me... um... live tonight." Cyrus clears his throat.

"I'm only eighteen! I haven't done a single wrong thing ever in my life. Ever. And I haven't had a chance to make it on Broadway yet."

I squint at the desperation in Adrian's voice, trying to decipher if it's believable or not. We're not here by accident. There's a reason we were all chosen—across many different states and backgrounds—to be here. He can't just be the comedic character. There has to be more underneath.

"I just really don't think I'm the reason we're here," Stacey shrugs, trying to act nonchalant. "Which means, if you kill me —which is what you'll be doing, may I remind you—you're going to be back in the same predicament tomorrow that you're in today."

Again, I look around the room, watching people consider her words. I think Stacey could be a number for me, if I needed her to be. If I don't make an enemy of her tonight, her chattiness might be the way I get the information I need as this goes on.

There's only one person left to offer their case, and my heart is in my throat while I wait for Tatum to say something.

Make it good, I plead internally, directing my thoughts toward her. *I need you to stay. For my sake and yours.*

It's as if time slows down while her green eyes pierce each and every one of us, slowly and meticulously.

"I'm pregnant."

ELEVEN

Nothing—*nothing*—could have prepared me for that.

"You're what?" Reese blinks.

Tatum folds her hands in her lap, voice trembling slightly. "You heard me."

Raven lets out a quick laugh, sharp and disbelieving. "Oh, come on."

Josh pushes back his chair. "You think we're going to fall for that?"

"I'm not asking you to fall for anything," Tatum snaps. It's the most direct I've heard her so far. "I wasn't going to say anything, but if we're all about to—if we're deciding who dies tonight—then you all should know it won't just be me you're killing."

"It's just a play for sympathy," Nick barks.

Tatum shrugs, but she's shaking underneath the motion. As everyone asks her a variety of questions—from when she's due to who the father is to the gender—I'm overwhelmed with the need to add my input.

"I believe her," I state. Her eyes meet mine, and the only thing I see within them is an immense amount of gratitude.

Good. Whether I actually believe her or not doesn't matter—her trust is what I need.

Josh rolls his eyes. "You would, little miss *reporter*."

I ignore the jab, pretending it didn't come from him. "Doesn't that make my opinion weigh more? Reporters deal with people making up things for a 'good story' all the time. And I believe her."

The silence that follows is heavy. No one says anything. It's as if we're all just waiting for another shoe to drop.

Kasey rubs her temples. "This is getting out of hand. We didn't get anywhere with this."

"It was *your* idea," Olsen wheezes. He's been incredibly quiet, and I'm hoping that's just because he isn't feeling good, and not because he has something to hide.

"What do you suggest then, bossy? That we should all just take a nap and hope we wake up from this nightmare?" Nick asks.

"Maybe we should take a break," Cady whispers. She has her hand on Tatum's arm in solidarity. "Before we say something we can't take back."

"We're strangers. I really don't care if I say something that hurts your feelings," Raven adds.

"Still," Reese interjects, always on Cady's side. "We should cool down a bit before we have to meet up again tonight."

"You mean before we vote on who's going to die," Drew deadpans.

"Just be happy it won't be you, pretty boy." Stacey flicks her blonde hair over her shoulder and saunters out of the dining room.

The rest of the group disperses unevenly, chairs scraping across old, wooden floors. The echo of footsteps fades down the hallway and up the stairs as I wait, hoping to catch Tatum alone somewhere. I could go to our room and see if she'll join me, but I'd rather be where people are talking.

So I can listen.

She gets up to leave, and I follow her out of the dining room. I'm about to whisper her name when suddenly, I'm nearly clotheslined by an arm blocking my path.

"Darling," Josh coos. "So good to get you alone."

Tatum disappears up the stairs without a look back, and disappointment swirls around in my gut. I try to keep myself from looking at Josh, but he's leaning in so close that I can't help it.

"You can't call me that," I snap. But then, to aggravate him, I muster a sweet smile, forcing myself to bat my eyelashes. "Did you need something?"

He shoves me on the shoulder, agitated. "Stop pretending you don't care. I know you do."

I grimace, dropping the act to look for a way around him. His free hand grabs my chin, forcing me to look him in the eyes, rendering me unable to pull away. When his thumb starts to move along my jaw, I fight back the urge to bite his finger.

"You've always been so pretty," he pouts.

I'm about to throw up on his shoes when my name is shouted from somewhere in front of me. I peek around Josh's stupid arm and spot Drew coming toward me from the library, questions and concern written across his face.

"Winter, hey. Olsen was hoping to talk with you. But if I'm interrupting something…" he trails off.

"You are," Josh snaps.

"You're not," I amend. "I'd love to talk with him. Josh and I can catch up another time. Right, Josh?" I give him a pointed look. I don't want this to be a big deal—us knowing each other. As much as I'd love to let people know *who* exactly Josh is, I don't want it to put a target on my back. Not here, not now, not yet. When I let other people in on this secret, it will be because it benefits *me*.

Josh gives me an annoyed glance, but he drops his arm and hand all the same. I give Drew a quick smile and take a few steps away from Josh to get to where he is.

A hand grabs my bicep, nails digging into my skin. I wince, pulling back, and turn around to tell Josh off. The look in his eyes chills me to the bone as he leans in to speak.

"You're not innocent," he whispers. "I know what you did."

And with that, he releases my arm, stalking back toward the kitchen as if nothing ever happened.

TWELVE

I plaster a smile on my face, shaking off the tremor that snakes down my spine.

"Sorry." I quicken my pace to get to Drew. "What does Olsen need?"

I follow him into the library. Immediately, I'm overwhelmed with the smell of pine and old pages. It smells just like my university's library, and I'm suddenly homesick. He stops in front of a bookshelf, looking back and forth, hand rubbing the back of his neck.

"Uh, about that. Olsen didn't actually say anything about talking to you. I just… I saw Josh grab your face, and you looked uncomfortable. I wasn't trying to eavesdrop or anything, I just happened to be leaving…"

Trying to keep a blush from spreading across my face, I put a hand in the air, stopping his ramble. "Thank you. Truly. I really appreciate you doing that."

He grins at me, hair falling in front of his eyes, a sparkle in them that wasn't present earlier today.

I shuffle toward two chairs in the corner and plop down. "So," I start. "How are you doing with all of this?"

He scoffs, choosing to sit on the floor in front of me,

clutching his knees close to his chest. "Not very good, if I'm being honest." He rubs his face, sighing. "I don't know why I told you that. I keep telling myself I need to put on a façade for everyone, but with you, it doesn't feel like I have to."

I nod. "It's the same way for me. I think it's because of your panic attack that first day. It's the most genuine thing I've seen out of someone since being here."

He lets a laugh slip, leaning back on his hands with his legs outstretched in front of him. "Maybe that was part of my ploy."

Winking, I lean forward. "I'm sure it was."

Drew laughs a bit freer now, and I join in, enjoying this little game we're playing. But soon enough, reality sets back in. He schools his features.

"So, you believe Tatum?" he asks.

I chew my bottom lip. "Yeah. I just think, if it was a lie, it's a bold lie."

He considers this. "So who are you going to vote for tonight?"

I shiver. "I hate acting so nonchalantly about all of this. This isn't us picking what we want to have for dinner—we're choosing who *dies* tonight. I don't want that responsibility on my shoulders."

"I can't even begin to fathom what kind of sick, twisted person is behind all of this. For your mind to work that way… something has to be seriously wrong."

His hazel eyes get a faraway look in them, glazed over almost, as if he's remembering something.

I hurry to speak to try and pull him out of it. "At this point, I don't know who knows anything. Everyone is up in the air. It could be me for all I know."

His gaze snaps back to mine, and as he tilts his head, his hair falls across his forehead. "You don't really think it's you."

I give him a half-shrug back. "For some reason or another,

we were hand-picked to be here. That makes everyone guilty until proven otherwise."

"I don't think it's you," he blurts. Then, as if wanting to make his point clear, he slows down his next three words. "For the record."

It's funny—he's acting as if he knows me. He knows nothing. I twist my mouth into something between a grin and a grimace. "Who do *you* think knows why we're all here?"

Drew pauses for a while, really thinking this question through. Finally, he says, "Faith seems like the obvious answer."

My eyes turn downcast. "The obvious answer is very rarely the correct one. But, she's all we really have to go off of right now."

"I'm going to keep my ears open to what everyone else is saying. If we're voting in front of each other… there's no need to put unnecessary targets on our backs by not voting with the group."

I quirk an eyebrow. "Our?"

He blushes, giving me an embarrassed grin. "I mean, if you want to work with me, I'd love to work with you. I understand if you don't, with the whole 'panic attack' thing and all…" he trails off.

This is better than I could have hoped for. *He* wants to work with *me*. I didn't have to approach him on my own. When I don't answer, he looks up, finding me standing above him instead of sitting.

I reach out a hand, offering it to my new ally. "Partners?"

He smiles, his large hand encompassing my own. "Partners."

We shake on it, and our hands linger a little longer than they should. Finally, I pull mine away, squatting to sit next to him now. We study the maroon walls and tall bookshelves, silent in the yellow glow of lamplight.

He breaks the silence. "Who else do you think is partnering up? I bet everyone does. Is that what Josh wanted to talk to you about?"

I can tell he's prodding a bit, wanting information from me about what was going on earlier. But even though we're allies now, that doesn't mean I can trust him with *that* yet. It hasn't even been a full day of knowing each other.

My fingers start picking at my nails absentmindedly. "No, I think Josh was just in the mood to bother someone. I'll bet he and Nick start teaming up. They seem to be cut from the same cloth."

"Do you think Reese and Cady will branch out and talk to anyone other than each other?"

"If they're smart, they will." I scoff. "They're lucky—they *know* each other. And unless there's some sort of sibling rivalry we don't know about, they'll be a tight duo until the end."

"Unless they get separated," Drew says, voice barely a whisper.

"Yeah," I purse my lips. "I'd like to work with Tatum and Olsen, too. I think at the beginning, the more people we have as numbers, the better. We need to secure our lives as best as we can."

"I agree. And not just because they're our roommates. They both seem like intelligent, level-headed people."

"Tatum's hot pink hair screams 'level-headed' to you?" I joke.

"She's clearly not afraid to express herself. That's an excellent trait to find in a person."

"Okay, Mr. Doctor. I trust your judgment."

"I'm not a doctor yet," he argues.

"You're closer to becoming a doctor than I am."

"Fair," he concedes, shaking his head back and forth. He looks at me as if studying my brain, heart, and soul all at once. "You make me forget reality."

My skin flushes, and I shrink back in on myself. His tone

sounds resigned, as if it's a bad thing rather than a compliment. "Sorry."

"No," he urges, placing a hand on my arm. "It's a good thing. Makes me think we might make it out of this with our brains mostly intact."

"I can't imagine walking out of this alive, if I'm being honest."

"I'm going to make sure you do."

The way he says it is so genuine, so insistent, that I nearly believe him. But belief in someone else isn't a luxury I can afford right now.

The grandfather clock starts to chime, and we look up, listening intently for what time it is.

Two chimes. Ten hours until one of us is gone for good.

"I might take a nap before dinner," I admit. "Maybe see if Tatum is up for talking a little. I want to feel clear-headed for our first night, so I can pay better attention to what everyone's saying and doing."

"That feels very journalist of you," Drew winks, standing up and offering me a hand.

I clasp his palm, letting him pull me from the ground with ease.

"I'll see you at dinner?" I ask as we walk out of the library.

"Sounds like a plan, Winter."

We split, and he walks toward the sunroom. I make my way toward the stairs, looking at him one more time before I head to the second floor.

Nothing in my gut is telling me he can't be trusted.

But if there's anything my high school experience taught me, it's that nothing is ever as it seems.

THIRTEEN

Tatum isn't in our room when I enter, so I make quick work of shedding my shoes and slipping under the cold covers. We don't have windows in our bedrooms, but I wonder, if we did, what I would see when I look out?

Is it still October? Or has the outside world not seen us in months? I didn't get a chance to check the window curtains earlier.

As I stare up at the white ceiling covered in ornate detailing, I wonder what my family is thinking. Do they know I'm missing? Or do they just assume I'm busy? We don't text all that often, anyway. My sister doesn't even have a phone. They probably aren't thinking anything of my silence.

I sit up quickly, a thought pouncing on my tired brain. I wonder if *all* of us have families who wouldn't think twice about our going radio-silent. It would be the easiest way to make sure no one is out searching for fourteen students across the United States who, all of a sudden, got kidnapped.

My hands itch for something to write on. I swing my legs over the side of the bed, wrenching open the nightstand to search for a pen and paper. First try, I strike gold. A maroon cloth palm-sized notebook stares back at me, a pen wrapped in an attached elastic loop.

Cracking open the notebook, I breathe in the fresh pages, fanning them in front of my face. There's nothing better in this world than a brand-new notebook. I write my first name inside the front cover, assuming that if I were to snoop through Tatum's nightstand, hers would have a matching book. Though I don't plan on letting this out of my sight, you can never be too careful.

On the first ruled-line page, in capital letters, I write:

QUESTIONS TO ASK:

And below it, I add my first.

– FAMILY DYNAMICS?

Writing this down fuels me, making me almost giddy at the prospect of being able to write down information and carry it with me. I slip back under the covers, lying on my side, clutching my new notebook against my chest.

If anyone is going to figure out what's going on and who's doing this to us, it will be me.

———

I wake to Tatum tiptoeing into the room, her bed creaking when she sits on it.

"Hey," I sleepily yawn, letting her know I'm conscious.

"Sorry, did I wake you?" she asks.

"It's probably about time for me to get up, anyway. How long until dinner?"

"An hour and a half or so." She stretches, pulling on her neck until it cracks.

I can't believe I slept, especially as hard as I did, for just over two hours. Apparently, my body and brain needed it.

My hands search my bed for my notebook, and my heart jumps in my throat when I can't find it immediately. I swing my arms wide, and my elbow collides with it. Relief floods my system. I sit up on my arm to pull it out of the safety of my covers.

"Look what I found," I start, offering Tatum a glimpse at my newest prized possession. "It was in my nightstand. I'd bet you have one, too."

She leans forward quickly, finding her own notebook. It's a twin of mine.

"I'm not really a note taker," she admits, blushing.

"That's okay, I can take enough for both of us," I offer.

"Us?"

"Yeah, I was hoping you'd want to work with me. Well, Drew and I. And probably Olsen."

Her smile brightens. "I'd love to. Thank you for trusting me. I'm not…" she pauses, searching for words. "I'm not the loudest, most rambunctious person in a room. But I'll have your back. I promise."

"I don't need *loud*. I need loyal," I wink. If she notices I don't return her sentiments, she doesn't say anything. Even though my goal isn't to betray or backstab her, I'm not one to make empty promises. "How are you feeling about tonight?"

"Like I have morning sickness again. Except this time, it's all-day sickness."

I frown. "I really can't imagine anyone would vote for you."

"Maybe not tonight. But later down the line, when all our other options run dry? Only one of us is getting out of here alive, Winter. And I really don't think it's going to be me." She places a hand on her stomach, rubbing it in soft circles, a faraway look in her eye.

I hop out of bed, slowly walking over to sit next to her.

"Let's go walk around together. Maybe we can find some clues that will help us get out of here." I tap my notebook with my pen, giving her a quick eyebrow wiggle.

She smiles softly. "I like that idea. I've been on the balcony. I needed some fresh air."

"We can go outside?" I exclaim, jumping up.

She nods. "I think it's the only place. It's enclosed by railing, but it was nice to get some sun on my face."

It's as if I'm a brand new person. I run back to my bed, sliding on my tennis shoes, ready to race out the door and down the hallway. She giggles at my enthusiasm, following behind me.

The minute I open the balcony door, I'm met with crisp fall air. The sun beams radiantly on my face behind fluffy clouds.

I groan, eyes shut, face tilted toward sunny rays like a sunflower. "This is exactly what I needed to feel human again."

I feel Tatum walk up beside me. "This property is massive."

Opening my eyes, I see what she means. There's an enormous expanse of land behind the house, spreading as far as my eyes can see. Colorful trees line the property behind a white picket fence. If you didn't know what was going on inside the house, you'd think this was a picture-perfect spot.

Light footsteps sound from behind us. "Hey, Kasey. Coming to enjoy the view?"

She looks back and forth between Tatum and me. "Yes. That was the plan. But I don't want to interrupt any conversations."

I shake my head. "We're just getting some fresh air."

Kasey stands to my right, breathing in deep. "So, Tatum. Do you think it'll be you tonight?"

Before Tatum can respond, surprise etched into her

features, I hold up a hand. "Whoa, that was ridiculously callous."

Kasey shrugs. "I'm just trying to understand what everyone's feeling. A good journalist knows how to ask the right questions, don't they?"

"A good journalist also knows when to stay quiet," I snap.

"It's okay, Winter." Tatum faces Kasey. "I don't think it's going to be me tonight. Faith basically offered herself up freely, and the Voice made that weird comment about Raven knowing why she's here. Which everyone has seemingly forgotten about, might I add. I haven't done anything to put suspicion on my name."

I keep my face toward the sun but nod along all the same, listening. She's a smooth talker.

"Yeah, we did kind of breeze over that Raven comment. Maybe it'll come up tonight."

I feel Tatum shrug. "Maybe it will, maybe it won't."

Kasey considers this. "I didn't mean to sound like a jerk. I'm just glad I'm safe."

I scoff, turning back toward both of them before I respond. "For now."

FOURTEEN

Reese serves us spaghetti for dinner, complete with buttered green beans and garlic bread.

"It's too bad we don't know who's being voted for *before* dinner. You know, so I can make their favorite meal as a last hurrah."

Eyes turn to look at him quizzically, and I'm surprised that it came out of his mouth at all. I can't help but cringe.

"You mean it's too bad we don't know who's dying tonight so they can have a death row meal?" Adrian asks, straight-faced.

Reese shifts, seeing our reactions. "Uh, yeah, I didn't mean for that to sound the way it did…"

I shake my head, focusing on my dinner. My plan for our first voting session tonight is to listen to what everyone else is saying and offering. Especially if Faith is the one people are gunning for, she might say *anything* to make us choose someone else.

And that information could mean everything.

I pat my back pocket, making sure my notebook is still there. I haven't told anyone else about the notebooks, other than Tatum and Drew. Drew is taking notes for both him and Olsen, as his hands have been really numb today.

We positioned ourselves around the large table so we could sit with a variety of different people. Unfortunately for me, Nick is to my left, and Stacey is to my right. Out of the corner of my eye, I see Josh sizing Drew up from beside him.

Nerves churn in my stomach. We don't know when the Voice will call us back to the game room, but we're less than six hours from midnight. This first pick—a murder, really—is *everything*.

And what if we pick the right person and we're already onto something? Will the Voice simply release us back into North Carolina and sentence us to live the rest of our days looking over our shoulders?

I gulp down the bile rising in my throat and take a bite of pasta. I hate to admit it, but Reese is really good at cooking.

Vote him out last, my inner voice says. *That way, you can eat good food every day.*

I shove that intrusive thought down, horrified that it came to my mind at all.

"Did anyone find anything new today?" Cyrus asks, mouth full. "I keep looking for a way out."

"I was thinking," Stacey starts.

"That's dangerous," Adrian jokes.

She stares daggers at him until eventually his smile fades.

"Anyway," she flicks her hair pointedly. "I was thinking… Maybe we shouldn't split up so much. Whoever's behind this has to be watching every move. We should show them we're a united front. Friends, even."

"Valid point. But if they're watching, they're probably also *listening*. Which means they just heard your grand plan."

Cameras, I think. *Microphones. Lots and lots of both.*

I'm going to need to tread lightly in my private conversations, and I *definitely* need to search our bedrooms.

Stacey rolls her eyes at Raven. "Okay, well, what if we just refuse to vote?"

"This, coming from someone who could be voted out tonight," Nick scoffs next to me.

"They'd probably just go ahead and kill us all if we don't play their games. Do you really want to risk all our lives?" Olsen asks, taking his time between each word.

"Don't give them any ideas!" Cady screeches.

"Face it—only one of us is leaving alive," Reese concedes. "Twelve, thirteen… what's one more death to them?"

"Maybe they're just really bored," Olsen wheezes. "If we offered them eternal friendship, maybe they'd let us out."

I almost laugh. What in the world is going on in his head?

"I don't remember ever watching a horror movie where the kidnapper just *let them out*," Kasey deadpans.

"Unless it was to chase them," Tatum adds.

The group falls silent, the tick of the grandfather clock echoing through the room.

"I just don't understand what they're waiting for," I murmur. "What do they want from us?"

"Maybe this is some sort of social experiment," Cyrus shrugs. "We're like rats in a maze, or whatever."

I shake my head. For some reason, that just doesn't fit the way I think the answer to all of this would.

How are the fourteen of us connected? Once I know that, everything else should fall into place.

I'm about to ask my first journalist question to the group when Drew speaks first. "We should be ready," he says quietly.

Raven snorts. "Ready for what?"

"For anything," he snaps. "As someone who's been in the midst of a life-or-death situation, something it taught me is that you can never expect what you don't expect."

I tilt my head, considering his words. He's giving us information about himself, but still withholding. I take out my journal under the table, flipping to Drew's page that I started earlier. Under his name, in the empty space, I write two things.

> **1. PANIC ATTACKS? "CAN'T DO THIS AGAIN"**
> **2. HAS BEEN IN A LIFE-OR-DEATH SITUATION**

Closing my notebook, I look up, catching his eye. He tilts his head toward the hallway. *Walk?*

I nod, grateful for the excuse not to go around and around with everyone again. As I finish dinner, the conversation dissolves into small clusters. I try to eavesdrop the best I can, but it doesn't seem as if anyone is really talking about anything of substance. I think for most of us, our situation still feels like an awful nightmare.

But at some point, we're going to wake up and realize it was real life all along.

FIFTEEN

My chair scrapes against the wooden floor as I get up to follow Drew out into the hall. It's darker than it was an hour ago, shadows pooling in the corners like spilled ink.

"You always this calm after being kidnapped?" he asks.

"Can't hear what others are saying if you're panicking."

He chews on the inside of his cheek. "Was that a dig at me?"

I smirk, trying to lighten the mood. "Maybe."

He laughs, rubbing the back of his neck. I think it might be a nervous tic of sorts, but I only notice him doing it when he's talking to me. "I thought we could set our plans before…"

I look around to make sure we're alone. Dropping my voice into a whisper, I lean in. "Have you talked to Olsen?"

He nods. "He's okay to vote for Faith if that's how people are leaning. But I told him we wanted to let everyone else decide first."

"Tatum and I are on the same page. Since she's the only one of the four of us that can be voted for tonight, I'm hoping we can stay quiet unless someone brings her up as an option."

He considers this. "We just need to remember that even

though we're safe from voting tonight, we might not be tomorrow. No need to put unnecessary targets on our backs."

"I agree."

Josh walks out of the dining room then, head on a swivel. When he spots me, forehead nearly touching Drew's in a secluded corner, I watch his body tense up. He pivots, about to head in our direction, when the intercom above us crackles.

My heart drops.

"Was that—" I whisper.

Before Drew can answer, the speaker comes to life.

"Houseguests," the Voice says. "It's time to return to the game room. The first vote is now underway."

My pulse thunders in my throat. Footsteps come from all directions, fourteen of us now huddled in the hallway, about to make a decision that will change someone's life for the worse.

Drew exhales slowly, giving my arm a quick squeeze. "I'm with you."

And yet, somehow, I've never felt more alone.

———

Around the table we sit. Josh, Nick, Kasey, Olsen, Drew, me, and Raven on one side. Cady sits next to Raven, with Reese, Cyrus, Faith, Adrian, Tatum, and Stacey finishing the rest of the circle.

The grandfather clock strikes 8:00 p.m., and the sudden chime makes my skin crawl.

"Houseguests," the Voice begins, tone cold and smooth. "Our roundtable sessions will go as follows: I will open the floor up for discussion. At that time, you may both accuse *and* plead your case. Once I feel all have been heard, we will transition into voting time. Everyone will vote, and the majority will rule. You must vote for one other houseguest, and one houseguest only."

The Voice pauses. "And let me remind you—only Cady, Reese, Cyrus, Faith, Adrian, Tatum, and Stacey may be voted on tonight. Houseguests, the floor is yours."

I sit still, waiting for someone else to speak first. Before time ticks by for very long, Nick slaps his hands down on the table.

"We've already discussed plenty. I don't need to hear anything else to know that I'm voting for Faith tonight. She's already been in this house before, which means she's gotta know something. And that's a good enough reason for me not to trust her."

Tears gather along Faith's eyelashes. I expect her to defend herself, but she stays silent. Perhaps she's already given up.

Murmurs of agreement ripple across the group. Raven pushes hard for Faith.

"She tried manipulating us from the very beginning," she urges. "Crying and letting us think she must have done some big, bad thing but only admitting that she came here on vacation? She's hiding something else. I don't trust that."

"Well, I don't trust you," Cyrus adds.

"But *I'm* not on the chopping block tonight. So keep your mouth shut."

I look at Drew out of the corner of my eye, and he gives me a subtle nod. Olsen is leaning back in his chair, but I know he's on the same page.

From across the table, Tatum looks to me for confirmation. I glance around quickly, making sure no one is watching me.

Faith, I mouth, making sure she knows how the rest of our little group is voting. Better to be seen as having numbers as opposed to being singled out solo.

"If I live tonight," Faith starts, clearly finding her courage. "If you don't vote for me, I promise to never vote for you."

"And what if none of us votes for you? Don't make promises you can't keep," Josh snarks.

"Okay, well, you guys don't even know anything! Which means you're—you're killing me for nothing."

"It's not for nothing," Kasey states, all business. "One less person to be suspicious of means one less opportunity to be wrong."

Faith looks at her, taken aback. "What does that even mean?"

"It means I'm voting for you too, Faith."

My chest pains for her as she slumps back into her chair, crossing her arms and refusing to make eye contact. It could be any of us in this situation, at any time. It could have been me tonight, and it could be me tomorrow. These games, and whether or not we win them, really do mean life or death.

"Houseguests, the time for talking is over. Please grab the chalkboard in front of you and write the name of the player you choose to vote for tonight."

I grab the board and a piece of chalk, hands shaking as I condemn her to death.

FAITH

I place it face down, scanning the room to watch facial expressions. Faith looks like she's one minute away from a breakdown. Adrian's sweating profusely. Cady and Reese's hands are intertwined.

Then I pivot to watching out of the corner of my eye at my team. Kasey sits with her hands in her lap, back straight and chin up. She voted fast. Nick has his arms crossed already.

Josh stares right at me, eyebrows furrowed, blue eyes burning a hole into my brain.

I shudder, snatching my gaze away.

The last chalkboard slams down onto the table.

"Houseguests, voting time is over. And we will start..." The Voice pauses, and I'm on the edge of my seat waiting for who will begin our first round.

Please don't let it be me. Please don't let it be me, I beg.

"With Josh."

SIXTEEN

Josh quickly sucks in air through his teeth. For a moment, he looks softer—almost like the boy I once knew.

My stomach curdles. The boy I once knew wasn't real. It was a lie, and he was full of nothing *but* lies.

His smirk returns, and his left dimple makes an appearance. He turns around his chalkboard slowly, clearly savoring this brief moment of attention and power.

"I voted for Faith. She's been here before, so she probably knows the person who owns it. Which means she could be in league with them for all of this."

Josh looks at Nick, supposedly assuming he'll be next. Nick clears his throat, placing his chalkboard face-up on the table. "I also voted for Faith, but I want to add onto what Josh said. I actually think Faith lied about being here for an Airbnb vacation—I think her parents own it and she's part of some sort of serial killer situation."

My eyes widen. I didn't think too hard about this first vote; I just wanted to go with the group. There didn't feel like any need to put an unnecessary target on my back so early.

I don't really think Faith is the person we should be voting for, but I only have so much to go off of. How much can you really know in twenty-four hours? This feels intentional, like the Voice wanted us to vote blindly at first. This little game… Whoever they are, they're enjoying it.

Blowing out a slow breath, I chew on the inside of my cheek. It's surprising to me that the boys even thought these points through. Are they truly convinced? Or are they just putting on a show?

And are Nick and Josh teaming up? Dread pools in my gut.

Kasey's next, elbows leaning on the table. "This is insane," she mutters, but she doesn't say anything else or refuse to go next. She just turns her chalkboard around gently, a grim smile on her face as she looks at Faith. "I voted for you, Faith. You didn't have to admit to us that you thought you were the reason, but you did. And that makes me think it might be true, and you were just hoping to gain sympathy. Or maybe even throw us off track with it. But it's not something I can easily forget."

Olsen's hands tremble as he shows his chalkboard. "Faith. She's been kinda wishy-washy in her emotions. Calm, but scrambled somehow. Makes me think she's trying to keep something else from us."

Drew's next, and while he pauses to take a breath, I take a moment to look at Faith. She's staring at the table, eyes full of tears, chest hardly moving. I can't tell if she's mad she got caught, or if she's resigned herself to her fate and is trying not to give in to the emotions that threaten to break through the surface.

Either way, my chest pains. It could be any of us at any given time. Nothing about this situation is fair. Nothing about this was something any of us expected.

Well, I guess one person *did* expect this. And I'm hoping it's the girl we're about to vote out.

"Faith. I honestly don't know what to think. But I've spent some time with people who were guilty of very bad things, and I've learned that they like to use distraction as a technique. If that's you, I see you. If it's not… then I'm sorry."

I tuck away Drew's words for something to mull over later. All eyes are on me as I wipe my sweaty hands on my denim jeans. I turn the chalkboard around, fingerprints all over the surface. "Faith," I say, bile in my throat. "I think maybe you're training to be a nurse to compensate for something." My own past and reasons for choosing my major echo in my brain. "You found Band-Aids for Cyrus' fists really easily that first day, and that's really all I have to go off of. I'm sorry, truly."

Before I've finished my apology, Raven cuts in, slapping her chalkboard on the table. She's so callous. "Faith. Faith. Faith. You're fishy, and you know it. You wanted to get us to look at it another way and feel bad for you, but instead, you're getting what you deserve."

Faith heaves, chest hitching as she does her best to hold back a sob. Still, she doesn't look up.

"Houseguests," the Voice interrupts. "Faith now has seven votes. One more vote, and she will be banished. Cady, your vote, please."

"Faith," she whispers. "I voted for you. Everyone else was and, I don't know. I just didn't have anything to go off of. I don't think we're right, but I don't think we're wrong about you, either."

And with that, we've condemned our first stranger to death.

"Faith, you have received the most votes and are banished from the house. Please stay behind to await further instructions. The rest of you—sleep tight, and don't let the bedbugs bite."

A chuckle is the last thing we hear as the intercom clicks off.

"So, that's just… it, then?" Adrian asks.

"She had the majority. Even if the rest of you voted for someone else, it wouldn't have mattered," Kasey states.

Raven salutes the group, leaving the room first. No one else makes a move to follow her.

"Should the rest of us share our votes?" Stacey asks.

I look around, gauging the rest of the losing team's reactions. Adrian shifts between the pads of his feet, as if restless, and Cyrus plays with the collar of his shirt. It seems unfair to talk about it in front of Faith, but what else can we do? If Faith doesn't have anything to do with all of this, we need all the information we can get.

And if people are willing to offer it up freely now, when we can check their words to make sure it's the truth, that's a luxury I can't afford to pass up.

"I voted for Faith too," Reese admits.

"Uh, yeah. Same," Cyrus says. The hesitation in his voice doesn't match his usual composed exterior. I quirk an eyebrow and look at his chalkboard out of the corner of my eye, but it's flipped over on the table.

Letting slip a quiet hum, I tuck that away for later. He shouldn't have any reason to lie, but… Again, I don't know these people. I can't trust my first impressions. And right now, my gut is telling me he's hiding something.

"Faith," Adrian squeaks.

Tatum nods. "Faith for me, too."

"And me. I'm sorry, Faith." Stacey walks over, leaning in from behind to give Faith a big hug. It's then that Faith's stoic demeanor breaks, and a waterfall of tears begins to overflow.

Most of us crowd around her chair to hug her. It might be the last bit of human contact she ever receives.

A tear slips out of my eye at that thought. The weight of our decision and what it means for her—it's too much right now. I can't imagine how she's feeling.

She sniffles, wiping snot on the back of her hand. "You guys should go. I don't want the Voice to get angry at you."

I hesitate, looking back and forth between a few of the girls. How can we just… leave her like this?

"It's okay," she musters a reassuring smile. "I really do hope you all get out of here. Truly. Figure out the truth." She waves her hand around, motioning toward the room.

We mutter our goodbyes, trying to act as if it's just a temporary separation. Realistically…

Well, I don't want to think realistically right now.

We shuffle out, the door clicking behind Cady once we're standing in the hall. We all pause for a moment, eavesdropping, but there's nothing to be heard. No screams, no more cries coming from Faith. Just stone-cold silence.

"I don't want to sleep alone tonight!" Cady cries. She's hysterical, snot bubbling while she tries to calm herself down. I place a hand on her back, rubbing in slow circles.

"Do you think the Voice would be mad if I switched rooms?" Reese asks the group, looking at his sister with the utmost concern. I watch others' reactions, but most of them just shrug. No one knows anything about this mysterious captor.

Someone does, my conscience reminds me. *And hopefully it's the person you just voted for.*

SEVENTEEN

When dusk comes, the house is quiet.

No one's seen Faith. The door to the game room is still shut, and none of us are brave enough to go in there and see what we might find.

I don't know how we're going to just wait patiently until morning.

The lights are working normally now, and the curtains—we found out this afternoon—are now movable. It's as if someone came in at some point and removed all the creepy, spooky details that were present at first. Whoever put this place together before our arrival wanted our first night to freak us out as much as possible.

And it worked. Very well, I might add.

A few of us are crowded in the upstairs hallway, freshly and not-so-freshly showered. Josh and Nick are who-knows-where, and Cady and Reese have been locked up in Cady's room since we left. Every once in a while, she lets out an ear-splitting cry. I wish I could say she's a pretty crier, but I'd be lying.

And I don't like to lie if I can help it.

Kasey comes up the stairs, spotting us sitting on the floor.

"About ten minutes until the clock will chime for midnight. We should probably get to our rooms."

My stomach twists. "I don't think I'm going to sleep tonight."

Tatum laughs nervously. "It won't just be tonight that I don't sleep." I lean my head on her shoulder, giving her the smallest bit of comfort that I can. At least she and I will be together. I can't imagine being Cyrus, Adrian, or Kasey right now, about to spend the night all by themselves.

"We've gotta be right, right? We'll be out of here tomorrow," Adrian says a bit hysterically, eyelids drooping. "The Voice will see that we figured it all out really quickly, and let us go."

"I don't think it's her," Stacey admits. "I don't think she actually knew anything, I mean. It just… doesn't feel right."

Silence is the only thing that responds to her statement. The group gets up slowly, and Tatum and I make our way to our door. Opening it, I'm about to follow her in when Drew whispers my name from across the hall.

I turn my head to look at him. He's leaning against his own doorframe, Olsen already inside. He's got one hand on the back of his neck, rubbing nervously.

"Stay safe tonight," he says.

My head nods on its own. "You too. Goodnight."

I close the door behind me, finding Tatum already under her bed's covers.

Taking off my socks, I throw them on the floor of the closet and click the lamp off.

My heart thunders as I stare at the dark ceiling.

"Tell me something," I say to my roommate, and to the endless black forming in front of my eyes.

"My favorite color is yellow," she says. "And I miss the sun."

I hear her change positions, rustling around on her bed. "You?"

"I miss homework. Bad coffee, classes, professors who sometimes have no idea what they're talking about. I love what I'm studying, but I've never wanted to go back more than I do right now."

She snickers a bit, a soft sound.

"What's your family dynamic like, Tatum?"

I hear her exhale, long and slow. After a few minutes of silence, I've convinced myself she either fell asleep or she doesn't want to answer my question.

"Messy," she answers finally. "I don't talk to my parents anymore. Haven't for a few years."

It might just be one person's answer, but it confirms my earlier suspicions. In the morning, if we aren't freed, I need to start asking questions. *Especially* this one, regarding people's families.

I look toward where Tatum is now snoring softly. I need to start with the people I want to work closest with. Olsen, Drew. If I'm going to make it out of here alive, I need to lean into the idea of trusting a few select individuals.

Sighing, I roll back onto my back. My body won't relax, and my brain won't rest. I keep replaying the voting table over and over—people's reactions, mostly. The things they said, and the things they didn't. Cyrus lying about who he voted for. But most of all, Faith's last minutes with us. Each time I revisit those memories is just a desperate attempt to make sense of something that probably never will.

I don't do well with things that don't make sense. There has to be a reason for everything.

My eyelids droop as I fight the pull that sleep has for me. But in the end, I lose the battle.

―――

My breath catches, something startling me awake.

Covered in sweat, I sit up, immediately looking toward

Tatum's bed. She's still, breathing quietly, one hand on her stomach.

Relief floods my chest. I'm glad she's getting some sleep. She needs it.

Once my breathing calms down, I flop back down onto my mattress, hair sticky on my forehead.

I close my eyes again, ready to attempt to succumb to sleep once again, when a faint sound catches my ear.

Holding my breath, I incline my head toward the door, listening intently.

Nothing.

I wait, patient, body and breath frozen from any sudden movements.

Just as I'm about to give up on listening, I hear it again.

There—just a sliver of something.

A sound I recognize.

A scream.

DAY THREE

EIGHTEEN

I blink away the sleep in my eyes as I look toward Tatum's empty bed. It takes a second for me to remember my circumstances. More importantly, what today is.

The day after our first elimination.

I rush to the bathroom, thankful it's empty, heaving over and over as dinner leaves my system. The taste of pasta sauce and cheese leaves an icky feeling in my mouth as I rinse it out with mouthwash.

Splashing cold water on my face and getting ready, I head straight for Drew's room. I pound on his door, not worried about waking him and Olsen up. If Tatum's up, they should be too. We all should be. I can't risk others sharing information and us missing it.

I cringe at my train of thought. Controlling circumstances, especially with the hope of gaining information, has always been a weakness of mine.

Light peeks through the balcony door, and I almost rush toward it, desperate for the feeling of something normal.

My fist nearly collides with Drew's face as he swings the door open, hair dripping wet.

He looks alarmed. "Hey, you okay?"

I exhale, calming my heart rate. "Just didn't want to go downstairs alone. Tatum is already out of bed."

He nods, chewing on his cheek. "Let me get dressed, and we can walk down together."

It's then that I register what he's wearing. My eyes drift toward his wet t-shirt and the towel slung around his waist.

I snap my gaze back up to his face, blushing. "Are you… Did you…" I clear my throat. "Were you in the shower?"

He runs his hand across the back of his neck. "Yeah. I thought it might be an emergency."

I gulp, embarrassed. "Uh, no. Sorry. I'll just… Come get me when you're ready."

Spinning on my heel, I stalk toward the balcony door, not bothering to turn around to see if he went inside his room or not.

My hands are shaking as I stalk through the hallway near the door. Stupid, stupid, stupid! I'm stuck in a life-or-death situation. I shouldn't be blushing around a possible suspect! And would it have killed him to put on some pants?

I chastise myself mentally. I never realized how many phrases use the word 'killed' until being one step away from being murdered against my will.

A few minutes go by before Drew comes to collect me, and I've since composed myself once again. A little crush isn't a bad thing—I'm human, after all. And if he feels the same way, it might make it easier for me to get information out of him. Even though I think I can trust him, I can't rule anyone out.

Not that I want to manipulate or take advantage of him, of course. I just want honesty.

Especially if we aren't freed today.

When we reach the dining room, it looks like everyone else is already there at first glance.

But no Faith. A ping of sadness bounces around in my head.

"Where's Cyrus?" Drew asks. I look around, sure that

Drew is wrong, and I was right in thinking everyone was already here. But upon second glance, no Cyrus. Odd.

Reese chews on a granola bar. "I don't know. I slept in Cady's room. He's probably still in bed."

"Morning," I croak, sitting next to Stacey. She's been a little off ever since we voted out Faith—rougher, almost. And I want to get to know her a little better.

She gives me a curt nod, hardly looking up from her eggs.

Okay, then.

I try again. "What's your favorite color?"

She shoots me a glare. "We just killed Faith last night, and you're asking me what my favorite color is?"

It does feel ridiculous. "You're right. Let's cut right to the chase—what's your relationship with your family like?"

Stacey meets my question with a quizzical expression. "I love my family. They're my best friends."

Going back to her eggs, she angles her body so that her shoulder is blocking my view of her face. Interesting.

We converse in small talk for a bit, all of us waiting for what is to come. We have no sense of direction, no clue how all of this works. If I'm forcing myself to find a bright side to all of this, it would be that if we weren't right about Faith, we at least have a sense now of how all of this works.

So we can do better next time.

But if we were right about Faith… maybe we can get out of here decently unscathed. And surely we'd be reunited with her too, right? If she's the one with information, she must mean something to the Voice. So they wouldn't *actually* kill her.

I sigh, putting my fork down on my plate, having not eaten a single bite. There's no way of knowing. And I'm not great with uncertainty.

The air feels silently heavy, like the house is also waiting for what's next. But really, if these walls could talk, the house would tell us what we already know. And what a gift that would be.

Should I mention the scream I heard last night? I could probably bet I wasn't the only one who noticed it. I'm not usually a light sleeper, but circumstances call for things that aren't natural to us. It sounded far enough away that it could have been a boy or a girl, but my gut is telling me it *had* to be Faith.

Right?

Who else would be screaming in the middle of the night? And what made her scream like that? What goes on behind the closed game room doors after we vote?

Will we ever know?

I rub my pounding temples. I'm confused and annoying myself with all these unanswered thoughts. It's too early for questions like this, and yet it's necessary.

"Winter," Nick snaps. I look up, tuning back into my surroundings. He's staring at me expectantly.

"Oh, sorry. What?"

"I was asking what you do in your free time at school," he offers. Everyone else is looking my direction.

"Um, study?" My voice pitches up like it's a question. I wasn't prepared to be interrogated. Not yet. I thought… Well, I thought we'd know by now. What is taking the Voice so long? "Has anyone tried the doors yet this morning?" I ask, changing the subject. "Maybe we were right, and we're supposed to just walk out."

"I did," Kasey says. "Nothing."

I slump, defeated. My foot taps absentmindedly, impatience getting the better of me. Maybe the Voice is waiting for Cyrus to get down here. Where is he anyway?

"Houseguests," the Voice calmly interrupts any remaining conversation. We all sit up, eager, ready to listen and hopefully be released. "Please report to the game room immediately."

Wide-eyed, I look at Drew, a confused expression on my face. His eyebrows furrow in response, a slight shrug in his shoulders. Lost, I realize. He looks lost. And scared.

"I don't like the sound of that," Adrian whispers.

NINETEEN

The game room is colder than it was yesterday. The scoreboard sits dark, turned off, and unused.

By chance, we all sit in our unassigned assigned seats. Cyrus and Faith's chairs stare back at us, glaringly empty.

"Where do you think Cyrus is?" I whisper to Raven.

She shoots me a mean side-eye. "Hopefully dead."

I'm so taken aback by that comment that I stutter. "Uh, wh—what?"

Raven just shrugs. "I thought he was annoying."

"You think *everyone* is annoying," I respond pointedly. What is her problem?

"Good morning," the Voice begins. "I'm sure you're all anxiously wanting to know if you were correct last night."

No one answers.

"Before we get to that, I'd like to know if there's anything *new* you have noticed today. Perhaps something… out of the ordinary."

"Where's Cyrus?" Reese asks. Cutting right to the chase, then. He's holding onto the edge of the table, as if for stability, but still trying to paint on a brave exterior for his roommate.

"Ah, you're finally asking the right questions, Reese."

A shiver runs up my spine.

"What happened to him? Is he okay?" Cady asks hurriedly. There's a twinge of guilt in her tone. I wonder if it's because Reese slept the night in her room, which meant Cyrus was left to his own devices.

"Unfortunately, Cyrus has experienced an unexpected extraction from the house."

Gasps collectively sound from around the table. Suddenly, it's really hot in here. Sweat runs down my eyebrow into my eye, and I blink the drop out of my eyesight.

"So, wait. We weren't right about Faith?" Stacey directs her question toward the ceiling. "You changed the rules! It's supposed to just be one person per night!"

A chuckle sounds over the intercom. "You misunderstand me—I can change the rules at *anytime*." They pause. "And no, you were not correct. Faith was the wrong choice, and she has met an untimely death because of your votes."

Before any of us can cut in and ask more questions, the Voice continues. "Cyrus attempted to remove himself from our game last night. Because he escaped the house, I had no choice but to take care of him. Both he and Faith are permanently gone. The rest of you are now *two* houseguests closer to figuring out this mystery. Consider yourselves lucky."

"He got out," Drew whispers to me. "Of the house. That means there's a way."

"Let me be clear," the Voice shouts, silencing the whispers that were spreading like wildfire. Our attention is captured once again. "Cyrus' escape route has been dealt with. And should any of you attempt the same, you will meet the same fate."

You could hear a pin drop. No one moves a muscle; no one dares breathe.

It's as if I can hear our captor smile from wherever he's watching us all. Peering, studying, memorizing.

"I will see you all this afternoon for our next game."

And with that, the intercom clicks off, the incessant buzzing of the speakers quiet once more.

———

No one moves. It reminds me of a military movie I can't recall the title of, when the soldier steps on a landmine and must do everything they can to stay as still as possible, or else they'll be blown to pieces.

The only difference is that *we* are the ticking time bomb. And our lives have already been ripped apart.

"What did we know about Cyrus?" I ask, breaking the silence. "Maybe he had figured something out. Anything you know might help us."

"All I know is that he was trying to get his pilot's license," Olsen wheezes.

"He was in the system," Reese cuts in, eyes downcast. "His parents were physically abusive. He ran away at thirteen after a bad run of foster families."

Cady sniffles. I tuck that information away. His family *definitely* wouldn't be looking for him if he were to vanish. Stacey is now an outlier in that regard.

"He was training to be a pilot so he could see the world," Reese finishes. He's grim, skin tone turning a sickly shade of green.

"This is sick," Tatum states. "First, they make us pick Faith. She dies for *nothing*. Then they take someone else? Just because he was smarter than them?" She scoffs, raising her voice toward the ceiling. "Should have thought of all the escape routes before dropping us into this stupid house!"

"It could have been any of us," Kasey adds. "He was left alone. He did what we wish we all could have done. It's too late for him, and for Faith. But it's not too late for us."

I can't stop staring at Cyrus' empty seat. Could he have been the scream I heard last night? He got out. He escaped from this nightmare we've been thrust into. And this is what he gets? He should have had *freedom*. A fresh start, a second chance.

He didn't deserve this. He had already been dealt a bad hand.

"It wasn't Faith," Stacey mumbles, head in her hands. "Which means we're all guilty of killing an innocent person. We're murderers!"

"I hate to be the one to say it, but we're going to be guilty of more than just her death by the end of all this," Nick says. He looks around the room at our appalled faces. "What? No way we're figuring this out. We're screwed."

A stone sinks deep into my stomach.

"I mean… What if Cyrus found more than just an escape route?" Adrian asks the group. "What if he found out what we're doing here? Or how they chose all of us?"

That thought pings around in my brain. I don't hate the idea, but I do hate the hope that's emerging within me.

"We need to turn this house upside down," I whisper to Drew. I don't raise my voice to the group because I still don't know who the person on the inside could be. I don't want any chances at finding information to be thwarted. And while I don't trust Drew completely yet—there's no way I could—I do think he's my best bet at helping me with this.

He nods in agreement, not making eye contact with me. Good.

Today, we'll make a plan for how to go about it. We can't be too sneaky, or that will raise suspicion. But we also can't freely search in the open. After all, the Voice is watching.

And if they come for me, I want to be ready.

Because if they can just take us in the middle of the night without any of us knowing how or why, I need to know how to stop it.

Before I'm their next target.

TWENTY

We stumble out of the game room in a daze.

Suddenly, unexpectedly, there are only twelve of us left.

Drew and I don't speak until everyone else scatters—some heading upstairs, others whispering urgently to each other in corners of other rooms. As much as I would love to join in on those conversations right now and glean from what people are saying, I have a different agenda to attend to.

I see Josh watching me from where he's shoving Nick around. He looks like he could pounce on me at any moment, but I do my best to make sure I'm never alone. Right now, Drew is my scapegoat.

I lean against the wall of the hallway, hands shoved deep into my jeans pockets. "Where do you want to start?"

Drew tilts his head, thinking. "What about where all of this started?"

I nod. "The parlor it is, then."

We creep across the hall, entering the room.

The first thing I notice is the portraits.

"Look!" I exclaim, my voice croaking as I rush over to point. "Cyrus and Faith are marked out."

A big red 'x' covers their faces, semi-fresh paint dripping down the glass.

Drew reaches out to touch it. "It had to have been done really late last night, or early this morning."

"Did the Voice do this? How did they get in here?"

Drew looks around the room. "I want to check the fireplace."

I cover him from wandering eyes as he moves in front of it, kneeling in the dusty soot. It looks like it hasn't been used in years. I survey the rest of the portraits from where I'm standing as he looks, but nothing catches my eye. All the photos look like something someone cropped and zoomed in on way too far.

Drew's photo is cute, honestly. It looks like he's got his arms around someone on either side of him, but they're cropped out of view. His smile is wide, free.

"What's your picture from?" I ask without meaning to.

Drew shoots a quick look up at his portrait, then resumes what he's doing. "Tennis buddies."

I stifle a laugh. "You played tennis?" For some reason, it doesn't fit my perception of him. He's all academics and thoughtfulness—not that tennis players couldn't be those things, I guess. I don't know, feels like a weird sport to be into.

I've never tried it, though.

"All my life," he offers. Then, he tries various bricks, pulling and tapping in methodical ways. Finally, he crawls into it, looking up toward the chimney.

"It's blocked off," he says, voice echoing. He reverses his way out, wiping his hands on his jeans and brushing off the evidence.

"That's going to leave a stain," I smirk.

"Good thing I have multiple pairs just like these," he quips.

I reach out a hand without thinking, using my thumb to wipe off a black smudge from his chin. His breath hitches, and my eyes jump to his. There's still something so guarded in his hazel gaze, and everything in me desires to crack open the box he hides things in.

Drew clears his throat, and I remove my hand from his face as if burned.

"Sorry," I blush. "You had something on your face."

"Thank you," he chokes.

I look over the rest of the room, nothing truly standing out. It feels fresher in here than it did the night we woke up. There has to be some sort of secret passage or something if someone came in to mark up those portraits.

Or the person working with your captor did it, I think. Not a terrible thought, but something that would be incredibly risky to pull off night after night. Although... it *is* required of us that we be in our rooms overnight. Cyrus is proof of that.

A half-hearted idea to sneak out of my room one night forms in my brain before I shove it away. I can't risk my life like that yet. Maybe I can come back to that later.

We search a few more rooms, careful to avoid the ones others are in, so we don't raise suspicion. Climbing to the second floor, I suggest we get some fresh air before figuring out what we want to do next.

I enter the balcony first, and immediately, something feels different.

Drew gasps. "This has to be it, Winter. This is how Cyrus got out."

He reaches out a hand to touch the netting that now encloses the entire balcony. It's thin, but tight as a cage around the space. There's no room to wiggle through the railing, and there's no chance of getting on top of the roof.

I wish I had thought about the roof access yesterday—why wasn't I looking harder for a way to escape? Shock shuts off parts of your brain. I wasn't as quick to think, and it shows.

Lost opportunity.

"Do you think he jumped?" Drew starts. "Or climbed?"

I peer below, sizing up the drop. "Jumped for sure. Probably made a run for the woods out back."

Drew nods. "Which means they have people stationed out there. They watched him, were ready, and caught him."

"Who are we kidding," I breathe, turning toward the small camera under the roof watching our every move. "They probably have people *everywhere*."

He looks at me sharply, but doesn't comment. For a long minute, we just stand there, the netting swaying with the slight breeze. I imagine Cyrus out here last night—what he saw, what he did. The fear he must have felt...

A shiver runs down my spine that has nothing to do with the chill in the air. I bury my head to my chest, resigning myself to head back inside. Drew follows soon after.

"I just keep thinking about them," I whisper.

He rubs the back of his neck. "Me too. And about our next game."

"I hope we're on the same team." I clutch my forearms, rubbing them to bring some warmth back into my skin.

"If we're not, I'll have your back. I won't be writing your name down, no matter what."

I offer him a pinky, and he takes it with his. I shouldn't be making promises like this yet, but I can't help myself. "No matter what."

———

After lunch, I sit on my bed with the lights off, listening intently to the surrounding sounds. The house hums faintly—pipes working, wind hitting the sides, electricity in the hallway buzzing. I close my eyes, imagining Cyrus and Faith's faces, not letting myself forget them.

I'm sorry, I think. *I should have done more for you.*

My thoughts shift unwillingly to an older memory. To a picture of someone else that I won't let myself forget.

Curly hair and dark eyes. A picture-perfect smile.

Reagan.

The scene shifts to a day I'll never forget—the day after the headline came out. The way everyone stopped talking when I walked by. The threats, the messages. My parents pulling me out of school…

I open my eyes, spine straight. Without bothering to put my shoes back on, I rush out the door and downstairs, my thoughts on the parlor. I pass Tatum and Stacey on the stairs, nearly knocking them over. They exclaim, Stacey shooting cuss words in my direction, but I ignore it.

I'm out of breath when I finally reach the wall of portraits once again, but adrenaline is carrying me. I find my picture once again, and something I haven't felt before settles in my chest.

I was right.

My portrait—I recognized it as a picture I posted on social media, which is true. But what's *also* true is that this picture isn't supposed to exist anymore.

This photo is from *before*. Before everything went wrong. Before I became a player in a game I didn't ask to be part of.

Which means the Voice knows what happened.

I gulp. And if they know that…

That means they know my real name.

TWENTY-ONE

I try to push my worry down deep within me as I stumble into the office. I lie down on the cold ground, trying to count my breaths. Every sound is amplified—the shift of the air vents, the faint hum of lights.

Plugging my ears, I close my eyes tight, willing away the fear that threatens to drown me.

I should have asked Drew to come with me. I shouldn't have checked my hypothesis alone. But I did, and there's no turning back now that this information is mine to hold.

I pinch my eyes shut tighter. If I had brought Drew, I would have to explain why I'm reacting like this to something that seems so simple. So I guess there's a blessing there I didn't see before.

It's only been a little over a year, but everything from before should have been erased.

But maybe what they say about the internet is true. Once it's out there, it's out there forever.

I lay my hand on my chest, forcing deep breaths. I'm okay. Just because they have an old picture of me doesn't mean *I'm* the reason why we're all here.

It doesn't mean *he* is the one doing this to us.

Across the hallway, doors open and close. I hear footsteps coming this way, then they stop and turn around, the sound growing distant with every step.

I sit up, listening, but I can't hear anything else from in here.

I'm about to get up and survey the office when the crackle of the intercom above me makes me wince.

"Houseguests," the Voice says. "Meet me in the sunroom. It's time for our second game."

———

We file into the sunroom like we're walking into a courtroom.

Unfortunately for me, I know what that feels like.

I pile onto one of the couches next to Cady and Reese. They're joined at the hip as always, and I hope that doesn't work against them. I could see some of us voting against one just to split them up.

If I'm being honest, I could see *myself* voting against them because of that. They have an advantage in this game, having someone they've known for longer than just two days here, whether they see that or not.

As if he can hear my thoughts, Josh catches my eye. He's definitely an example of someone you can't trust, even if you've known them most of your life.

Sunlight bleeds through the glass wall, giving off the illusion that it should feel warm. But it doesn't. Instead, it feels like I'm sitting under a spotlight.

Once we're all in a seat, the speakers come to life once again.

"Welcome to your second game, houseguests. Once again, you will be split into two teams. Each round, one player from each team will step forward. You will both be asked the same question. Once you answer, the opposing team will guess whether they think you're lying or not. If they're correct, they get a point. If they're not, your team gets a point. The team with the highest points will remain safe. The losing team…" There's a long pause. "Well, you already know the stakes."

"Do we have to answer?" Nick asks from the floor.

"If you refuse to answer, your team will immediately lose the game in its entirety."

I shudder. Not only do we have to trick the opposing team, but we also have to trust each other not to forfeit the game for us.

The person who is responsible will make their team lose, my brain squeaks.

I shake my head. That would be too easy, too noticeable. The person who knows things will make this as hard for us as possible. They've been preparing for this, planning for who knows how long.

Whoever they are, they're ready to put us through the wringer.

———

We split into two teams, with Reese and Cady chosen as captains this time. I'm glad to split them up, but I also feel bad. Cady did *not* want to be a team captain again.

But it was all of us against her. And the majority rules.

Reese chose first, picking Adrian, Raven, Kasey, Nick, and me. Cady's team has Stacey, Drew, Olsen, Josh, and Tatum.

Anxiety claws at my chest that all three of the people I trust the most are on the opposite team. If Cady's team loses, there's a high chance that I'll be saying goodbye to one of them tonight.

The first round begins, Tatum and Nick up first.

"Our first question," the Voice says. "Have you ever caused someone's death?"

"Yes," Tatum answers quickly, voice small.

"No," Nick states. He's got a wide grin on his face, like this is all just fun and games.

We're given thirty seconds to decide as a team about Tatum's answer.

"I think she's telling the truth," I offer. At this point, three days in, I think I know her best out of everyone here. Like me, I don't think she'd lie unless she had to.

No one objects. "Okay, we can go with that if you really think so."

I nod. We wait for the other team to stop talking. I have no idea if Nick is telling the truth or not, and I'm thankful for a brief moment that he's on my team.

Something rings above us, cutting off conversation.

"Time is up. Captains, your answers?"

"Tatum is telling the truth," Reese states. *Ding.* Relief momentarily floods through me. We were right. But that feeling only lasts so long when I realize the horrible truth. Tatum has been responsible for someone's death before.

My first question is, I wonder if she would tell me about it? That thought feels so gruesome, but the more I know about these people, the better.

"And Nick is also telling the truth," Cady responds. I look at her teammates' faces, and none of them seem confident in that answer.

Buzz. Incorrect. Our team gets the first point, and I pull out my notebook while a mixture of celebration and frustration coats the room. Nick's laugh reverberates in my brain at tricking the other team. I won't fool myself—there's no way he's going to freely offer me information about the death he was responsible for.

GAME TWO

TATUM AND NICK: HAVE BOTH BEEN RESPONSIBLE FOR SOMEONE'S DEATH. HOW? WHEN?

Nick stumbles back to our side of the room. He sits on the floor, his laughter fading with every second.

The group will have questions for him later, I'm sure. For now, we're just focused on winning.

Josh and I stand up for round two. Of course, it just had to be me against him.

"Have you crossed paths with anyone here in the past?"

My eyes widen. *No*, I think. No, no, no, no, no. How did they—

Josh gives me a little smirk, but I can tell the question has shaken him, too. It's in the slant of his eyebrow and the lack of gleam in his eye. I hate that I can still read him, that knowing what he's feeling is still second nature. But when knowing those things meant survival at one point, it's not so easily forgotten.

It doesn't matter if I lie or tell the truth. Either way, everyone will know that there is someone here from my past. But the same could be said of Josh, and that could be very dangerous for both of us. If that secret gets out… it could put targets on both of our backs.

I have to answer first. What would the other team believe more? That has to be how I answer this. My team needs these points. I can't think of anything else—just them. Me. Our survival.

Drew, Tatum, Olsen, my brain chants. I shut it down.

"No," I answer quickly. Maybe too quickly. Only time and their answer will tell.

Josh smiles. "No," he says slowly, dragging out the 'o'.

Our teams debate quickly, but I can't focus on what they're saying. I just want to turn around and scream at them that he's *lying*. But Josh is probably thinking the same thing. And how would I know he was lying if I didn't know him before this?

I can't tear my eyes away from his as we await their

answers. There's a gleam in his eye again, like he knew this was coming.

It's like I'm struck. *Did he?* Josh knew me before. He knows who I am. He knows my *name*.

He would have had access to that photo. In fact, I'm sure I sent it to him at one point.

My blood runs cold. Is this just a scheme to get back at me? I've paid my debt. My life has already been ruined.

The ring sounds. "Winter is telling the truth," Cady offers first. A buzz goes off, marking that as incorrect. They groan. I keep my eyes away from my friends and their reactions, not wanting to give anything away. Instead, I keep my eyes on Josh, jaw firmly set.

Please say he's lying, I beg to anyone who might be listening. *Please.*

"Josh is… also telling the truth," Reese says, voice quiet.

My shoulders slump in defeat before the buzz sounds again. It's an action that could cost me everything, but I can't help it.

Incorrect.

"No points for either team," the Voice barks.

Kasey and Olsen are up next.

I can almost hear the Voice smiling behind the intercom. "Do you know why you're here?"

TWENTY-TWO

I watch the rise and fall of Kasey and Olsen's chests. Kasey's is steady, whereas Olsen's breathing pattern starts to pick up a little bit. Nerves? Or fear?

Picking at my nails under the table, I wait for their answers.

"No," Olsen squeaks. He looks like he's struggling to get air in.

"No." Kasey shakes her head, spine straight, looking past Olsen toward the view outside the windows. The sun continues to reach toward us, as if inviting us into a welcoming embrace we can't reciprocate.

"He's lying," Raven urges our group. "What are the odds that he doesn't have *some* sort of idea?"

Adrian considers this. "I mean, I don't have any idea why I'm here."

I look at him, eyebrow quirked. He rushes his words when he's scared. It's as if, when he has a second to put on a character and play a part, he's as confident as can be. Otherwise? Not so much.

"What?" he asks the group. "I don't!"

Nick scoffs. "Right. Anyway, I say he's lying just like Adrian is right now."

"I'm not lying!"

Reese holds up a hand, silencing Adrian's cries. The other team is staring at us, clearly trying to hear what the commotion is. They must have come up with their answer already.

I hate being last.

"Olsen is lying," Reese says.

Buzz. Wrong.

I take out my notebook quickly, flipping to my earlier page.

OLSEN DOESN'T KNOW WHY HE'S HERE.
<u>BUT HOW WOULD THE VOICE KNOW THAT?</u>

I can't help the groan that leaves my throat. Frustration is not my friend—I make irrational choices when I'm frustrated. So instead, I underline that last question, marking it as something I'll need to come back to.

When I'm calmer.

Maybe Olsen can help give me some insight into that. I feel relieved knowing that he's on my little team. And I think —hopefully?—he would be honest with me.

Or at the very least, with Drew. Who could then relay it to me.

This feels like a messy group project I didn't ask to be a part of. Everyone always expects me to do everything myself. Which is fine, I guess. My control issues feed off of that.

I tune back into the other group's reactions. Cady looks shocked, eyes wide. She stumbles as she gives their answer. "Uh, we think Kasey is lying, too."

Ding. Point, Cady's team.

They celebrate for a moment, but then the room goes quiet as both Olsen and Kasey sit down.

Kasey knows why she's here. And yet, she hasn't offered

that bit of information to us. Is that because she doesn't want to be seen as a target? Or is that because she *is* our target? Faith offered up information freely, and we killed her for it.

I guess I can't blame her.

There's no time to ask, and no time to come up with hypothetical answers.

Because Drew and Raven are next. And our score is one to one.

"Has death ever had its hands on you?"

It's as if the room's temperature drops twenty degrees. First of all, that's a weird way to phrase that question. Second, the fall sun shining through the windows disappears behind gray clouds, leaving us in a bleak darkness.

Drew's gaze flicks to me once—something fragile in his eyes. I take a deep breath, hoping he will follow suit. I don't know for sure that a panic attack was incoming, but just in case.

"No," Raven answers quickly.

"Yes," Drew breathes, shutting his eyes for just a moment to focus on his breathing.

I look at him as my team starts to discuss, peering into his soul. He makes eye contact with me again and gives me a quick nod. It's so subtle that if you weren't looking for it, you wouldn't have seen it.

"He's telling the truth," I say to my team, keeping my eyes locked on Drew's. His breathing grows shallow, and I make sure to overemphasize my own deep breaths again. Eventually, he calms down a bit.

"Winter was right about Tatum," Kasey states. It catches me off guard—I appreciate her vote of confidence.

I feel my team nodding. Tearing my eyes away from Drew, I look at his team, trying to get an understanding of what they think of Raven's answer.

Josh is staring daggers at me, eyebrows low against his eyes, not taking part in his team's conversation at all.

His look gives me the chills, and I force myself to tear my gaze away. *Jerk.*

Cady speaks for her group. "Raven's lying."

Ding. Another point for them. Part of me wants their team to win so I don't have to face the reality that one of my friends might be killed tonight.

But I also don't want to fear for *my* life.

"Drew is..." Reese looks at me one more time. I encourage him to keep going. "Telling the truth."

Ding. Point, us. Everyone's shoulders sag, our relief so visible you can almost taste it. I add those two little tidbits to my journal page, closing it quickly before my teammates can peek.

No one else seems to be utilizing a journal. Maybe they haven't found theirs yet. Or their memories are just really good. Unfortunately, mine is sub-par at best.

Tied back up. The Voice has been overwhelmingly quiet other than to ask the questions. I wonder if that means something.

Raven doesn't look at us as she sits back down, face dark.

Adrian smiles as he faces Stacey, but she doesn't return the gesture. She takes her glasses off to rub her eyes, then puts them back on, fixing the wire-rim so they're perfectly placed on her nose.

"Just two fake people competing for their lives," Adrian jokes, popping his teeth out. Again, Stacey just stares, not giving him a reaction. Even I thought it was a little bit funny.

"Have you ever abandoned someone to save yourself?"

Immediately, Adrian's posture changes. The time for fun and games is over.

"Yes," Stacey exhales.

"Yes," Adrian says, trying to muster a smile.

I wait, listening to see what my teammates think about Stacey's answer.

"She's really closed off," Kasey says.

"I feel like that's a broad question. Could be taken a lot of different ways," Reese adds. "Like maybe you left your sister at home so you could go have fun."

Raven shrugs. "I think the important part of that question is *to save yourself.*"

"We all just abandoned Faith last night," Nick says. It might be the smartest thing I've heard him say so far, and it is a very, very good point.

"Whatever you guys think," I offer. I've done enough talking. Time to let others take the front seat in driving this thing.

Reese nods. "Stacey is telling the truth."

Ding.

"Adrian's lying."

Buzz.

Their team curses each other. It's three to two, with one pairing left. Reese motions for us to lean in before he stands up.

"I'm going to tell the truth," he whispers. "If she answers the same way I do, there's a very good chance it's also true. We do everything together."

He leaves, and as he does, Nick scoffs. "He wants her team to win. He's probably lying to us."

I consider this, but something about it doesn't feel right. I don't think Reese would forsake our lives—his own life—just for Cady's.

Right?

My head pulses. This game has taken too long. I need a break and to get away from the thick air surrounding this room.

And away from these people.

"Do you think you deserve to be here?" The Voice's question rings around the room as we end this game once and for all.

Reese's shoulders tense. His hands are clasped behind his

back, as if fighting himself from reaching out to embrace his twin. Her eyes are beginning to fill with tears.

"Yes," he chokes.

"Yes," she whispers.

If we're wrong and they're right, we'll tie.

And I do not want to know what the Voice will make us do if that happens.

TWENTY-THREE

"Reese is telling the truth," Josh shouts without talking to the rest of his team.

Ding.

I look at Nick right away. "He did what he said he was going to do. That probably means Cady is telling the truth, too."

He just crosses his arms. "I don't trust him."

"You can't trust *anyone*," Kasey says, exasperated. "That's the whole point of all of this."

"If we're both right, we win," Adrian adds. "It's a chance I'm willing to take."

"Vote. If you think Cady is telling the truth, raise your hand," I say, raising my own.

Everyone but Raven and Nick raises theirs. With Reese being questioned, that technically makes up the majority.

Nick opens his mouth. "Cady is telling the truth!" I shout before he can beat me to it and say something other than what the group decided.

I hold my breath, waiting.

Ding.

We were right.

We won.

And Nick's an idiot.

For a moment, there's sweet relief. I'm safe tonight. I don't have to play defense. I can sit back, listen, digest, and make notes on everyone.

But then my stomach drops. It could be Tatum, Drew, or Olsen tonight. Chances are very good that it will be one of them.

I can't let that happen.

The Voice sighs over the intercom, as if pleased. "Reese's team wins. Cady, Stacey, Drew, Olsen, Josh, Tatum. One of you will be voted out tonight. Prepare your goodbyes."

With that, the speaker clicks off, and we are left with silence.

None of us moves right away, unsure what to do next.

"I don't want to do this again," Tatum says, tears spilling from her eyes.

"None of us do," Raven scoffs.

I make a mental note to update my notebook and share what I learned with Drew. My biggest desire right now is to hear what *his* group was saying during that game.

I would have never guessed that honesty could be so dangerous.

But I'm starting to believe that may be the whole point.

———

"Well," Raven says as we leave the sunroom. "Does anyone want to offer any explanation regarding their answer?"

"Only if you go first," Stacey quips.

Raven rolls her eyes in response. Begging for answers without being willing to let go of some of your own is not how you'll win this.

Drew heads toward the stairs, and I aim to follow, wanting

to get his thoughts. As I walk away from the group, someone grabs my forearm tightly.

I yank my arm away, looking back at Josh. "What?"

"Can we talk?"

"No."

"Darling, please."

I keep my eyes on his, but I can feel people watching us interact. I take a second to cool down, even though it feels like steam is blowing from my ears.

"Leave me alone," I grit out, mustering a fake smile. "They're going to start getting suspicious."

If they aren't already, anyway. And after how we answered our question earlier… It's only a matter of time.

He relents. "You can't avoid me forever."

"Watch me," I say back, tossing my hair over my shoulder as I walk away. Drew is waiting for me on the second floor.

"What's his deal with you?" he asks, cutting right to business.

"What do you mean?" Covering up my shock, I try to feign innocence, but I think I'm failing. Josh's hand left marks on my skin, and his grip really hurt.

"If you can give me one of your truths," he says slowly, "Then I'll give you one of mine."

I hesitate. It's tempting. The story I have with Josh, though… It's a can of worms I'm not ready to open.

But Drew could be killed tonight. And my secrets would die with him.

I wince, and he tracks the movement. I didn't mean to think that.

"He called you 'Darling'," he adds. "And it didn't sound like it was the first time."

I exhale, caught. There's no way I can talk myself out of that one. *Josh, you idiot.* "Okay, okay. You win."

He tries to hide it, but there's a spark in his eye. He wasn't expecting to get this out of me.

You and I both, I think.

I follow him into his room. He sits on his bed, patting the space next to him. I relent, leaning against the wall, kicking my shoes off so I can pull my legs up and tuck my chin into my knees.

It's silent for what feels like hours. I don't know how to start this story without telling him everything. And I just…

I just can't.

"I don't mind going first," he offers.

I swallow, thankful for the kind gesture of faith. "Sure."

He traces his fingernail on the leg of his jeans in a circle, over and over again. "My question," he starts. "If I've ever been touched by death. I told the truth."

I nod. It's nothing I don't already know. What I want to know is *how*. And I can't believe I'm about to get the answer to that so easily and without even having to ask.

"When I was eight," he begins, voice already shaking. "There was this day at school. We had a sub, I remember. And our teacher told us we'd get to watch a movie in class."

He pauses. I'm careful not to move, so I don't disturb this memory he's conjuring.

"There was a shooting. At my elementary school. I was in the hallway, getting a drink of water, or something. I don't—" his breathing grows shallow, eyes shut tight. "I don't remember much else but the pain. And the sounds—"

Drew clutches at his ears suddenly, as if reliving that moment over again. I place a hand on his shoulder, shaking him a bit. "Hey, you don't need to tell me anything else. You're not there anymore."

"Except I *am*," he bites. "I can't keep pretending that what's happening here doesn't remind me of that day. The hiding, the fear, the loss of control."

I silence, rubbing his shoulder in slow circles, letting him say what he needs to.

"I almost died," he whispers finally, opening his eyes. "I

was in the hospital for weeks. I had to relearn how to walk, to talk. I should have died. But I didn't."

He chuckles, a dark and indistinct sound coming from his throat. "And now my life is out of my own hands again. And I can't do anything about it."

"I'm so sorry," I say softly.

"I'm so afraid, Winter."

My arms move on their own, wrapping him up tightly in a hug. His body shakes a bit within my cocoon, but I don't mind. I just hold him tighter.

There's something in his tone that tells me he's been *waiting* to tell someone this. And it's for that reason—and the sheer desperation in his tone—that makes me trust him even more than I already did.

Something cracks from far away, making him jump. The sound of rain pounds against the roof out of nowhere.

He pulls away, wiping at his eyes with his t-shirt.

"I won't let anything happen to you," I offer, taking his hand.

He gives me a sad smile. "Don't make promises you can't keep. I'm on the chopping block tonight, after all."

The room quiets as that reality sets in.

I sigh. I guess that means it's my turn to tell the truth.

"Josh and I know each other," I say, mentally steeling myself for the story to come. "We've known each other for a while."

TWENTY-FOUR

"How?" he asks when I pause.

I chew my bottom lip. "He was… uh, he's an ex-boyfriend."

Drew makes a sour face. "Like, recently?"

"We broke up two years ago after dating for a little over three years."

I can tell he's doing mental math, just as everyone does when I start the story this way. "So he was… You were…"

"Yep," I cut him off. "Eighteen and fourteen."

His upper lip curls. Unfortunately, this is only the tip of the iceberg of the story that is my time with Joshua Damon.

"I was one girlfriend of three," I continue. "At the same time. Everyone warned me about him, but I didn't listen. I was just—"

My voice chokes, and I pull back from Drew, not wanting to look him in the face. I'm still so ashamed of how easily Josh took advantage of how young I was.

Sighing, I finish my sentence. "I was just so excited an older boy looked at me and thought I was pretty. He pulled me in, broke me apart, and left me."

"What did he do to you?" Drew whispers, clearly testing the waters between us.

I gasp for air, choking on a sob. "Enough."

He's silent in response, and tears begin to form on my lower lashes. Josh isn't *worth* crying over, I try to tell myself. But still, the betrayal and anguish he put me through are a knife to my still-healing heart.

Especially because of everything that came after.

"You were together for three years?" he asks.

I nod, pulling my misty eyes back to his, scared to find contempt in them. Instead, all I find is a kind understanding.

"Why did you break up?"

Breathing in deeply, I pull my shoulders back. This is a question I can handle. "I tried to break up with him a few times over the years. He always convinced me to get back with him, usually claiming he'd, uh, harm himself if I didn't. But as I got older, and I became less compliant, he became angrier. I started losing memories after hanging out with him…"

I exhale, rushing the rest of this part of the story. "He was drugging me. Because I stopped doing whatever he wanted me to do. My parents didn't know, and it felt like it was too late to tell them. So I threatened to press charges, submit a restraining order, *something*."

Looking back, I think he knew I was bluffing. "But before my senior year, *he* dumped *me*. I think he wanted to hurt me, but I was just overwhelmingly relieved. It felt like the war was over."

"Winter, *what*?" his voice is dripping with disbelief. "You have to tell someone. This is crazy."

"That's the thing," I whisper. "Someone already *knows*." I move my eyes toward the ceiling, gesturing. We don't know if there are cameras or recording devices in the bedrooms. The ethical part of me wants to say no, but nothing about this situation is ethical.

He nods, realizing. We're both against the wall, shoulders touching. Eventually, he starts tracing patterns on his jeans again.

"You didn't have to tell me all of that," he says. His hair falls into his eyes as he looks up at me, and I resist the urge to push it back out of the way.

"You were honest with me," I respond. "I simply returned the favor."

Drew leans his head back against the wall, knocking it a bit as he sighs loudly. "This game is messed up."

I mimic his posture, overwhelmingly resigned. "So are we."

"Mostly you," he teases, a small, crooked smile on his face. A breath of relief enters my lungs. As much as our pasts suck, I appreciate him not spending a lot of time dwelling on them. I've had years to dwell—I'm tired of giving it power over me.

I knock my shoulder into his, continuing the joke. "You're the one who almost died."

He chuckles, a light but stressed sound. I scoot down to lean my head on his shoulder. Just for a minute, I want to feel like I'm back at college with a friend, procrastinating on a homework assignment.

But still, a countdown sounds from somewhere inside my brain, reminding me that this moment of peace is fleeting.

"For the record," he breathes, words hardly audible over the rainstorm drenching the house outside. "You *are* pretty."

I feel my chest slowly unclench, butterflies swarming my stomach. "Thank you."

———

At some point, sitting there with each other, we accidentally fell asleep.

The sun is setting now, and dinner is beyond cold. After

heating something up, we find Tatum and Olsen with Adrian in the parlor playing cards.

"Hey guys," Drew greets. "Olsen, you okay? You're looking a little pale."

"He's been burning up all afternoon, but he won't do anything about it," Tatum responds for him.

"I'm fine," he wheezes.

"That was very convincing," Adrian teases. His tone might be light, but his eyes bounce back and forth between Olsen's in rapid motion.

Olsen moans, shifting his posture. "It's your... turn."

Adrian places a card down on the table.

We sit across from them on the floor, watching the game. I notice Olsen's hands shaking, so I try to pivot the conversation. "Have you guys been talking about who you're going to vote for tonight?"

"I mean," Tatum starts, not looking up. "Two of us sitting here are safe. Three of us sitting here are not."

"I'd be okay voting Josh," Drew says, a smirk on his lips.

"Done." I can't help the smile I give him back.

The others look back and forth between our brief exchange, obviously lost. Before anyone can ask questions, Olsen groans again.

"Hey man, maybe we should have Faith check you over."

"Faith's dead," he reminds us. The room goes silent.

Right.

Olsen then peeks a closed eye at Drew. "Aren't you studying to be a doctor?"

Drew chuckles, clapping Olsen on the shoulder lightly. "I never said I was studying *well*, buddy."

Olsen laughs a little in response, slumping back on the couch, one hand on his chest. The laugh turns to coughing, which turns into wheezing. He's bent over, gasping for air.

"Is it just me," Adrian says. "Or is he looking a little blue?"

I stand, rushing over to grab his hand. "He's ice cold."

Olsen tries to get up, but he collapses nearly on top of me, and I can't catch him in time.

"Hey!" Drew shouts. Tatum stands next to him, clearly unsure of what to do.

I get Olsen off of me with help from the boys. His cheeks are hollow, and his eyes are shut tight, but he's at least standing with our support.

"I'm fine," he whispers, swaying, shoving our hands off his arms. I take a step back, trusting that he knows his body and his capabilities.

"Let's just take it easy," I respond. "We can help you get upstairs to bed."

He opens his mouth to respond, a rasping inhale grating against the silence.

But then his knees buckle, and time slows as he goes down again.

We lunge for him, but we're all too late. He hits the floor with a soft, sickening thud. His head lolls, body limp.

"Olsen!" I scream, hands shaking as I grab him and try to roll him over. Adrian and Drew rush past me, out the door, yelling for help.

Motion blurs around me as I focus on getting Olsen on his back, my heart pounding in my ears.

Tatum kneels next to me, clasping my hand. We make eye contact, hers full of resolve.

"We're going to have to ask *them* for help."

TWENTY-FIVE

"No," Olsen groans. "No, you *can't*."

His voice is full of sheer desperation, and something else. Fear.

"They won't help," I urge. "They *want* us to die, remember?"

"But not like this," Tatum adds, hopeful. "It shouldn't be like this."

Footsteps rush back into the parlor, a horde of people following Drew. There's a mix of voices and commotion happening out in the hallway. None of us knows what to do in a situation like this. Olsen is *sick*. He should be in a hospital—not stuck in a mansion with a bunch of strangers.

Drew looks at me—tired, worried.

Olsen's breathing grows more labored.

"Hey," I whisper, my hands on his cheeks. He's so cold. "Deep breaths if you can. Stay with us."

His eyes roll into the back of his head once more, and I can't help the panic that sinks in.

I look at Drew, at Adrian, at Reese and Cady, and everyone else crowding into the parlor.

"We need to get their attention," I cry. "*Now!*"

Stacey is the first one to shout. "Hey!"

Olsen's head is in my lap now, so I keep my hands on his face, but everyone else is waving their arms, screaming at the top of their lungs.

It feels like years pass before we get a response.

"Houseguests," the Voice crackles. Is that worry I hear in their tone? Or is my mind playing games and giving me what I want to hear? "Please head to the game room."

We freeze in our tracks, looking at each other in shock.

I motion for Nick and Drew to come help me get Olsen up when the Voice cuts in.

"Leave the boy."

———

My leg bounces as I sit at the round table once again, anxiety gnawing at my stomach.

We moved Olsen to the couch, hoping he would be more comfortable. He didn't make a sound or move a muscle. He was completely limp.

There are three empty seats now with Olsen missing.

"Houseguests," the Voice interrupts my thoughts. "Here is how we will proceed. You claim Olsen needs medical help, and that may be true. But what is also true is that it's time to vote."

I hold my breath, waiting. I haven't had a chance to prepare—I'm not ready.

"You have two choices. Vote Olsen—I will put him out of his misery. Or you can vote for someone else. Olsen will be leaving the mansion tonight either way."

"Leaving like, you're going to get him help?" Cady asks, voice small.

Silence is the only answer we receive.

I'm sitting between Tatum and Drew, and I reach both of

my hands out to squeeze theirs. Olsen is our *friend*. The last thing I want to do is write his name down.

"I don't want to kill two people tonight," Stacey says.

"But how can we condemn the sick guy?" Adrian asks.

Nick scoffs. "He's already dying. We're just speeding up the process."

Josh laughs from the other side of the table, and I resist the urge to glare. Read the room, dude.

Tatum opens her mouth to speak, but I shake my head at her. We need to let the group decide. Both she and Drew are up for voting tonight—I can't lose *two* of my allies.

"What would Olsen want us to do?" Reese asks. He aims the question at Drew.

He sighs, contemplating. "In the short time I've known him, I've realized he's the most selfless person here. Honestly, if he were sitting here, I think he'd tell us to vote for him. I hate to say that, but I think it's true."

Taking a deep breath, Drew continues. "But we should also remember that he was telling the truth in the game earlier. He has no idea why he's here."

"That probably means we're murdering an innocent man," Tatum adds on my left.

My gut churns. I force myself to let go of their hands so I can wipe my sweaty palms on my jeans.

"Houseguests," the Voice begins. "The time for talking is over."

We grab our chalkboards, our writing utensils screeching against black paint. I pick at my chalk with a fingernail, biding my time until I *have* to write his name down.

Maybe they'll help him, I let myself hope. *They just... don't want to tell us, for obvious reasons. Can't have us thinking the bad guys are actually good.*

Drew sets his chalkboard down on the table, covering his face with his hands.

For my friend, I will take this chance. Nick was partially

right earlier—Olsen is dying. And he knew it the moment he woke up here. We can't lose two people in the same night again.

I have to believe there's a reason for this happening.

I scratch his name onto my board, making sure my handwriting is neat and pristine. Only the best for my new friend.

When I look back up from my board, everyone is staring at me. I was the last one left to vote.

Tatum starts to cry, so I reach out to rub her back in slow, methodical circles. It seems to calm her down a bit.

"Thank you," she whispers. I just nod, offering her a small smile.

But the only thing on my mind is that whoever is behind this is absolutely sick. Sick to include Olsen at all, *knowing* he has Leukemia. Sick to kidnap us and make us play their games.

I swallow the bile rising in my throat.

Time both speeds up and slows down as we go through the motions of reading our vote.

All I can hear is his name in my brain repeatedly.

Olsen.

Olsen.

Olsen.

Olsen.

It's not fair, but it's not supposed to be. In some awful way, we've convinced ourselves that we're doing what's right. That we're helping him somehow.

None of us states why we think it's him. We know it's not, deep down. And the Voice doesn't say anything about it. There are no monologues in between or sly jokes.

I watch myself read my vote to the group from somewhere outside my body, lingering nearby to not feel the grief that surrounds me.

She looks like a traitor. An excuse of a human being.

"Olsen received the most votes and is now banished from the house. Goodnight."

The intercom clicks off, just like that. Hurried, rushed, and not a moment too soon.

Fresh air is calling my name, but it's still raining outside. A dreary gray evening to match my mood. All our moods, probably.

"What now?" Josh asks.

"I'm going to bed," Raven states, rising from her chair and leaving, just like that.

"She's always the first out of the room," Kasey remarks. I couldn't have said it better. Kasey says out loud what we're all probably thinking, and I appreciate that. There's an honesty to that.

I look at Drew and Tatum, a question written across my facial features. It's as if we share a brain in that fleeting moment, rushing to our feet and running to the parlor.

I need to tell him I'm sorry, I think. *I need to talk to him one more time.*

But when I get there, I stop in my tracks.

It's too late.

Somehow, he's already gone.

DAY FOUR

TWENTY-SIX

Olsen's portrait is painted over when I enter the parlor the next day.

It's just after noon; I laid in bed, wrapped in grief, for hours this morning. Eventually, Tatum brought me a plate of food, which coaxed me to get up and take a shower.

I wasn't built for this. It's only going to get harder and harder to vote people out.

Olsen's absence hangs around me like a fog. This morning, everyone is unusually silent. Even Nick and Raven, the two I would say are the most unaffected by our circumstances on a normal day, ease up on their usual snide comments.

We sit in the game room, waiting. Waiting for the Voice to give us more instructions, waiting for someone to fess up and get us out of here.

Waiting for a miracle.

My head is pounding. My eyes feel dry and puffy, the result of spending the entire night crying.

The silence is deafening.

I need a second alone.

Mumbling something about a headache to the group, I slip away before anyone can ask more questions. Let them be suspicious of me—I don't care right now. I can't *make* myself care.

I race up the stairs, longing for the privacy of my room. But when I step foot over the threshold, something feels *off*.

Pausing, I look around before shutting the door, ready to bolt at a moment's notice.

Nothing looks out of place.

Except—

There.

Something is peeking out from under my pillow.

A sliver of cream sticking out just far enough to catch my eye.

My heart stutters as I creep slowly toward it, pulse thundering in my ears. I can't help the tremor in my hands as I lift the pillow, only to find it's just a simple piece of paper, folded into thirds.

The rough, uneven edges tell me that someone ripped it out of a notebook. I grab mine from my back pocket, testing if the page lines are the same.

A perfect match.

For a moment, I just stare at it, as if it will disappear before my very eyes. I'm terrified to open it, because deep down, I feel like whatever is hidden inside will change *everything*.

Finally, I peel back its layers, steeling myself for what's to come.

I KNOW WHY YOU'RE HERE.

The words knock the air out of me.

There's no name, no signature, and no explanation. Nothing but a sharp statement that threatens to tear me to pieces.

I read it again, and again, trying to make sense of it.

Trying to force air back into my lungs. Trying to decipher whose handwriting this could be.

How could anyone here know this about me? I'm not even sure *I* know why I'm here.

Yes, you do, my inner voice whispers. My throat suddenly goes dry. I gulp.

A knock at my door jolts me so violently I almost drop the note. I tuck it into my notebook quickly, forcing both of them into my back pocket.

"Hey," Drew's voice calls through the door, soft. "You okay?"

I swallow down the panic threatening to suffocate me. "Yeah. I just needed a second."

He hesitates. "Can I come in?"

Against my better judgment, I say, "Sure."

The door creaks open, and Drew steps inside, hair messy from running his hands through it.

I muster up a small smile for him, the sight of his worried expression hitting me hard in the chest. Did something else go wrong while I was gone? Did I miss something from the Voice or—

He closes the door behind him gently. "You sure you're okay? You look like you're going to be sick."

I might be, I think.

But no, I'm not okay. Someone here is watching me. Someone knows something they shouldn't.

I want to believe that it's Josh—that would be the easy answer. But something inside me says that's not it. I want to believe that I could tell Drew about this, but my inner warning bells go off. What are the odds this note would show up the day after I admitted to him part of my past?

Could he just be putting on a front, tricking me into sharing truths with him? Do I even *know* him?

I do my best to keep a suspicious glance from shifting my facial features.

"I'm fine," I lie.

He doesn't believe me, not even for a second. His eyes drop to my hands, where they pick at my fingernails, then drift back up slowly. "We did what we had to do last night. We can only hope that they're getting him help."

My throat tightens. In my panic and momentary selfishness, I forgot all about Olsen. This is what Drew expects me to be worried about, though, so I'll go with it. "Still doesn't feel right."

He steps closer, voice gentle. "Hey." He grabs my chin, pulling it up to meet his gaze, trying to catch my eyes. "We're in this together."

For a moment, we stay just like that, locked in a standstill. The silence between us feels different from the silence we have with everyone else. It's less… suffocating. More like a tether connecting us to each other.

"We should probably get back," I choke.

He removes his hand, nodding. "Come with me?"

I make sure my notebook is tucked securely in my pocket. As we leave my room behind to head back downstairs, the folded note burns a hole through my jeans.

Someone knows.

Someone *wants* to scare me.

And whether I want to admit it or not, it's working.

TWENTY-SEVEN

The Voice still hasn't spoken by the time we eat dinner.

Reese made us food again: burgers and hot dogs on a griddle he found.

"Do you think they're still killing Olsen?" Josh mutters. Apparently, he's done pretending to be sad.

"Shut up," Adrian snaps. He's been bolder ever since Olsen's death. Mostly, I think we're all just fed up with each other.

A squeal sounds from overhead.

We all look up.

"Houseguests, report to the library. It's time for our next activity."

Activity—not a game. That's new. I'd try to decipher the meaning behind that, but I don't have the energy.

We leave our half-finished dinner where it is, not wanting to risk an angry captor. Drew tries to walk beside me, but Josh shoves his way by my side instead. I try to slow down so he walks ahead of me, but he matches my pace.

He's so aggravating.

The library is darker than normal, only lit by the one window in the back and a multitude of lamps.

There's a long table in the middle where the chairs used to be, covered in a deep green tablecloth.

And on it, eleven wooden boxes. One for each of us, unlabeled and identical, shut tight with a small brass clasp.

My skin prickles.

The Voice purrs through the speakers once we're all in the room. "Welcome to the past. Each of you will open one box. Inside is something connected to each of your stories. You will share what you find with the group and choose whose item you think you hold. If you get it right, you are safe from tonight's vote."

Silence permeates the air while we wait to see if that's it.

"The vote will take place once our game is finished. Additionally, you won't know if you got it right or wrong until everyone has gone. There's no need for any unfair advantages."

I blow out a deep breath as a strange hush falls over our group. Even though this is our third time now playing these games, it still hits hard thinking about my life being on the line.

Not only that, but with the vote happening right after this, we won't have any time to talk or prepare ourselves for our inevitable doom.

Anything could happen.

The boxes sit there, staring back at us.

The Voice chuckles. "We will begin with Winter."

I nearly laugh, not expecting my name to be first. I don't want to step forward, but my legs move anyway.

Reaching out with trembling fingers, I unclasp the box directly in front of me. There's no rhyme or reason for why I chose this one. I just want to come across as confident to the Voice.

My stomach drops.

Inside is a book. I turn around, showing it to the group, doing my best to watch their reactions, but no one gives me anything. The book is navy and black, and there's a bird on the cover, but nothing else. It's large—at least four hundred pages as I flip through it. I can't tell what genre it is, and there's no description on the back.

I survey the group, head spinning. Something from everyone's past...

Raven shifts on her feet, just once. But it's enough to catch my eye. She never shifts.

I look back at the bird on the cover. It's an abstract piece of art, but I swear that's a raven. My eyes survey her body language once again.

I'm going to be guessing regardless. And black and navy both seem to fit her aesthetic.

"This is Raven's," I say, mustering confidence.

Nothing sounds to tell me if I'm right or wrong, just as the Voice promised. I set the book back down in the open box and rejoin our line.

Josh is next to me, of course. He strides right up to the boxes, thinking carefully about which to choose.

He flips open his chosen box with a smirk, then freezes.

The smirk slides right off his face.

Josh holds up a white leather glove covered in a substance that looks like dried blood. It looks like it may be a sports glove of some sort, something you'd wear to give yourself more grip.

My immediate thought is Nick. He's the only person here that I know for sure plays a sport.

Josh hesitates. "I think this is Nick's?"

Nick doesn't say anything as Josh takes the glove and throws it back into the box.

Stacey goes next, holding up an empty, clear bottle. It doesn't have a label, but it looks like something alcoholic.

She surveys us through her fake glasses.

"Uh," she starts. "Do you think I can say someone who's already been said?"

I shrug, looking at the rest of the group. We're always given the bare minimum of rules and instructions. Everything else is up for interpretation.

Seeing our unhelpful expressions, she decides for herself. "I think *this* one is Nick, actually."

He scoffs. "You think I'm some sort of alcoholic?"

She doesn't respond with words, just shrugs. With that, she puts the empty bottle back in its box.

One by one, people make their choices.

Drew holds up a photograph of two girls arm in arm, smiling at each other. He guesses it's mine before I can give him a subtle head shake. It's not a terrible guess, considering he knows I have a sister.

But I've never seen that photo before. So, unless the Voice knows something I don't, that means Drew should be up for the vote tonight.

Adrian picks a box with a single tree leaf. It's wet and bright orange, and *huge*. He looks around at everyone, but I don't think anyone gives him anything, because his shoulders slump.

His voice wobbles. "Kasey, I guess."

TWENTY-EIGHT

I'm starting to get distracted. It's not super helpful that we don't know if we're right or wrong when we make our guesses. But I guess that means none of us gets the advantage of going last. Instead of zoning out, I force myself to pull out my notebook.

I nearly let the slip of paper from earlier drop out of it when I open it to a new page.

I had forgotten all about it.

Looking around briskly, I tuck it into the front of the pages, hoping it'll stay secure there.

As I'm writing down the items that have been pulled out so far, I put all our names on the other side of the paper so I can draw lines connecting things and people.

"This is Cady's," Reese says grimly.

I look up, having tuned out Reese picking his object. He's already put it back, so I can't see what it is.

Begrudgingly, I lean over to Josh. "What was it?"

He scoffs. "Some stupid library card or something."

I purse my lips. For a second, I thought I might have been wrong in picking Raven, and that the book was for Cady instead. She's studying to be a librarian, after all. But if Reese guessed his sister, I would assume he's probably pretty confident in that answer.

What is it with him always getting her things? Does he have an unfair advantage somehow?

I put a star by his name. I wouldn't be surprised if they end up making it to the end together. And if that happens…

Nick pulls out a little phone from one box—one of those that you have to pay for minutes on.

Without looking at the group, he tosses it back into the box, mumbling Kasey's name.

I don't know what it is he knows about Kasey that would make him think that, but she *is* a mystery to me right now. She intentionally keeps from talking about herself in our conversations.

Though I can't complain much. I've been doing the same thing.

Kasey's next, picking the box furthest to the right. I'm making notes on what everyone has picked up and whom they've chosen, writing these details as fast as I can so I don't miss any other items.

Once the Voice tells us who is up for the vote tonight and who isn't, I'll fill in the empty gaps. And hopefully be able to place the right items with the right people.

Kasey's item clinks against the box as she pulls it out, and reveals a dented steel water bottle that looks like it's seen better days.

Something about it makes my arm hair stand up. Why is it so… smashed?

Her green eyes pierce each and every one of us as she decides on whose she thinks this is.

"Drew."

My blood runs cold. It does look like a kid's water bottle—could it be from the shooting he survived?

Tatum grabs a colorful theatre mask out of the box, beads dangling from the open eye holes. "Uh, Adrian, maybe?"

I nod, impressed. Not a bad guess, considering he wants to be on Broadway.

Nothing that has screamed 'me' has been pulled out of those boxes yet, and with only two left, it has me nervous. Drew's the only person who has guessed my name for anything. That means someone might get it right and show that they know something about my past.

Which could lead me right toward whoever left the note for me.

Cady and Raven are left. Cady pulls out something that looks like an earpiece from a spy movie. It's clear, with a coil attaching one piece to another. She throws up her arms in exasperation. "I don't even remember who's been guessed so far. Whatever. Josh."

I tilt my head. I don't think that's his, but I guess I can't count anything out. We haven't talked in years, after all.

Raven opens the only box left, showing us a piece of paper.

Goosebumps erupt on my arm. I try to keep the chill from running down my spine at the sight of that cream sheet.

"What is that?" Adrian asks.

Raven takes another look at the paper. "Some report card. History class." She lets out a low chuckle. "Perfect scores on everything. Some teacher's pet."

Eyes roam, pausing for a brief moment on me before moving on.

"I'll guess Reese."

I breathe out a quick sigh of relief. Is Josh looking at me from the corner of his eye, or am I making that up? I try to look at him from my peripheral vision, but I can't tell.

"Houseguests," the Voice croons. "Our activity is completed. Those that are up for the vote tonight are…"

We pause, not a single person breathing as we await our fate.

"Drew, Nick, Adrian, Stacey, Cady, Raven. Meet me in the game room in fifteen minutes. I look forward to it."

The intercom clicks off, but all I can hear is a buzz in my ears.

Nick tries to open the boxes back up to look at the items, but they snap locked as if controlled remotely.

Okay, then. I'll go off my bad memory.

Finding a spot to sit on the ground, I grab my notebook again, scribbling down who got things right. That means Raven's *was* the book, Cady had the library card, Nick had the bloody glove, Drew's was the water bottle, and Adrian is connected to the mask.

I can count the report card out, because I *know* without a doubt that it's mine. That leaves the photo, alcohol bottle, burner phone, earpiece, and leaf.

Running my pen down the names left on my list, I try to pair things up in my head to make it make sense. With only fifteen minutes and counting until voting, I need some sort of idea of what to go off of.

Someone slides down the wall next to me.

"I could tell you mine," Josh whispers.

I glare at him, wanting to tell him off, but it *would* be helpful to know which one was his. My heart was hoping I could decipher it myself easily, but none of it makes sense for him.

Staying quiet while he stares, I pair things together with his name in my brain before asking for his help. If he's anything like he used to be, help will cost me something.

Photo of two girls? No, I would have recognized the girls if that were the case.

Alcohol? He was a notorious drinker, but that feels too... easy.

Burner phone? That one makes me pause. A memory pings in the back of my mind of me years ago asking him, begging him, to tell me how he hid his other girlfriends from me. It came out of nowhere. I had *no* clue he was seeing other people.

The earpiece and leaf don't bounce around in my head as the phone does for him. I decide to take a chance, making sure to watch his reaction.

"I already know which one is yours," I smirk, connecting his name to the burner phone on my paper. I lift a hand to my ear, acting as if I'm taking a call.

He grinds his jaw, his eyes angry again.

Bingo.

He scoffs, standing up. "Looks like we'll both be here tomorrow. Can't say I'm upset about that."

I smile sweetly. "Not if I have anything to do with it."

Josh squats next to me, grabbing my wrist so hard he pinches my skin. "You can't get rid of me this time, Darling."

I look past him at the small crowd watching this interaction. Forcing a scared expression on my face, I wince, showing everyone that he's *hurting me*.

He follows where my eyes are looking, realizing we have an audience. Letting go of my wrist, he grinds out something that sounds like both a promise and a warning. "I'll get you alone again one of these days."

With that, he stalks out of the room, leaving red finger-marks on my arm.

TWENTY-NINE

On our way to the game room, Tatum told me hers was the photograph of the two girls.

"I'll explain it later," she whispered to me.

That leaves three items and three people left to put together. I'm hoping the voting table will help me gain some insight, because right now, Reese, Kasey, and Stacey are the people I know the least about. Which means they are going to be very hard to pair with objects.

We're quiet around the table at first. The Voice reiterates what they already said—that six of us are up for the vote tonight. The air feels heavy, but charged at the same time. No one wants to look at each other.

I'm not up tonight, I remind myself. *And I don't think they'll vote for Drew.*

At least, I hope they don't.

"We have to start," Kasey says. The safe ones, like myself, are always the most outspoken. We can afford to be.

Nick speaks first. "I don't like that our twinnies over here," he waves toward where Reese and Cady once again cling to each other, "Get to know things about each other that we don't."

He makes a good point. It's something I've been thinking about over the last few days. I can tell that hits a spot for some others, because they're nodding along to what he's saying.

Reese and Cady shift in their chairs, trying to be still and not look guilty.

"You've had it out for us since the moment we arrived," Reese bites back.

"Nick's had it out for *everyone* since the beginning," Adrian adds.

"We can't just let this be about grudges," Stacey whines. "Do you guys remember the whole point of why we're here? That we're trying to figure out which one of us knows more than everyone else?"

"I don't have any guesses tonight," I admit. "I'm just… tired."

"None of us wants to die," Cady whispers. "Please."

"That's the point," Nick snaps. "But someone obviously has to. And I think it should be one of the twins."

The tension tightens. I think back to our previous votes. Faith was voted out because we thought she was our perpetrator, and we were wrong. Cyrus was ejected because he escaped. Olsen was taken because he was sick.

We don't exactly have an impressive track record of voting so far.

Someone has to know something. We can't all be this stupid. Josh is still a top suspect in my mind because of the note and what he knows about me, but I can't say that tonight. He's safe. And if I start down that train now, it'll also point fingers toward me.

So I'll save that for a day when he's not safe. And hopefully, at that time, I will be.

"This is getting ridiculous," Raven declares. "We can debate all night, but we still have to vote. Unless someone has information we haven't heard and wants to share with the group, we should just get on with it."

A rustle of clothing sounds from my right, a shift in breathing. Then, silence once again.

"Okay," she announces. "Should we just tell the Voice we're ready, then?"

"Wait."

Drew's voice splinters through the room.

Everyone freezes, myself included. All eyes snap toward him. What could he know that I don't? We're allies.

He looks up toward the group slowly, face pale, expression carved from weathered stone. He's up for elimination. His speaking up against someone could turn everyone against him instead.

"Drew," I mumble to myself. "What are you doing?"

If it's worth risking his life, then that means… whatever he's about to say must matter. A lot.

I hold my breath.

"There's something everyone needs to know about Cyrus' eviction," he says, voice unsteady. "His death."

A ripple of panic goes through my body.

"Stacey," he says slowly, "Care to share?"

THIRTY

Immediately, she bursts into tears.

Drew slumps back in his chair, arms crossed, waiting for her confession like the rest of us. He's trying to look tough and unafraid, but I see the tremble in his fingertips.

"Cyrus got out," she chokes, sobbing.

No one says anything. We all assumed that was the case, but to hear it be a known fact… that hurts. He got *out*. He was *safe*.

But he got caught.

"The night he was… evicted," she continues. "He climbed over the balcony and dropped to the ground."

I look at Drew out of my peripherals and he nods subtly, not looking at me. Just as we thought.

"We were, I don't know. Talking a little. Allies, I guess. And he had made it to the woods behind the house when he turned around and—"

She cries harder, head in her hands. I can't hear anything she's saying.

Finally, she raises her voice, completely broken. "He came back for me! He brought me a leaf, trying to prove that he had gotten out. But I thought he was trying to trick me. I—we can't trust anyone. He begged me to help him wake everyone up, but I was scared. I thought it was some sort of test. So I told him no."

A gasp comes from Kasey at the far side of the table.

Stacey nods slowly. "That's what the leaf is for, I think. Proving that the Voice knew he came to me."

She wraps her arms around her body, shrinking in on herself. Adrian places a hand on her shoulder.

"He left. He left again, got out, and then he got captured. And I think it's—it's my fault. If he hadn't come back for me…" She squeezes her eyes shut.

"If he hadn't come back for you," Tatum continues. "He might have made it out alive."

Stacey's chest heaves, deep cries leaving her mouth.

"I have a question," Josh begins. He points at Drew. "How did *you* know?"

My heart flutters, nervous for him, but Drew doesn't bat an eye at the question. He must have been expecting it. "That night, I heard them talking outside my room. Between the new netting on the balcony and the leaf in the box, I made an educated guess."

A few people murmur around the room. My chest aches. For Cyrus, for Stacey. For all of us.

"I'm sorry," she whispers. "I'm so, so sorry."

"You can't change what happened," Kasey adds. "Cyrus made his choice, you made yours. And we are about to make ours."

In moments of sorrow and confession, it's so easy to forget about the voting part of all of this. Especially when it's not my life on the line.

I try to make eye contact with Tatum and Drew, but neither of them looks at me. I don't want to vote for Stacey— her story sounds believable, and if anything, the leaf makes me think the Voice is trying to scare her. That probably means she's a victim like the rest of us.

"Stacey hid the truth from us," Reese says. "So I'm going to vote for her."

"She thought it was a trap!" Adrian defends. "You would have too."

"Everything is a trap," I interject. I didn't mean to speak; it just happened. "From the moment we woke up that first night, every moment has been watched, listened to, digested, and used against us."

Gripping the table, my knuckles turn white. I try to shove the anger that hit me out of nowhere down deep into my heart where it belongs. Out of sight, out of mind.

"Houseguests," the Voice interjects, and not a moment too soon. They always know just when to push and pull. "The time for talking is over. Vote."

The room holds its breath, waiting to see what is going to happen.

I hold my chalk, closing my eyes, letting my gut tell me who I need to vote for tonight.

In the end, it seems as though there is only one right answer.

I scratch the four letters onto my board, then place it face-down on the table.

Then I watch. I wait.

And I hope we are not wrong again.

THIRTY-ONE

My fingertips feel like ice as I wait for everyone to write their vote.

No one talks for a long time. Finally, the Voice breaks the silence.

"Adrian, we will start with you."

He holds up his chalkboard. "Cady. One twin has to go, I think."

Stacey's next. "I'm voting with Adrian. Cady."

Kasey votes for Stacey. Tatum votes for Stacey.

The scraping of the chalkboard against the table makes me wince as Drew shows his. "Sorry, Cady. Something about you guys… it doesn't add up."

I blow out a slow breath. He and Tatum must not have looked at each other's chalkboards, or they probably would have voted for the same person.

Raven slaps her chalkboard on the table. "I voted for Cady because she's annoying."

I frown. We're never going to get anywhere if we keep letting petty things like this decide how we vote.

"I voted for Stacey," Nick says, taking his time. "Because she lied about Cyrus, and the leaf feels like the Voice is trying to warn her. Maybe she was supposed to do something and messed it up."

Nick hasn't been my favorite person so far, but he's obviously thinking these things through. And I appreciate that.

I turn mine around, refusing to look at her. "Cady. Something about your story doesn't make sense. And I'm hoping that, by voting for you, Reese will become more honest."

It's as if I can feel her flinch next to me. "Stacey," Cady mumbles. "If it has to be you or me staying alive another day, I'm choosing me."

I count up the votes in my head. Only two people are left to go. Cady has five, and Stacey has four.

It could be either of them at this point.

Reese is quiet for just a moment too long, and a ripple goes around the table. "Stacey, obviously. Cady isn't why we're here, and I don't understand how you guys can't see that."

"Maybe because we don't know anything about you," Adrian snips.

He stiffens, gripping the arms of his chair so hard his knuckles turn white. Cady places a hand on his arm, and he takes a deep breath.

The votes are tied.

Josh revels in this moment, where he gets to break it, a smile lit on his face.

"I voted," he pauses, slowly flipping his board around, "For Cady."

Cady bows her head. She doesn't cry, she doesn't shout. She just lets out a tiny, broken breath.

My heart pinches at her reaction. Was this the right choice? I don't know that we are any closer to discovering the truth than we were—

"NO!" Reese screams, voice overlapping the Voice's as they try to wrap up our voting session. "You don't get to take her! You can't pick her!"

He lunges toward her, grabbing her in his arms as if protecting her from what may come.

It's like something snapped. And now, there's no going back.

"Cadence has received the most votes," the Voice yells overhead. "Houseguests, go to your rooms. All will be revealed in the morning. As for Cady—you will stay."

"I won't let you!" Reese roars, red-faced, spit flying. His eyes are wild in a way I've never seen.

Cady is trying to calm him down, but it's no use. His chest is heaving like he can't get enough air.

No longer the quiet, protective shadow he's been. Now, he's something else. Something broken.

She pushes him away, resigning herself to the corner to cry. "Leave, Reese. Leave! Someone *get him*!"

We all stand, ready to grab him and take him away if needed. There's no need to forfeit his own life. We've already had too many taken from us unfairly.

It's all unfair, I remind myself. I shake my head. Sometimes, I can almost convince my brain that my situation is reasonable. It's hard to wrap my head around the fact that I was just a normal college student five days ago.

Finally, Josh and Nick grab him, hooking their arms around Reese's elbows. He thrashes, trying to get free.

"You killed her," he snarls, voice dropping low as we leave the game room. "Every single one of you. You killed my sister."

The boy we thought we knew is gone—replaced by something furious.

Something none of us know how to stop.

THIRTY-TWO

The hallway feels too narrow, too loud, too full of everyone's distraught fears. Reese's shouts still vibrate my bones as Nick and Josh drag him upstairs.

He didn't even get to say goodbye, I think, wiping a tear forming on my lower lashes. The game room door slammed shut behind us, a lock clicking into place once we stepped out of the room.

I don't know what to do with my hands. I need out. Out of this hall, out of this moment, out of this house. There's a suffocating pressure tight against my chest that threatens to bury me alive.

Kasey catches my eye—just for a second—like she's checking whether I'm about to crumble.

And honestly, I might. Part of me wishes I would.

I force myself to keep walking toward the stairs. No part of me wants to go listen to Reese cry and scream all night, but what choice do I have? Where else can I go?

A warm presence falls into step beside me.

"Hey," Drew murmurs, low enough that no one else hears. I know he's noticing the way my hands are shaking and my shallow breathing. He's lived through enough panic attacks to see the signs in someone else.

I don't answer him. He jerks his chin toward a door right before the staircase, and I follow him inside. My feet lead the way before my brain can make a decision.

A tiny coat closet. There are no windows, no witnesses, and hopefully no cameras.

Let the Voice see how this is affecting us, I think. They clearly enjoy it. Our lives are simply for their enjoyment at this point.

The moment the door closes behind us, the noises outside dull to a muted throb. It's not complete silence—I couldn't expect that—but it's the closest thing to calm I've felt since we got here.

I lean against the wall, exhaling slowly, regulating my breathing patterns. My legs feel rubbery, like they might have collapsed had I gone upstairs.

Drew sinks onto the ground in front of me, elbows resting on his knees. The closet is so small that our legs touch.

Something bangs upstairs.

"That doesn't sound good," I remark.

"I don't even want to know."

I chuckle a bit, and he huffs out a laugh in response. Just something small and quick, but it's real. His eyes flick up to mine, overwhelming gentleness in them.

Leaning my head back against the wall, I close my eyes. "Thank you."

"For what?" There's genuine surprise in his voice.

"For getting me out of there."

"How do you know," he teases, "That I wasn't just looking for a way to get you alone?"

I open an eyelid, peeking at his sarcastic expression. "You could have just asked."

"What's the fun in that?"

I smile. "Right. Because this whole thing is just *so* fun."

We quiet, teasing over. The closet feels oddly warm, but maybe that's just him.

Every time I'm with Drew, I feel something close to normal. We're just two people hiding from the chaos, trying to steal a moment of peace like teenagers sneaking away from a party they didn't want to be at in the first place.

"I can't believe Reese lost it like that," he says.

"Somehow, I can. But for some odd reason, I don't think Cady would have reacted the same way if roles were reversed."

He looks at me. "What objects do you still have left to pair with a person?"

I pull out my notebook, squinting at the page in the dim light. "Bottle of alcohol. Earpiece. Just Reese and Kasey."

Drew chews on his lip. "I don't get the earpiece."

"Me neither." I tilt my head, waiting to see if he will continue. "But?"

"But," he starts. "I kinda think the alcohol is for Reese."

"Why?"

"Just a feeling."

My fingers twitch, my hands wanting to pick at my nails. He was right about his hunch about Stacey. Maybe I can trust his intuition. Before I can think, I move my feet out further, intertwining his knees with mine.

He doesn't move, doesn't flinch. If anything, I think he leans into it. He lets out a slow breath, like he's steadying himself.

This closet feels very tight all of a sudden.

"This is hard," I admit.

"You'll get through it."

"Just me?" I try to muster a teasing tone in my voice, but it falls flat.

"I'm just here to pay for my mistakes."

"What mistakes could you have possibly made in your life

that would require *this* as a payment? You're like, if golden retrievers could get 4.0 GPAs."

He lets out a surprised laugh—loud enough that I reach over and cover his mouth without thinking.

"Shh!"

He nods, giggling silently, eyes bright again.

My stomach does a stupid little flip at the sight of his dimples as I move my hand away slowly.

We're losing our minds.

But it *does* feel good to laugh.

I don't know how long we sit in that tiny closet, breathing in dusty air. Outside, voices shout and doors slam. We should probably head to our rooms soon and get some sleep, but I just don't want to go back into the games just yet.

"Can I ask you something?"

"Anything," he responds.

"Do you think we can win this?"

The question hangs in the air like a blade suspended from a rope.

"Will any of us really *win?*" he responds. Then, slowly, "Some of us will just… last longer."

My eyes drift to the floor. "And you're okay with that?"

"No," he whispers. "Of course not. But is there any other choice?"

———

We slip back out into the hall, somewhere between minutes and hours later. I've calmed down, and my brain feels rational again. There's no one out and about, and I'm thankful for it.

It's just us. I'm not ready for our time together to be over.

Just before we reach our bedroom doors, Drew slows.

"Winter?" he breathes.

I look up at him. He searches my face intently.

"If it comes down to you or me—"

"Don't," I interrupt, slicing my hand through the air. "It won't."

But I don't believe that. And judging by the look in his eyes, neither does he.

His jaw tightens. "You don't know that."

We stare at each other, reality stretching thin between us. The games, the house, our fear... it curls around us like smoke.

I turn my doorknob, the hinges creaking open. But before I can step inside, I decide to give him one more piece of me. Because deep down, we both know that if it came down to the two of us, it wouldn't matter.

There will only be one left standing.

"Call me Winnie," I whisper.

And with that, I slip inside.

DAY FIVE

THIRTY-THREE

Morning arrives in a haze.

A dark, dreary, gray haze.

Sleep barely came to me, but my body feels wide awake and alert. Leftover adrenaline coats my bones, my brain replaying every second of last night. The voting, Reese's reaction.

Drew's knees brushing mine.

I keep hearing Drew's voice above everything else.

If it comes down to you or me...

I don't want to think about that. Or the way he looked like he was ready to sacrifice himself at the thought.

Besides, chances are good that *neither* of us will be the last two standing. Our fate is not in our hands.

I push my blanket off my body and sit up. My heart thuds at the sound of knocking at my door.

It could be him.

I open my door, expecting Tatum or Drew.

Reese spits in my face.

"That's for voting for Cady."

He stalks off, leaving me both stunned and impressed. I didn't know he had the gall to do something like that.

After washing my face, I head downstairs, careful to avoid eye contact with Reese, who is pacing back and forth down the hallway. His hair is wild, his face pale and blotchy. There are shadows under his eyes so big they could be bruises.

Drew appears at my side the moment my feet hit the first floor, as if he was waiting for me. He gives me a quick, reassuring smile.

We walk into the dining room together, receiving a huge eye roll from Josh.

"Great," he deadpans. "*You* guys are here."

I open my mouth to snark back, but Drew's hand grabs my arm, tugging on me.

"Don't react," he whispers. "He's been on something all morning."

I nod slightly, taking a place at the table. Reese didn't cook this morning, it looks like. Cereal and toast it is.

Small talk floats between us like snow on the wind.

Reese storms in like a blizzard.

"You all think I'm stupid," he yells, spiraling. His bony finger points at every single one of us. "You want me gone."

Adrian stiffens. "Reese—"

A chill crawls up my spine. *This is it*, I think. *The moment we all go crazy.*

Kasey tries to calm him. "That's the name of the game. It's the Voice who wants all of us gone."

Reese barks a humorless laugh. "Not just the Voice."

I tilt my head, watching as the color drains from Kasey's face.

Drew's fingers brush my elbow lightly. A small, grounding touch. I don't look at him, because if I do, I might miss everything.

And right now, I can't afford to miss a single thing.

"What are you accusing us of?" I ask, baiting him. "If it's your life or mine, why should I choose yours?"

Reese turns to me. "You're hiding things. You're *all* hiding things. We pretend to be on each other's sides, but we're not. No one is."

"And you don't have any secrets, Reese?" Stacey asks.

His gaze hardens. "None. Of. Your. Business."

"Right," Nick says slowly, drawing out the 'i'.

"Why alcohol, Reese?" Drew asks.

The room quiets.

"What did you just ask me?"

Drew gets out of his chair, creeping toward Reese like you would a wild animal. "What does the alcohol have to do with *your* story?"

Reese stutters for a moment, but he recovers quickly. "Did you come up with that last night in your secret closet?"

Heat flares up my neck. "It's not a secret closet," I grind out. "Anyone can go in it at any time."

"Go in it with me?" Josh smirks.

"Shut. Up." I bite. Not the time nor the place. Scraping my chair against the wooden floor, I remove myself from the table, wanting a better position to watch everyone from.

But also to get away from Josh.

"Okay," Stacey begins, hands up in surrender. "What is going on here? Do you two know each other?"

I open my mouth to deny it, but Josh beats me to it.

"Go ahead, Darling."

All eyes land on me.

Before I can fluster my way out of this, Drew steps in front of me. Not blocking me exactly, but purposefully shielding me from penetrating eyes. "Back off."

Raven's eyes narrow. "Don't act all innocent and mighty, schoolboy."

"Wish I had some popcorn for this," Adrian interrupts. We snap our heads in his direction, and he shrugs. "What? Do you think there's some in the kitchen?"

He gets out of his seat to go look when Reese says, "There's not."

Adrian throws his hands in the air. "What good is morning entertainment if I can't have a snack to go with it?"

"You're an idiot," Stacey groans, facepalming.

"A cute one," Adrian smiles.

The corners of my mouth twitch, but my shoulders are still tense.

"Who's the earpiece?" Nick asks. "I don't understand that one."

I murmur along, watching reactions.

"I think it's Drew," Josh says, voice cool but tense.

Here we go again.

"I don't know what it means either," Drew responds quickly.

Josh hums. "Maybe you're just good at hiding things. Like how you talk to the Voice at night like a good little pet."

The accusation hangs heavy.

Too heavy.

Drew's shoulders tighten, like he's holding himself back. "What are you talking about?"

Suspicion glides into the room like an icy breeze.

"I think we need to take a breather—" Tatum murmurs.

"No," Reese snarls. "No more pretending. No more secrets. Let's do this."

He grabs an opal-colored plate from the table, throwing it down onto the ground so that it shatters into a million pieces.

I gasp.

"Reese—" Stacey starts, hand reaching out slowly like he might bite.

He cuts her off with a sharp gesture. "Adrian sneaks around at night."

Adrian yelps, taken aback. "I—what?"

"Kasey controls things way too much to not know anything," Reese continues. "And Nick isn't actually the jerk he wants us to think he is."

My head is spinning. What is happening?

"Stop," Nick growls.

"Hit a nerve! Pay attention, everyone." Reese is dancing around the room now like a madman. "And someone—" Reese taps Drew on the shoulder. "Knows more than they say they do."

THIRTY-FOUR

Drew doesn't move.

My heart thunders in my chest almost painfully.

"Drew?" I whisper, barely audible.

He looks over his shoulder at me, from where he's still shielding me from the group. His eyes close for half a second. Then, carefully, he responds.

"Don't give him the reaction he's looking for."

Not an answer.

"And somehow, we've forgotten all about the alcohol, haven't we?" Stacey cuts in. I appreciate her directing it back to Reese. This is becoming too much for me to keep track of.

"We're all hiding something," Kasey snaps. It's the first time I've heard genuine anger in her voice—or any emotion, really. "This is what the Voice wants from us. They want us not to trust each other."

"Of course I don't trust you people." Raven throws her hands in the air. "You have the power to *kill me*."

"And you have the power to kill me," Tatum quips. "We're all connected. Somehow."

Yes, I think. *But how?*

Josh scoffs. "You guys are just mad he figured you out."

"Maybe," I respond. "Or maybe some of us care about our fate in this game. It's suspicious that you don't."

We stand locked in a silent battle, chests heaving.

I break first, grabbing Drew's hand without thinking.

He startles, just barely, but doesn't pull away. His fingers curl around mine instinctively as I pull him out of the dining room.

Enough of accusing each other. It's not going to get us anywhere until someone actually opens up and decides to be honest.

It just won't be you, my inner voice critiques. *Hypocrite.*

"Shut up," I murmur.

Drew glances at me, a flash of something confused and worried. Warmth shoots through me so fast I forget how to breathe for a moment.

I just squeeze his hand, pulling him into the office.

"We need to trust each other," I say weakly. "And we need to keep from putting targets on our back."

He considers this. "You think they'll start targeting us because we are working together."

"Look at the twins," I whisper.

He responds with silence.

Before I can keep talking, a crackle sounds from the ceiling.

I freeze.

The Voice floods the house, tone crisp and emotionless.

"Houseguests," they begin. "Report to the parlor immediately for your next game."

I swear the temperature drops ten degrees, the lights flickering in response.

Drew's whole body shakes. "I'm not ready."

I grip his hand tighter. "You're okay."

He takes a deep breath, chest shuddering. His eyes are turned toward the ceiling, avoiding eye contact with me, as if steeling himself for what is to come.

I rest my hands on his shoulders, and he flinches. The distance between us feels unreachable. We're splintering, cracking, shattering into fragments that cannot be mended.

Just like the Voice wants.

Shutting my eyes tight, I picture my dorm room. Rest, safety, *life*. I shove those images into Drew's brain mentally, hoping he can find some sort of respite himself.

His thumb brushes the inside of my wrist. Just a tiny motion, barely there at all.

But it sends peace into my soul, and I choke on a sob emerging from my throat.

I shut my eyes tighter.

"Winnie," he murmurs, and I feel him lean down slightly, his breath tickling my ear. "Stay close to me. In this game, for the rest of our days here. Stay with me."

"I will," I whisper. "That goes for you, too." Opening my eyes, I find his hazel gaze sparkling in the light. "You're shaking."

"I'm always shaking," he teases.

He steps slightly in front of me toward the open door as voices emerge on the other side of it, heading into the parlor.

His hands go to my waist, and it's as if he's leaning in…

"You two think you're safe because you have each other," Raven's voice cuts in from behind us. "But you need to watch your backs."

I whip around, separating myself from Drew, hands tucked behind my back.

My face burns.

She opens her mouth as if to say something else, but then seems to think better of it. With a small grunt, she leaves.

"We, uh. We should go," I stutter.

"Stay with me for a second," Drew chokes. "Look at me."

I pull my embarrassed gaze back toward his.

My world narrows, and suddenly, all I see are bright eyes —ones that reflect golden rays and summer fields. They're filled to the brim with worry and chaos and *goodness*. How could I have ever doubted him?

Before this, I didn't know someone could look at you like you're both their lifeline and a danger at the same time.

But they can. I know that now.

His voice drops lower. "Whatever happens in that room… You stay with me."

My chest tightens. "Yes." That one word is all I can say. Let him use me just as I am using him. We need each other to make it through.

He lets out a deep exhale, one that shakes him slightly.

We start walking across the hall, the last ones to arrive at the parlor.

Reese is muttering to himself in the corner, and I swear his eyes are freshly red from crying. Josh keeps running a hand through his hair, pinning his eyes on me the minute I enter the room.

Drew stays by my side.

I look at the wall of portraits as we find our seats, awaiting the instructions the Voice will have for us.

Cady's portrait is marked out, the red paint fresh and dripping down the glass pane.

Drew notices my line of sight, reaching over to squeeze my hand quickly before letting go.

"I've got you," he whispers.

My heart stutters painfully. He thinks he knows my full story. He thinks he knows *me*. But if he really knew why I believe I'm here…

Would he feel the same?

You don't know his full story, I remind myself. *Would you feel the same if you knew?*

If I'm being honest with myself, I don't know the answer to that question.

THIRTY-FIVE

"Houseguests, welcome back to where it all started."

I focus on my breathing, trying to find the mental capacity to be ready for whatever curveball the Voice is about to throw at us. We are five days in, and there's ten of us left. I'm not sure I can take nine more days of this.

I'm not even sure I can make it through today.

Breathe in.

Breathe out.

"Today's game is a bit different. You will not be split into teams. Your fate—and whether you will be safe from tonight's vote—is entirely in your own hands."

My head bobs at his words, internalizing them and mulling them over. On a team, it's easier to hide and hope that everyone else comes through. When it's just you…

Well, there's no longer a place to hide.

"One by one, you will tell the group why you believe you've been chosen to be here."

The house groans against the gust of wind blowing outside.

My breath hitches. This game… it could be everything we need to figure this out.

For good.

"You have a choice: tell the truth and find yourself safe tonight. Choose not to speak… and you will not be. Lie, and you'll also be up for the vote."

There's a pause. "And let me be *very* clear: all of you are here for a reason. Deep down, you know what that is. Kasey, you're first."

She stumbles a bit standing up, clearly not ready to be the one to start us off. "I think…" She looks at us, hesitating. Will she be the first to deny saying anything? What if we all decided not to share and allowed ourselves to be up for the vote tonight? I bet the Voice wouldn't be expecting us to band together in that way.

Really, it's too bad. I know we won't. We aren't a team. I'm not sure we ever will be.

"I'm here because I've covered things up at my job. Abuse cases, stolen finances. My boss threatened me. I… I had to." She gulps, sitting back down. I've never seen her so shaken.

"Very good, Kasey," the Voice purrs.

Without pondering what everyone will think, I whip out my notebook, adding these notes under Kasey's name. The pages are slowly filling in as I've been scribbling down everything that might be important for someone.

Information that could mean life or death.

Stacey stands, itching at her bare arms, leaving red marks. She opens her mouth to speak, but nothing comes out.

We wait, expecting the worst.

Finally, she just shakes her head and sits back down.

"I see you, Stacey." Intercom systems crackle as the Voice reminds us that they are both watching and listening.

My eyes widen. I don't understand why she would choose to say nothing at all. Even if she had lied, that would be better than *nothing*. Whatever it is she's hiding… it must be big.

And that means I need to watch her closer.

Adrian doesn't bother to stand. The Voice never did say

that was a requirement, after all. It's just something we've done on our own. Maybe it makes this feel more natural—like we are just kids again, doing show and tell.

"I used to be… not the person I am today," he breathes. "Bullying was something I became very familiar with at a very early age. But I mean, I get it. I'm goofy, and kinda look weird…"

He trails off, eyes searching for some faraway place and time. "I became what I despised. *That* is why I'm here."

"Correct," the Voice cuts in.

Interesting. Adrian has never given me any reason to think he's anything but what he is. Funny, kind, meek.

Which means that he is a very, very, *very* good liar.

I jot thoughts down in my notebook, my pen scraping against the worn paper. It's warm from living between my back pocket and my hands. I've probably read these pages hundreds of times by now. If I had a better memory, my written words would be stuck in the folds of my brain. Once upon a time, I would have been able to memorize these facts.

But it's hard for me to remember things now. Trauma does that to you.

Tatum holds her stomach, looking a little green. "My sister has been missing for ten years." That's what her photograph was from in the last game—it's the last picture she has of her and her sister. "Well, about ten years. The anniversary should be coming up soon… I don't know what day it is anymore." Tears spill down her cheeks. "Am I here because of her? Is this something to do with her disappearance?"

She's hysterical now, eyes shut tight and face blotchy.

"Tatum, that is incorrect."

She turns pale, eyes wide and surprised at the admission. Before we can say anything, she rushes to the corner of the room where Reese is slumped against a potted plant and pukes in it.

"What the—" he scoots away in anger. "You can't just throw up wherever you want!"

"You're lucky men can't get pregnant," she mumbles between heaves.

Nick is next, surprisingly shifting between the balls of his feet. Is he… nervous? Unsure?

"I'm here because I've killed someone."

I'm taken aback, but his admission shocks the entire group. Tatum runs into a lamp on her way back, clearly distracted. It hits the ground with a *clink*. Drew jumps up, grabbing her arm to steady her before she trips and falls. Together, they put the lamp back where it goes, no harm done.

I cannot say the same thing about Nick's truth.

"Thank you, Nick."

The Voice's words send a chill down my spine. I'm learning more about these people now than I have in the entire five days we've spent together.

And it's because we are being forced to choose between honesty and our lives.

Which leads me to one question that I desperately need answered.

I grab my pen again, flipping to an empty page near the back cover to scribble down my new thought.

DOES THE VOICE WANT US TO FIGURE THIS OUT? IF SO, WHY?

THIRTY-SIX

Reese wipes his hands on his jeans like he's getting ready to fight someone. The air grows heavier with every secret confession, and each refusal to. It's as if the walls are shrinking with every truth.

Rolling his neck, Reese gives a half-smile that doesn't fool me.

"Hmm, why do I think I'm here?" he mutters, glancing at the ceiling cameras like he's ready to call them out. "I'm here because I'm a liar. An addicted liar with no mother, no future, and now—"

He chokes on a sob he wasn't planning on letting slip. "And now, no sister."

The intercom crackles. "That's right."

My stomach churns. The alcohol *must* have been for Reese. So that means… Is the earpiece for Kasey? I wonder if it has something to do with her job. Maybe her boss talked to her with that, somehow. When she was being controlled by him.

I wish she'd just tell us.

Silence stretches, and none of us choose to fill it.

Josh swallows loudly on purpose. "I'm here because the

Voice is obsessed with me. My hair, my face. The person behind this is probably one of my many, *many*," he looks at me out of the corner of his eye, "Admirers."

I look deeper than the smirk he's giving the group. He's shaken a bit, I think.

"Wrong."

Others gasp, but I just nod my head. He's hiding something. I refuse to forget about the note that was left for me. The *only* person that could have come from is him. I'm sure of it.

Raven moves on quickly, not giving me time to process my thoughts on Josh's incorrect admission. Her expression is flat and unamused as usual. Her face says she's bored, but her fingers tell a different story. They tremble where she's folded them across her lap.

Raven never fidgets.

She looks at us like we're nothing.

And she doesn't say a word.

An uncertain amount of time passes before the Voice decides to cut in as they did for Stacey.

Except, unlike Stacey's turn, Raven doesn't even *try* to say anything. Her mouth doesn't open, and there's no hesitation in her body language. She's certain of her choice.

That lands like a punch to my stomach as confusion ripples around the room.

"Noted, Raven."

She clutches her hands together tighter at the Voice's warped tone, skin turning a pale white.

I update my notebook furiously, making note after note of my thoughts. I take extra care to add questions that need answers, even if they'll never receive them.

My pulse picks up before I can try to stop it as all eyes land on Drew for his turn. He's steady and composed, just as he always is. But right now, he's also something else. Hollowed out and maybe even a little weary.

Perhaps the calm nature he presents is just a show, and this act is draining him day by day.

He doesn't stand, but he doesn't open his mouth either. For one terrifying second, I think he might choose not to say anything at all and do what Stacey and Raven did.

Then, he breathes in deeply.

"I'm here," he begins. "Because I survived. And I shouldn't have."

My pen pauses over my notebook as the air in the room stands still.

He rubs the back of his neck, waiting, refusing to make eye contact with me.

"Correct, Drew."

A shadow crosses his face as he comes back to himself.

My throat bobs. Something twists painfully inside my chest. A wanting. And a fear. A longing to make things right for him, and a panic about what that means for me.

But I don't have the time or safety to unpack that right now. Not when ten more days of this nightmare, and the Voice's control, hang over our heads.

I close my eyes. Besides, it's my turn now.

And I've spent years preparing to never say what I'm about to admit.

THIRTY-SEVEN

I stand. It's necessary in ways I can't explain to them right now.

My knees almost give out all the same.

Everyone watches me, but I shove my fear of their judgment deep down. I can't be afraid of them. No, I can only allow myself to be afraid of the Voice. Of being wrong. Of letting a truth slip out that might not matter after all.

Most of all, I'm scared of speaking a truth that has stalked me across towns, identities, schools, and years.

I can't look at Drew. I *can't*. I can't, I can't, I can't—

Inhale.

Exhale.

Repeat, over and over, but not for so long that the Voice deems my silence as a non-answer.

Steady, I remind myself. *You've done this before. Find your voice.*

Josh laughs at me, the sound low and cruel. I ignore him.

"I'm here because I told the truth. But I told it too late."

My voice wavers, but I don't stop. Something within me *needs* to let this out.

"Truth sets us free, yes. But it also destroys lives. And I've destroyed more than I'd like to admit."

My notebook is heavy in my hand. I await my fate, vision blurring.

"That," the Voice pauses as if to torture me, "Is correct."

I sag, visibly relieved. No part of me cares if that's held against me. I made it another night. *Safe.* I'm safe.

For now. But right now is all I can focus on. Because right now is all that matters.

As I sit, the Voice concludes today's game.

"Stacey, Tatum, Josh, Raven. You will be up for the vote tonight." Something about the Voice's tone makes my skin crawl. "Enjoy your afternoon, Houseguests."

The speakers click, and the sound rings consistently in my ear as I go back to my room.

———

Being safe, one might think the dread of this experience would fade.

It doesn't. If anything, it thickens.

Something begins to spiral in my head as I lie on top of my bed covers—connections, inconsistencies, things that just feel wrong.

Pieces of stories I've been picking at over and over again.

"Can I talk to you?" Drew asks from my doorframe. His presence catches me off guard. My brain and body need a moment alone, but I guess that's what I get for leaving the door open.

"Yeah. Yeah, that's fine." I sit up, scooting over so he can join me on the bed. Tatum is in the bathroom, cleaning up after throwing up a few more times. Today has not been kind to her.

And now she's up for the vote. *Again.*

My head starts to pound.

"Uh," Drew begins. "I just wanted to give you the rest of the story. My story, that is."

"Oh," I say, surprised. Not at all where I thought this was going. "Sure, yeah. Please."

"I was the only survivor of my school's shooting."

He says it quickly, as if it's been on the tip of his tongue this whole time.

"Wow." I don't know what else to say. I try to school my features to be nonchalant, but I can't help the shock that bleeds through. "Wow, Drew. The only one?"

"I wasn't supposed to live, I think. The person who did it —their goal was everyone. But by some miracle, I lived."

"And now," I drawl. "Now, that's the reason you're here."

He nods. "The Voice confirmed my suspicions."

We sit next to each other for a moment, and all I can hear is the sound of his breathing.

"What if," he starts. "What if *I'm* the reason we're all here? What if someone is here, tormenting me, to finish what they started?"

"Don't say that."

"It's a possibility, Winnie. You can't sit here and tell me you haven't thought the same thing."

I have. More times than I'd like to admit. We all have, I think.

If we're being honest, anyway.

"You can't be the reason we're here," I start. He opens his mouth to contradict what I'm saying, but I hold up my finger, signaling for him to wait. "Because I think *I'm* the reason."

"No."

"You can't just say 'no' to that—"

He laughs, short and humorless. "I can, and I will."

I furrow my eyebrows at him, unamused. "You didn't let me finish. You can't just say no until you've heard *my* full story, too."

He sucks on his teeth. "You don't need to tell me."

Chewing on my lip, I avoid eye contact. "I think I do."

He's silent, allowing me space to gather my thoughts and decide how I want to start.

"I told you about Josh," I begin. He nods. "Josh was just the start of it for me, really."

Taking a deep breath, I continue, closing my eyes as I transport myself back in time.

"There was a history teacher. That's what my report card was for in the item-matching game. To signify… that time in my life."

I can see it so vividly in my mind—how he treated the other girls in the class and me. The icky feeling I got when he leaned over my shoulder to check on my work. The way he said my name.

"Everyone loved him. Mr. Pearson is his name. He was charming, smart, and kind. *So* kind. He took a special liking to the girls in the high school, especially the freshmen. But they liked the attention, and it was all in good fun. At least, that's what we all thought."

I start to pick at my fingernails, and Drew lays a steady hand on top of mine to stop the habit. I look at him, giving him a quick smile of thanks.

"My senior year, just after my breakup with Josh, it felt like I had come out of a fog I was living under. For the first time in a few years, I was free. And I started to notice things."

Sighing, I start to doubt telling him this story. It's so complicated, and there are so many moving parts.

"Sorry, you didn't come in here to hear this. I won't continue if you don't want to. We can talk about something else."

"Winnie, no. I *want* to hear. I want…" he trails off. "I want to know you."

Chewing on the inside of my cheek, I look away to keep my eyes from tearing up. Not yet, not now. I need to get through the story first.

"Because of my experience with Josh, it opened my eyes to situations that other people weren't seeing. In the end, we found out that Mr. Pearson was having inappropriate relationships with many of the girls at my school. But there was one freshman who had caught my eye, and it was she who started the snowball effect that would change my life."

THIRTY-EIGHT

Curly hair. Dark eyes. Perfect smile.

"Her name was Reagan, and she was *so* fun. Like, if you could put summer in a bottle, that was her. We had a photography class together. Slowly, day by day, I noticed that the color she usually exuded began to fade."

"Eventually, she confided in me. Little pieces at a time. It wasn't until… after… that I put the complete story together."

I can't help the tears that begin to fall now as I remember the day I got the news. "I started watching him more closely. In his interactions, his words. There were a few days I followed him from school and watched him meet up with girls. One day, it was Reagan."

Sweet freshman Reagan, who I thought was telling me about boyfriend trouble she was having. But it was so much worse.

"I leaked it anonymously to our police station, asking them to look into it," I sob. "I thought I would save her and the other girls he was doing these disgusting things to."

My vision blurs. Drew squeezes my hand. I almost forgot he was here.

"They were too late. *I* was too late. She… S-she took her

life the week before they arrested him. Reagan died because of him, but the guilt I carry surpasses any anger I could *ever* feel toward him."

I should have been faster. I should have recognized the signs or told an adult when she came to me about her troubles.

"Her mother had come to the school that day, looking for Reagan. A search party went out, and when they found her..." I shudder. "You said a few days ago that you remember the sounds on the day of the shooting. Her mom's scream—the guttural, overwhelming sound of her scream—it's something I'll never, ever forget."

My chest cracks open.

"He went to prison. It wasn't his first time doing this at a school, and it wouldn't have been his last." I swallow hard. Do I finish the story? Do I tell Drew the rest?

I have to. It's important to me that I see this through.

"My identity was slipped to the public, somehow. That I was the one who ruined his career and life. He swore that when he got out, he'd find me again."

Wiping my eyes, I finish with the part I'm still coming to terms with. "He got out just a few months ago. He's coming after me, if he hasn't already."

Drew's eyes widen. "You think he could be behind all of this?"

I shrug. "I don't know. I mean, what part do all of you play in this if Mr. Pearson *is* the Voice? It doesn't make sense to me. Not when he could have just tortured me and me alone."

He ponders this, removing his hand from mine to lie back on my bed. I follow suit, placing my hands on my stomach.

"I know what it's like to be manipulated. More than that, I know what it looks like when other people are being lied to and used." I flip over to lean on my elbow, facing Drew. "Being here feels like that."

"Something's been bothering me," he whispers, eyes darting around the ceiling. "When Olsen disappeared. He was just… gone."

"Right. But how?" I respond, somehow knowing that's the question he's asking.

"Someone came to get him while we were in the game room."

I sit up. "There are passages. There has to be. And people on standby, maybe."

We stare at each other.

"Do you think they're lying to us?" I ask.

He closes his eyes, nose wrinkled. "I don't know. But it feels like we're being baited."

"Why would they have us tell the truth about why we think we're here? What could they possibly gain from that other than us figuring out the connection between us all?"

He shivers, peeking at me from behind long lashes. "What if this isn't punishment?"

I breathe out quickly. What if this isn't revenge? What if we're simply rats in a lab, being watched to see if we can get ourselves out?

Pieces start clicking together like a key in a lock.

The Voice *wants* us to talk. They want us to confess to each other, unravel, and split apart.

But why?

I flip through my notebook, pages filled with worst moments, private secrets, and decisions others have made. The words begin to blur as my head swims.

"It wasn't just Olsen," I whisper. "*Everyone* we've voted out has disappeared. No blood, no body."

I look at him, tone serious. "No screams."

Except for that first night, I don't say out loud. He props himself on his elbows, leaning in a little to read over my shoulder. We aren't close enough to touch, but if he moved over to the right just a little…

My heart races.

"Who is moving them?" he asks, posing the question just to himself, rather than to me.

I grab my pen, writing those four words on the back of a page, underlining them three times.

"Someone here knows the full story already. They know us, our secrets, and why we're here. They aren't being fed pieces like the rest of us. They already have it all put together. If we can find them, I think everything will make so much more sense."

Drew's eyes lift to mine. "It's like a test."

I swallow, scared to admit what I'm about to. "I'm not sure the deaths are real."

A weight is lifted off my shoulders at that admission. And he doesn't look at me like I'm crazy. If anything, it seems like he's had the same thought.

"Is that your theory?"

"My theory," I close my notebook, "Is that either someone is pretending to kill us to scare us, or people really *are* dying. And the Voice is trying to break us either way."

Drew shifts closer, whispering quietly and carefully. "We need to be sure," he says. "About the deaths. About these games. About everything."

THIRTY-NINE

My heart feels lighter than it has in days. Drew might not know the full story, but he knows enough to know *me*. And that is everything to me right now.

Now I just need to get through tonight's vote.

We all congregate in the game room, playing a few rounds of UNO. It's moments like this—the mundane, easy minutes—that hurt me most of all. If we all went to the same high school—if we were enrolled in the same college classes—would a lot of us be friends?

Out of the corner of my eye, I look at Josh. I wonder if it would be too much to hope that he gets voted out this evening. If he did, I wouldn't mind if the deaths were real.

Just for tonight, of course.

As I play, he snorts out of his nostrils, drawing my attention again. He's smirking, laughing to himself as if he doesn't have a care in the world.

"Dude," Nick says apprehensively. "What's your problem?"

"Good question, buddy." Josh plays a yellow three, calling out UNO. "Winter, Darling, I think it's time you share a few facts about yourself with the group."

I tilt my head, my eyes darting back and forth between his own. He knows exactly what he's doing. What I don't understand is why. Why now, why like this? I'm safe from tonight's vote, and he's not. How does he not realize I can pin things on him and sway people's opinions?

Dumb move, Josh.

I smile sweetly, playing a reverse card when it's my turn to keep him from playing his last card. "Which do you think everyone would prefer—facts about me? Or facts about *us*?"

His face pales a bit, but he regains his composure quickly. Placing his card on the table facedown, he grabs something rumpled up from his jeans pocket, smoothing it out and showing the group.

"This is the fun fact I'm referring to."

I shift, peering at the worn paper in his hands.

The article is familiar. It's burned into my brain, every line memorized to the point where I could probably recite what it says verbatim.

"What are you doing?" Drew asks, shifting in front of me protectively.

"I can't see the words from here," Stacey says. The game pauses, everyone leaning in to read.

"Winter is very clearly the reason we're all here. She got a teacher arrested, and he went to prison—"

"That's enough," Tatum speaks up, voice small.

"—someone leaked her identity, and now he's out and looking for her." He gives me a wicked grin. "Or should I say, he's already found her."

I shake my head, throat strangled.

"This says someone died," Adrian whispers, looking over the newspaper. "You killed someone?"

A tear slips from my eye. "It feels like I did."

Josh's voice continues to rise, but I try to drown out the noise. He had to have been listening to my conversation with Drew. But the article… where did *that* come from?

Unless…

"How do you have that?" I ask, voice cutting into his monologue about how I'm a liar.

He pauses, stumbling. "Uh—"

"Did the Voice give you that?" My tone is sturdy, despite how shaky I feel.

"I've been suspicious of Josh since day one," Kasey says calmly. While I appreciate her being on my side right now, the admission feels out of place. We've had five days' worth of voting, and she brings this up now?

Reese steps closer to the paper, breathing heavy. "I don't care who dies next. I don't want to be here anymore."

With that, he walks out, clearly done playing UNO and talking to us.

"Winter's a threat now," Raven says nonchalantly. "Regardless of where Josh got this, it's obviously a hint for us. And hopefully one in the right direction."

Drew shakes his head. "She's not up for the vote tonight. This conversation isn't helpful for any of us."

"And Winter would never do anything to hurt us," Tatum says softly.

"Don't be dense, Tatum," Nick scoffs.

My head whips back and forth as people argue about my involvement and the newly presented information.

Josh crosses his arms. "She can't be trusted. And neither can Drew. They've been working together this whole time— too closely, if you ask me."

Ah, so *that's* what this is about. I should have known.

"You can't weaponize her trauma," Drew snaps.

I stand, hands outstretched so my palms are facing the group. "Stop!"

"What if the Voice is the teacher?" Stacey asks the obvious question.

Suddenly, the room is alive with voices overlapping each other.

Josh creeps next to me in the chaos, grabbing my arm. "You might want to keep this on you."

He slips me the ripped piece of paper through icy fingers.

"How do you have this?" I ask.

Leaning in, he whispers directly into my ear, sending shivers down my spine. "It was a gift."

Walking away, I shove the paper in my pocket, about to leave altogether when Adrian's voice cuts out above the rest. "This is ridiculous. I'm ready to vote. I'm done waiting."

I freeze, slowly turning back toward him.

No. The Voice couldn't have heard that.

The intercom crackles.

No, please—

"Houseguests," they say. "It appears we have grown restless. Take your seats. It's time to vote."

FORTY

We begrudgingly take our seats as we wait for Reese to come back.

He never does.

I shoot a glare in Adrian's direction. I appreciate the honesty—truly, I do—but he seriously couldn't have waited another few hours? This part—the voting, the arguments, the anxiety—is the hardest part.

"Stacey, Tatum, Josh, Raven. The four of you are up for the vote tonight. Please begin."

Tatum's name rings louder in my ears than the others.

She's trying to hide her panic, but her hands flutter toward her stomach once again. Nausea begins to swell inside me like a restless storm.

"I guess we're starting without Reese?" Stacey asks.

The Voice does not answer.

"Maybe he'll join us later," Drew shrugs.

I steel my nerves, pulling the newspaper back out. I don't want to be put on display again—and I definitely don't want to give Josh more fuel for his fire—but if I'm going to rip away my peace, now's the time.

"Has anyone else received something mysteriously?" I hold up the newspaper. "A clue to the other players, perhaps?"

Heads shake as Josh turns an evil eye toward me.

"Josh and I know each other. Quite well, to be honest. I'm assuming he hasn't shared that information with you all?"

Nick raises his hand like he's in school. I roll my eyes, making a gesture like I'm calling on him.

"He, uh," he looks at Josh, as if nervous to say what he's about to. "He says your name. In his sleep."

I keep myself from blushing in embarrassment. Real cool, Josh.

Keeping my wits about me, I continue. "I received a note yesterday." I pull it from the folds of my notebook, showing the room. No one speaks, no one moves a muscle. For the first time since this game started, I feel like my words are worth something.

And for the first time, I think they're listening.

"'I know why you're here', it says. To me, there are only two people who could have known that information before today's game."

Taking a look around the room, I breathe in deeply. "Josh," I pause. "And the Voice's pawn."

As I say that last sentence, I make it a point to make eye contact with Josh. "This got me thinking—what if they're connected? What if they're the same *person*?"

I really have their attention now. Josh's face gradually turns more and more red with anger, but I don't let it stop me. He started this, and *I'm* going to finish it.

Holding the newspaper article back up, I continue. "There's no reason Josh should have this. None. Unless—" I trail off, as if still thinking. Tapping my chin, I pretend to have come to a conclusion. "Unless, of course, he's been working with the Voice this whole time."

"Winter," he grinds out. "Stop."

I ignore him, my rage a fire that cannot be contained.

This is why I chose news reporting as my major. To bring a voice to stories that need it. And if it has to be my story this time, I'm okay with that. There's no better person who can do this than *me*.

"I think Josh is the reason we're here. He's been working with the Voice all along, and his 'I don't care' attitude is real, because he doesn't have anything to care about." I sit back down. "I'll be voting for Josh tonight."

Silence rings throughout the room. Finally, the spell breaks.

"Wow," Adrian breathes. "You're a dead man, my guy."

"You guys don't seriously believe her," Josh argues. "What about the article? Why would I be the reason we're here when it's obvious all the information we've been given thus far points to *her*?"

He points at me, frantic.

"Winter isn't up for the vote tonight," Kasey says. "But you are. And if it's not you, I'll vote for Winter tomorrow."

Heads nod. A shiver runs down my spine at that thought, but I guess I couldn't have expected anything else to happen. I'm putting my life on the line for this.

"Can I cut in?" Raven asks, not waiting for any of us to answer before continuing. "Great, thanks. If I'm being honest, I'm tired of being here. I don't want to do this anymore."

Tatum gives her a puzzled look. "What are you saying?"

"I'm asking," Raven pauses. "No. I'm *begging* you all to vote me out tonight. I'm ready."

"To die?" Adrian exclaims.

She doesn't answer. Her face—which for a brief moment, held a sliver of emotion—is once again stone cold.

I tilt my head, taking her in. "What's your story then, Raven? If you're so done."

She sighs. "I think this is about me. Us being here, anyway. Plus, I don't buy Josh's act—I think he's just jealous." Raising an eyebrow at him, he shrinks back a bit in his chair. Interesting. He doesn't stand down to anyone.

"I've been kidnapped before. Almost died, actually. That's what the book was about—it's my story. And right before this complete fiasco, I got a letter in the mail telling me to watch my back. The kidnapping didn't take me by surprise. All of you being here did."

I suck air in through my teeth quickly and sharply. "W-what?"

She just nods, as nonchalant as ever. "I beat death once. I'm not interested in trying to do it again."

Voices rise as I put those pieces together. Peering at Raven, something is swimming beneath the surface of her unamused attitude. Something like… sadness. Maybe regret?

"If we're bringing up other names…" Stacey begins. "I want to vote for Tatum tonight. I know that makes me the worst person in the world, especially because I know *I'm* up for the vote tonight too—"

Nick huffs a laugh, raising his voice. "Get to the point!"

Stacey startles. "Right. Uh, she got the reason why she's here wrong. And the Voice said that if we really thought about it, we'd know. So I just think, she's not as dumb as she wants us to believe."

I quirk an eyebrow at her, and she catches it, blushing. "Not that I think she's dumb, of course…" she mumbles.

"That's an interesting point," Kasey adds. She's so shortly spoken, it's getting on my nerves. I wish that, for once, she'd say what she's thinking. Or what she really means.

Nick leans forward, placing his elbows on the table. "I guess if we're throwing everyone's names out there, I want to vote for Stacey. Blah, blah, blah, she talks too much. And then she doesn't. I can't get a read on her, so I want her gone."

I huff in annoyance. Did everyone just forget about my entire monologue presenting evidence against Josh? I shoot him a quick look, and he's smirking, like he *knows* he's getting away free tonight.

My brain wants to throw a fit, scream, cry, and yell at everyone to listen to me again, but I know I can't. I did my part—I planted the seeds that needed planting. Now, I just need to wait.

And hope.

FORTY-ONE

"Houseguests," the Voice intercedes at just the right—and wrong—time, as always. "The time for talking is over. Place your vote on your chalkboard."

Inhaling deeply, I do what I must and write Josh's name on the chalkboard. Looking out of the corner of my eye, I try to catch a glimpse of other people's boards, but arms and heads block my view.

I guess I'll just have to be surprised. Great.

Reese still hasn't made an appearance. I'm not sure if I should be worried or relieved. What does it mean that he didn't make it to the mandatory voting time? Surely that will be punished.

Once everyone's boards are facedown, the Voice says, "Kasey, we will start with you."

She turns around her board, placing her hands in her lap. "I think it's Tatum. She's playing a smart game, but it's not enough." She looks around the room, peering at us. "Also, I'd like to offer a show of trust to you all. I heard some of you questioning which object was mine. It's the earpiece. I often coordinate job fairs and other company-related conferences.

That earpiece is used to keep me in touch with my boss and follow their orders."

Looking straight at me before moving eye contact elsewhere, she continues. "I just, I know there's been some talk concerning that, so I wanted to set the record straight."

I chew my lip. I'm grateful for the clarification, but this didn't feel like the time or the place.

Stacey flips around her board, revealing Tatum's name. "I think this does have to do with your sister. Maybe you were blackmailed into doing this because you want information or something. If that's the case, I hope you get it."

A tear slips down Tatum's cheek. I can't believe she has two votes already. This is going so, so wrong.

"Stacey," Adrian says. "I voted for you. Your energy doesn't feel right."

She squeals. "My *energy*?!"

He just nods, not making eye contact or provoking her further.

Tatum's turn. "Josh," she says. "I believe Winter."

He rolls his eyes, waiting for Nick to show his vote.

Turning his board around, he shows us Raven's name sloppily scrawled on his board. "She wants to go. Who am I to deny her that?"

Drew and I are next, both voting for Josh. He doesn't look surprised, but he does look irritated.

Good.

So far, Josh has the majority. Now if we can just keep it that way…

"Raven," Josh says, showing his board. "I'm with Nick. You want to die so I don't have to? Fine by me."

Disgust boils in my throat, threatening to come up in a blind rage.

Raven's the last vote left, and I prepare myself to see Josh's name written on her board. She can't vote for herself, and for a moment, I feel incredibly smug at that rule. I know I convinced her—

"Tatum," she winces.

"No!" I scream, unable to stop myself. *What?* Where did I go wrong?

Raven gives me side-eye, waiting for me to be done. "If I can't vote for myself, it's gotta be you. I'm more convinced that it's Winter than Josh. Didn't feel right to vote him out."

Josh smiles at me smugly as I begin to hyperventilate. Tatum's breath hitches as her fate rushes toward her like a car unable to be controlled. Her hand flies instinctively to her stomach, and she looks like she's about to throw up.

"No," I whisper. "No, no, no."

Drew grabs my arm, stopping me from standing up and rushing over there. I wrench it out of his hands as the Voice comes back to life.

"Tatum, you have received the most votes and are banished from the house. Please stay behind to await further instruction."

I run over to her seat, where she starts to whimper. "It's okay, Winter."

Folding my body over hers protectively, I'm at a loss for words. She's about to lose her life, and she's comforting *me*?

A warm hand finds my back as the rest of the group leaves awkwardly, silently, as if they didn't just condemn her to death for no reason.

"Remember your theory," Drew whispers to me. "Hold onto that."

Tatum leans in and hugs me tightly. The kind of hug that could be nothing other than a goodbye.

My knees buckle as I walk away, and Drew catches me before I hit the floor.

The door slams shut behind us.

"She'll be okay," he whispers, but his voice is shaking too.

I want to believe him, but I can't.

All I can think is that if the deaths are fake, she's alive. And I'll see her on the other side.

But if they're not… If the deaths are real and I'm completely wrong…

Then we just killed a girl carrying a life inside her. A baby that will never know its mother's embrace. Tatum will never hold her child in her hands, or hear their first words, or watch them take their first steps.

I clutch my theory tightly with both my hands.

I have to. I have to stay strong and hold fast to it.

Because if I don't, the alternative option just might break me completely.

DAY SIX

FORTY-TWO

Every time I close my eyes, I picture Tatum being killed. Echoes of her soft breathing as she slept torment my mind. It's as if she's still in the room with me. I feel her arms around me in our final, impossibly gentle hug.

But every time I gaze back at her bed, the pit in my stomach grows larger.

Exhaustion eventually drags me under, but it's not true rest. No, it's something between drowning and grief. Heavy, dark, slow. I'm being pulled underwater with no hope of resurfacing.

And I want to stay there. Forever.

I wake in the middle of the night, darkness surrounding me. The room feels colder than it normally does, but maybe that's just the absence of Tatum's presence. My world is now dipped in everlasting fog.

"Winnie."

Drew's voice is soft from the doorway. I lift myself on my elbows, motioning with my head that he can come in. A sliver of light enters through the hall, illuminating his features.

Sitting on the edge of my bed with his knees pulled up, I make out dark circles under his eyes. He's not sleeping either.

"I can't believe they're both gone," I rasp. Olsen and Tatum, Tatum and Olsen. Two people I had full trust in. Two people I wanted to protect until the very end.

I know the point of all of this is for only one of us to make it to the end. But somehow… I don't know. I thought I could keep us safe. Keep *them* safe. It's what I'm supposed to be doing, keeping other people safe—

Somehow, I keep failing.

Drew nods, knowing exactly what I'm thinking. I'm sure he's been thinking it too.

The air in my room feels wrong. Empty, just like my heart.

"Do you need anything? Water?" he asks gently.

I shake my head. My hands are trembling, so I shove them under my covers. There's no reason for him to worry about me.

"What time is it?" I ask.

"Early," he chuckles softly.

I push myself more upright, but the motion sends a rush of dizziness crashing over me. I've been lying down since we said goodbye to Tatum—forsaking the idea of showering and putting on fresh clothes. It didn't feel right, cleaning myself of her death.

Drew leans over, ready to steady me, but I wave him off.

"I need air," I murmur.

"I'll go with—"

"No." The word comes out too fast, too sharp. "I just… I need a minute alone."

He hesitates. His jaw tightens like he wants to argue.

I gulp. "Please."

Finally, he relents, moving back to let me slip out of the room.

The hallway must also be mourning my friends. The lights are dim, and it's more silent than I've ever heard it.

And cold.

My bare feet pad against the floor—I *did* take my socks off before climbing into bed. I'm practical, at least—as I make my way to the balcony.

The door is open, letting in a cool night breeze.

No wonder it's so cold in here.

I freeze for a moment, peeking, making sure someone else isn't already out there.

Empty.

I take my time, deepening my breath against the chill. Goosebumps erupt on my arms as I peer out into the night sky, watching stars emerge and disappear within the same breath. There's hardly any moon, and visibility is low.

But it's quiet. Serene.

And that's exactly what I needed.

As I walk back to my room, a faint sound pricks at the back of my mind.

Clink.

I tilt my head, pausing, waiting to hear it again.

There—softer, like something in the walls.

It's an old house. Probably just the pipes…

Again, to my left.

My pulse jumps. I should ignore it. Nothing good ever comes from investigating weird sounds—especially on your own.

But I think my time for worrying about self-preservation is over. I'm never making it out of here alive. If the Voice wants to speed things along…

Well, be my guest. There's nothing left in here for me to live for, anyway.

Drew is here. I plunge my nails into my palm, ripping that thought from the forefront of my brain.

Instead of dwelling on that thought, I follow the sound, and it leads me to a painting hanging on the wall. It's large— about half my size—and hangs to the left of Drew's room.

There's nothing too special about it—just a painting filled with chaotic splatters of black and maroon.

The sound murmurs again from behind it.

My breath hitches. Should I go get Drew?

Before I can answer my own question, I reach out and touch the frame. It moves slightly, like a door might if it were left open.

Lifting the edge carefully, I pull the painting aside, opening it all the way.

There, built into the wall, is a matte-black rectangular panel. It's a smooth surface, hardly noticeable even with the painting removed.

The sound rattles closer this time.

Holding my breath, I look back toward the hallway. Empty.

Pressing my fingers to the edge of the panel, it shifts. I push harder, and it slides open.

Cold air rushes out, brushing my skin.

A crawl space beckons me forward, and without thinking twice, I wriggle inside.

It's narrow and cramped. Dark, but ribbed with wiring. Bundles of red, blue, and yellow cables snake along the small space toward other parts of the house.

The sound goes off again, coming from a small box in the corner. On it, one word is lit up in bright red, reading 'recording'.

I breathe out, slow and quiet.

We know they're recording us. Both through cameras and microphones—probably everywhere.

But this. This confirmation just makes it feel so…

Different.

I crawl back out of the hole, making sure to replace the painting exactly how it should be. One wire holding it in place had been removed from its hook. Was that intentional? Did someone knock it loose?

Burying the question I really want to ask, I head across the hall to my room.

Or was the Voice here and simply made a mistake?

FORTY-THREE

When I return to my bedroom, Drew is instantly alert.

"What happened?"

How he knows I'm shaken, after only knowing me for less than a week, is insane. I guess that's what a trauma bond can do to people.

Sitting on the bed, I let my head hang toward my chest.

"Talk to me," he whispers.

"I found a hidden panel in the wall," I say softly. "Wires and stuff, something that said it's recording. Next to your room."

He blinks, startled. "Did anyone else see?"

I shake my head.

He mumbles under his breath, words I can't catch. My brain is shutting down again, ready to succumb to the fog that is Tatum's absence. The box and hole in the wall don't matter to me anymore. I just want to disappear.

I lay back on my bed, not bothering to cover myself back up. Drew notices my shiver.

He grabs my blankets, pulling them around me and up toward my chin. "I just wanted to check on you. I'll go." He gets up, heading back toward the door. Before I can talk myself out of it, I shout after him.

"Wait!"

He turns, eyes curious. I blush, embarrassed. My voice came out more desperate than I meant for it to.

"Will you," I hesitate. "Uh, would you stay? We don't have roommates anymore, and I know it might be weird to sleep in Tatum's bed, but it would be really nice to have—"

He cuts off my rambling. "I'd love to."

Without another word, he moves toward me quickly, kissing me on the forehead. I sink into my mattress, heart warmed.

He slips into Tatum's bed, lying on top of her covers. "Goodnight, Winnie."

I whisper back, eyes already drooping. I'm safe with him. "Night."

<hr>

Lunch comes too early.

Drew left the room sometime around breakfast, offering to grab me a plate. I declined, stating I wanted to shower and get cleaned up.

I lied. I haven't left my bed.

Somehow, he knows. Because when the grandfather clock chimes noon, he's at my side, pulling me to my feet.

"You can't stay in here forever," he says, pushing my sweaty hair back off my forehead.

"I want to," I mumble.

His mouth is set in a frown, not sure how to bring me back from the brink of this depression I've surrendered to. "Shower, Winnie. I'm not leaving this room until you do. *Please* don't make me come into the bathroom with you."

I huff, shoving him off of me. That sentence alone propels

me into action. He grabs me new clothes from my closet and pushes me toward the bathroom.

I pause as I shut the door behind me, realizing that I now have this bathroom all to myself. Now that Tatum's gone, there's no one to share this space with.

Tears threaten to rain down my cheeks, but I shove them back. I don't want Drew to hear me crying—I can wait until I'm in the shower.

Turning it on as hot as it will go, I strip my old layers, carefully folding them and placing them on the sink. This is the last shirt I hugged Tatum in. I will not discard that.

I melt as I step into the shower stream, letting the steam fog up the bathroom mirror. I don't want to admit it, but Drew was right. I *needed* this. Time to grieve, space to think.

All I can do is hold on to hope that the deaths aren't real, for whatever reason. It doesn't make sense to me, not yet, but I'll figure it out. I have to.

Once I'm changed and cleaned up, Drew smiles at me. "I'm proud of you."

I ignore the praise and head back toward my bed. "I'll take that plate if the offer is still open."

He laughs. "Oh no, you're coming with me." He grabs my wrist, tugging me gently toward the door.

I look back at my bed, arm extended, reaching for my safe space. "I don't want to see people yet. Drew! No!"

Wrapping his arms around my waist, he flings me over his shoulder like a sack of potatoes. I kick and flail, hoping he'll set me down. Finally, he relents, pulling me in close so I can't get away.

Breathless, I look up at him, frustrated and ready to turn on the charm. Whatever it will take for him to let me go back to bed…

"Winter," he murmurs. "I can't do this without you. I can't go back down there without you."

My breath hitches, body frozen as his thumb slowly moves

back and forth on my cold skin. Regret pools in my stomach. I've only been thinking about myself—I never gave a second thought to how this might be affecting him, too.

I can't win this fight. He's right—we need each other right now, more than ever. My shoulders slump in defeat. "Okay. I'll go."

He smiles again, and it's blinding. "You promise?"

I hold out my pinky, offering it as both a joke and a very real agreement. "Promise."

We lock fingers, and he pulls my hand in for a quick kiss. It's sweet, and the butterflies in my stomach aren't protesting the gesture. But at the same time, worry threatens to overtake my giddiness. We don't know what the rest of our time here will bring. We don't even know what's waiting for us *today*.

Have we gotten too close, too soon? Am I letting this… crush… distract me?

My heart sinks. The possibility that he's the Voice's pawn isn't zero.

And oh, how that betrayal would sting.

I steel my spine. I just need to be careful. Maybe take a few steps back, not ask him to sleep in my room again. Even though I *did* sleep better than I have all the other nights we've been here…

Something is off when we enter the dining room. Everyone else is already there, and they look wrecked.

Stacey's hands tremble in her lap. Adrian is pacing and muttering under his breath. Raven stares at her empty plate, dead-eyed. Kasey is leaning forward on the table, observing intently.

And Nick and Josh won't stop fidgeting, knees bouncing, and knuckles tapping.

Reese isn't here, which still worries me. We haven't heard anything yet about him. Could he still be in his room? I should have checked.

Pasta sits untouched in the center of the table.

"What's going on, guys?" Drew asks, taking his usual seat. I grab the one next to him, eyes bouncing between others.

"I can't do this anymore," Stacey declares.

"Literally no one cares," Josh mutters.

Stacey stiffens. "Excuse me?"

"You think we're having *fun?*" Josh says, rolling his eyes. "None of us wants to be here anymore. Get over yourself."

She stands. "We should have voted you out last night."

"And," Adrian interjects. "Let's all remember that *one* of us is having the time of their lives."

"You're enjoying this," Raven says flatly. "Don't pretend you're not."

Adrian laughs, the sound empty and hollow. "Yeah, because this is just a vacation to me. Sorry, guys, totally forgot."

"You want to go on a vacation? I can make that happen." Josh cracks his knuckles. "Better you than me."

Stacey's chair screeches as she stomps her foot, face red with fury. "Shut up, shut up, shut up! You don't care about anyone but yourself."

I snort. Josh gives Stacey a lazy grin. "Been told that my whole life. Try something new for a change."

Stacey's breath shudders as the room stands still.

And something inside her breaks.

She grabs a knife from the table.

My heart stops.

"Stacey—" I gasp, Drew and I already running toward her.

But she's already lunging.

Everything erupts. Her body slams into the table, dishes clattering and breaking as they fall. Josh leaps back in surprise, but she's already on him. He's bigger and stronger than she is, but she has the element of surprise on her side.

"Get off!" Josh snarls, both of them crashing to the floor.

She screams, a feral, guttural thing, swinging the knife wildly so that none of us can get too close.

Finally, Nick grabs her left arm, and Raven surprisingly moves in to restrain her right.

Stacey raises the knife again—

A piercing alarm detonates from the ceiling.

Everyone freezes, hands clamping to ears at the sound, Stacey included. Screams and sirens penetrate the air.

Kasey kicks the knife away from Stacey.

"Violence outside of my own will not be tolerated. This will be your first and only warning." The Voice booms forcefully from the speakers.

Stacey begins to cry.

Josh rubs blood from his cheek, stunned. There are drops on his white t-shirt.

No one speaks.

"Because of this, today's game will be altered. You will all remain in designated areas until you are called upon."

A chilling pause.

"Do not test me."

The speakers click off, and silence suffocates the room.

FORTY-FOUR

We leave the dining room in shocked, fractured pieces.

Still no word about Reese, but my brain doesn't have much room left to wonder what's going on with him.

All I can see is the knife glinting under the fluorescent light as it moved toward Josh's throat.

He has a napkin pressed against his cheek, eyes darting. A storm is gathering in this house. In us, around us. As Drew walks beside me down the hallway, I feel it pressing in from every direction.

"We're gonna make it through tonight," he murmurs into my ear.

I don't answer. Somehow, deep down, I know:

The Voice has reached its breaking point with us. And tonight is going to be something much worse.

I can't believe I'm about to admit this to myself, but I'm incredibly bored.

The Voice ordered each of us to go back to our rooms

until called upon. Stacey is now in Cady and Faith's old room, and Josh was ordered to move into Reese and Cyrus'.

An announcement came on as soon as Josh protested moving into Reese's room. "Why isn't he in there?" he had shouted.

"Reese is dead. As of last night, Reese took matters into his own hands."

We didn't get much else other than that. The Voice's tone was frustrated, annoyed even. We were forced into our rooms with little else to go on.

The fact that the Voice gave us that tidbit of information makes my head spin. Reese wasn't a friend, exactly. But he was still one of us. And if the pressure of the house got to be too much for him, what's stopping it from becoming too much for the rest of us?

What will the Voice do if we kill ourselves before they get the chance to do it?

I hope, above everything else, that he and Cady have been reunited with their mom. I hope they're at peace.

The intercom crackles to life, finally jarring me from my mind's wandering. It's probably for the best—I'm ready to get whatever is about to happen over with.

"Before tonight's game," the Voice says, calm and controlled. "Each of you will receive a personal hint. These hints are designed to give you a strategic advantage—as long as you're clever enough to use them. Should you not..." They laugh into the microphone. "Well, that's entirely up to you."

My room goes dark, all the lights shutting off on their own. I sit on my bed, picking at my fingernails, awaiting whatever this hint might be. Do I listen to the Voice's advice? Or should I risk my life in this game and do things my own way?

It could be a trap. A way to test our confidence and resolve.

"Winter."

I shoot straight up, hands stuck at my sides, waiting. That was quick.

My gaze finds the intercom hidden in the ceiling.

"Your hint is: Do not pair with an ally."

I tilt my head, eyebrows furrowed, not expecting this. Do they mean Drew?

The Voice doesn't give me long to process, and I don't have the opportunity to ask clarifying questions. They've already clicked off the speaker and surely moved on to the next person when my brain finally catches up.

My stomach drops. Pair? We're pairing up for the next game?

Why wouldn't the Voice want me to pair up with Drew? Unless…

Unless we're onto something. And they don't want us getting the same information.

I won't make my decision on who to partner with tonight just yet. I want to wait to see what the game entails and what's at stake if I lose. Plus, others might be getting different hints. Their hints might tell me something if they choose to share.

Drew and I trust each other. If my fate lies in my partner's hands, I'm not sure I could say the same about someone else.

Eventually, the lights come back on. My door opens on its own.

I guess that means we're free to walk around again.

Immediately, I walk across the hall to Drew's door, but he's nowhere to be found. I frown. Why didn't he come see me first? Where is he?

A pit forms in my stomach as I return to my room and shut the door. Something about him just leaving doesn't feel right. Leaning against the door, I sink to the floor. There's no one else I want to seek out right now. And if he didn't come find me… What does that mean for what he learned? Maybe the Voice told him the same thing.

My brain does a complete flip on my train of thought.

Maybe I need space. From him, anyway. From our partnership. Maybe I *should* trust the Voice's advice tonight.

I'm relying too much on this one person to get me through this game, and he might not even make it out tonight alive. Tatum and Olsen didn't. What makes me think Drew would be any different? I can't lose another person close to me.

And the solution to that would be to not be close to him anymore.

A tear falls down my cheek. I know what I need to do. I just really, really, *really* don't want to.

FORTY-FIVE

I head to the parlor, just to be around people but not necessarily *with* them. Kasey nearly runs into me on my way.

"Winter!" she exclaims. "Hey, actually, I'm glad I ran into you. Can we talk?"

I give her a tiny nod, apprehensive. Out of everyone, she's kept to herself the most. Always watching, taking in information. A bit like I've been playing, I guess. Maybe we're more alike than I realized.

She steps closer. "I just wanted to say… I'm, uh." She rubs the back of her neck. "I'm really sorry about Tatum."

Her name hits me like a punch to the stomach. This is grief I'll never get over, not until my last breath.

My friend. Gone.

"I know that might not mean anything," she continues. "But I didn't… I know we haven't talked much. I haven't been very outgoing, really. But—"

A tear pricks her eye. "I don't want to be enemies. We're alike, you and I. And I'd like to be on your side. If you want that." She rushes the last four words, as if worried I'll shoot her down.

Her sincerity throws me for a bit of a loop. I tilt my head, assessing her.

"Thank you," I say softly. Relief floods her face so quickly that it hurts to look. "I'd like that."

"If you need anything, I'm here. Okay?"

I nod as a strange pang hits my chest. Maybe I should have tried harder at the beginning to get to know more than three people.

She could be faking it, my inner voice yells at me. *Everyone else got hints too, remember?*

I shake off that thought. What purpose would the Voice telling her to get close to me accomplish? But then again, why is she choosing now to reach out to me like this, rather than a few days earlier?

Something I'll digest later.

We part ways, and I'm grateful for that exchange. Maybe it wouldn't hurt that badly to get closer to her, seeing as we only have a few days left. It could give me space from Drew and give us a chance to rely on other people.

A warm body slides onto the couch next to where I sit.

Speaking of Drew.

"Winter," he says, a little frantic. His eyes are darting back and forth between me and the door. "What did the Voice tell you? What was your hint?"

I open my mouth, but quickly shut it. He feels really on edge right now, and I don't like it. I could lie. Or, I could tell him the truth and be honest about needing to pair up with someone else tonight.

But both things require us to be close, and right now, that's something I can't afford. Not anymore.

I shake my head. "I can't tell you."

His face falls like I've hit him. "What? Why?"

Pinching my lips together, I look at my lap. "I need some space, Drew."

He hesitates, clearly confused and taken off guard. "Space? Now?"

I nod. "Yeah. Please." I don't want to beg, but I will if I have to.

Before I can change my mind, and before he can decide to argue my request, he leaves.

I flop down onto the couch, wishing I had never gotten myself into this mess.

———

We're led into the dining room for our game. The chandeliers glow softly and honey-warm, as if we are safe here.

We're never safe. We haven't been since we woke up that first night.

The Voice comes on over the speakers, instructing us to get into pairs.

Drew makes eye contact with me immediately, and I see him heading my way. Panicking, I do what I have to and grab the arm of the person closest to me.

It just so happens to be Josh.

I wince, removing my hand, but quickly recover as he looks down at me with a confused look on his face.

"Partner?" I ask.

His eyes widen. "What?"

"I need a partner," I grind out slowly, trying my best to smile. *Please take the bait.*

He grins triumphantly. "Of course. I knew you'd come around."

I resist the urge to throw up. Or roll my eyes.

Or both.

I let my arm hook with his, and something shifts in his eyes. Already, I've snared him. He's too easy.

Over Josh's shoulder, I see Drew watching. His jaw is tight, and his eyes gleam with something wounded and raw. Because of me.

I look away. I can't have him coming over here.

It has to hurt for this to work. For both of us.

I soften my voice—my body language, *myself*—into the old version of me. I morph into the person Josh dated. The one who looked at him as if he hung the moon.

Somehow, he falls for it.

He leans into me slightly, drawn by muscle memory and the need to prove something to those watching.

And I let him. I let him think he can trust this—us. For now, I have to believe that the Voice was giving me good advice. My survival just might depend on it.

I look around at the other pairings, wondering what hint everyone else got. Adrian is with Nick, and Kasey partners with Raven.

Drew is standing next to Stacey, and a ping of jealousy rings through my brain.

I ignore it. He's just… doing what he has to. Because of me.

Glancing at them from the corner of my eye one more time, I breathe out, expelling all care from my body.

I have to win this. Something within me is saying that tonight is big.

"Tonight," the Voice purrs. "Four of you will die."

FORTY-SIX

My knees buckle. I can't form a cohesive thought, and it doesn't seem like anyone else can either.

Josh holds me up while my jaw stays firmly planted on the floor.

A panel in the table opens up, four switches rising from a platform to sit in the middle.

Two red, two blue. A black panel divides the switches, putting one red and one blue on either side.

"The game is simple. Each round, either the red or blue switch will be considered safe. Once your partner decides which they'd like to flip, you *must* choose the other color."

Josh looks at me, searching my face like there's an answer written somewhere on my skin. I give him a small, hopefully reassuring nod. There's no way this game is going to be strategic. We are in the Voice's hands.

Still, I can't panic. I don't want Josh to think something is up or that I want to switch partners. For whatever reason, I need to be *his* partner today.

"Whoever picks the safe switch will live to see another day. The other will die. Tonight."

I blow out a slow breath. These are… the biggest stakes we've had yet. I thought we had at least another week of torture left in this house. After tonight…

We'll be down to four of us.

Something chills my blood. My heart pounds so hard in my chest, I can't hear anything else the Voice says.

Josh tugs on me, leading me toward the table.

I guess we're up first.

Taking my seat on one side, I wait for him to sit. Red or blue, blue or red? I need to make my choice before he does. I don't want my fate in his hands.

The divider between us feels like such a small wall in comparison to the war zone we've been living in.

Without thinking twice, I switch the blue on. It's a calming color, which maybe is why I chose it? The switch lights up, illuminating my face. Gasps sound from behind me, but I don't look around. I just wait for Josh to pick the red, knowing he has to. If he had chosen the safe color, I would have been forced to flip the unsafe one. If he had chosen the unsafe color first, then I would have survived, but only by his hand.

It's better this way, I tell myself. That I made the choice first. This way, he didn't sentence me to my death. It was my doing—my own stupidity—that did it.

Soon, we'll know.

Josh and I stand back up at the Voice's direction, going back over to the other pairs to wait.

The room is suddenly flooded with a blue so vibrant, it's blinding. Every lightbulb has changed color, coating us in overwhelming cobalt.

"The correct color," the Voice remarks, "Was blue."

Relief floods my body. Safe—I'm *safe*, again!

And Josh isn't just unsafe. He's marked for death.

His time in this game—in this life—is over.

Part of me feels regret. But it's only a very small sliver. My heart can't help but feel a small bit of relief that I might finally be rid of him. I'll no longer think that I see him in the grocery store, or expect him to text me out of the blue. It feels like winning.

I gulp. How can I think that? I don't even recognize myself anymore. He may have hurt me, broken my heart, and done things to me I wouldn't wish on another person, but I've *never* wanted him *dead*.

Josh's hand slams on the table, but he doesn't say a word. His jaw is firm, a muscle twitching as he grinds his teeth together.

I stay by his side as if in solidarity. Really, I just don't know where else to go. I don't know what else to do.

As the lights turn back to their normal yellow coloring, Drew and Stacey take their respective seats at the table.

As I watch them, waiting for them to make their choices, a realization hits me like a ton of bricks.

The Voice told me not to pair with an ally for this. If I had, either Drew or I would be killed tonight.

Someone—the Voice, perhaps—wants both Drew and me to still be in this. Together.

But why?

Drew doesn't look around—he just stares at the switch. It's weird that we can see everyone making their choices. It gives me a funny feeling in my stomach, something unsettling.

Drew takes after me, hurriedly flipping a switch. He chooses blue.

I blow out a slow breath. If my hypothesis is correct…

Stacey licks her lips, flicking the red switch because she has to.

They get back up, their turn taking much less time than ours did. Or maybe that's just my brain anticipating what's coming.

The room floods with navy light again, marking Drew as safe.

I knew it. The Voice wants us in this game. We were going to be safe no matter what.

I let out a relieved sigh, melting a bit. It feels good to know that, for whatever reason, a hypothesis of mine was correct. I try to catch Drew's eye, but he doesn't look at me. And why would he? I've not been the person that he's gotten to know over these last few days. He has every right not to have any trust in me right now.

Maybe I can tell him my clue after this. We need to work together now more than ever if the Voice truly does want both of us alive.

Raven's eyes are sharp and calculating, but Kasey hesitates behind the divider. Her hand hovers over the red switch, but Raven gets to it first. Kasey is forced to choose blue.

We are bathed in blue lighting again. Kasey is safe, and Raven's time is up. It's been blue every time.

Raven's shoulders slump for a moment, but then she turns calm. She's ready, I think. Ready for this to be over. For some reason, this is the ending she wanted.

I can't blame her.

Finally, Adrian and Nick make their stand. Nick flips the blue one quickly, not waiting a second to see what Adrian might do. Adrian is left with red, and red was the right choice this time.

Nick is as good as a dead man.

It doesn't feel real—that so many of us would be immediately out of the house like this. There's no need to scramble tonight—no need to plan for who you're voting for.

Our lives are incredibly expendable. This game has proved that.

As I look around the room, a thought hits me like a lightning strike, burning me up on the inside.

One of the other three remaining people has more information than the others. They know what we're all doing here.

I know we didn't get rid of the person causing all of this in the game we just played. The Voice wouldn't let that happen. Tonight was calculated by the Voice—likely controlled by them, too. They hand-picked who they wanted to kill and who they wanted to keep alive.

FORTY-SEVEN

When the dining hall doors reopen, I feel Drew's gaze across the room.

He doesn't speak, doesn't approach. If anything, he moves backward from where I still stand with Josh.

"Congratulations," the Voice begins. "We have a final four. Those of you who were not marked safe are expected in the game room immediately."

And with that, silence.

Somehow, I'm still standing.

The eight of us start to congregate toward the hallway, about to part ways. I feel numb—like I'm watching myself experience this moment from outside of my body.

Raven gives us a salute, then immediately heads for the game room. I watch her sit down in one of the empty chairs surrounding the round table, arms crossed, waiting.

She has a spine made of steel. I would be a nervous wreck right now, giving myself as much time as possible to *not* enter that room.

"Winter," Josh murmurs. The hair on the back of my neck stands up. "Darling, can we talk? Please?"

Something in his voice—desperation, maybe?—pulls at

me. My body protests, but I give in. I can give him this one last thing, can't I? After all the years we spent together, even after how it all ended. If this is how he dies, I don't want to be left with regrets.

We move toward the far end of the hall, out of earshot. Stopping a few feet apart, I wait.

"I need you to listen to me, okay? Don't interrupt. Just listen."

I nod.

"Someone gave me the newspaper article."

My heart stutters. My mouth opens on its own to say something back, but I remember his request and quickly shut it.

"It was lying on my bed last night. There were no instructions—I didn't know what to do with it. It had to have come from the Voice."

A question nags at the back of my mind. I know he said not to interrupt, but I haven't listened to Josh in a long time. "Did you leave me a note a few nights ago?"

His Adam's apple bobs. "Yes."

My mouth feels dry. I knew it. "Were you just trying to scare me? Or what?"

He looks down at his feet. This is a version of Josh I've never seen—one that's embarrassed. "I was jealous. Of Drew. And thought… I thought, if I made you question him, you'd find someone else to be close to."

I tilt my head. "All that did was make me suspicious of *you*."

He rubs the back of his neck. "Yeah. I was also kinda hoping you'd confront me."

I'm about to walk away in frustration when he catches my arm. "Wait! I wasn't done."

"You have to go, Josh."

"I *know*," he whines. "Da—er, Winter. I don't know how to say this. But I was invited to be here."

My stomach drops. An incessant buzzing sounds in my ears. There's no way he just said…

"I got a letter in the mail. Anonymous. Asking if I'd like to see you again, but that I would have to participate in a life-or-death game. I said yes." He blows out a slow breath, slightly laughing. "I thought it was from you, honestly. I don't know. I wasn't thinking, I guess. Because the next thing I know, I'm here. I don't remember much between that and this, like the rest of you—I'm being honest about that."

"Idiot." I shake my head, searching his eyes. There's sincerity there, and a bit of panic. I will my brain to think otherwise, but unfortunately, I believe him. "Why didn't you tell me sooner?"

"You hate me."

"Yes," I respond quickly, though that might not be entirely true. "And no." Hurt by him? Yes. Ready to never see him again? Also yes. But this information could have changed everything for us these last six days.

"Part of me felt like I was invited to be here because I had a part to play. I was the guy who knew your secrets—the one who knew you before. So I acted the part, hoping it would keep me alive until the end. Thought maybe the only reason I was brought here was to make your life harder." He looks toward the open game room door. "It wasn't enough."

I don't know how much more of this I can take. "I don't know what you need from me."

He gives me a quizzing look. "What? Nothing. No, I'm just—" Stacey walks inside the game room, and Nick barks out Josh's name, motioning for him to follow. Josh gives him the 'one minute' finger. Nick huffs. "I just wanted to warn you."

I take a sharp breath. "Okay." I'm at a loss for words. I don't know what else to say. "Thank you."

He nods, looking back at Nick.

We've put it off long enough. It's time for them to go.

As he turns from me, it's my chance to catch his wrist. "Josh. Thank you. Seriously."

"You're welcome, Darling."

I roll my eyes, but I let him go, watching as the game room door shuts tightly behind him.

Stepping back toward the rest of the group, I can feel Drew's eyes on me again—wounded, questioning.

Concerned.

I don't meet them. I can't yet. There's so much I don't know—so much I need to make sense of.

———

None of us talk as we drift toward our bedrooms. Kasey comes up beside me, quiet, as we reach my door. The boys part ways, mumbling goodnight to us.

"That was hard," she says softly.

I look at her. Part of me wants to believe she's just buttering me up for strategy. But her eyes are too earnest, too trusting, for that to be true.

"I'm glad you're still here," I respond.

She smiles. "You and I, we know what it's like to be manipulated. We know what it feels like to lose."

I grab my doorknob, turning it as I consider her words. The metal is cold under my fingertips. "I'm not losing this," I whisper. Whether that's a threat or a promise, I'm not sure.

She smirks at me, pleased with the fire in my tone, offering me a curt nod. "Good."

Leaving for her own room, I slip inside mine, eyes immediately landing on Tatum's still-made bed.

I sit on the edge of my bed, chest tight. Ten of us are gone. They won't be sleeping in their beds tonight or eating breakfast with the rest of us in the morning. We'll never hear their voices again or learn more about their past. They don't have a future, and their goals and dreams have been erased all too easily by someone with a sick mind.

Whether we die or not, we are changed completely by these games. If I'm right that our deaths are fake—and I hope so badly that they are, somehow—then everything we've felt, risked, and lost has been for someone else's entertainment.

And that feels just as bad.

I lie back, staring at the ceiling, heart hammering under my ribs.

The Voice wants chaos, and they're getting it tenfold.

Tomorrow, we'll bleed all over again.

DAY SEVEN

FORTY-EIGHT

Morning leaks in slowly, unannounced gray light filtering through narrow windows, painting the walls in a wash of despair.

For a few seconds, I forget where I am. I actually slept last night, though I can't remember the dreams that ran through my tired mind.

I turn my head, seeing Tatum's bed.

Oh yeah. Right.

I sit up slowly, my body protesting the movement. My limbs feel heavy, like they're stuck to the bed. I swing my bare feet onto the cold floor and let the chill ground me.

There's no one in the dining room as I grab breakfast. The house is far too big for just the four of us, and I suddenly don't know what to do with myself. The long table stretches farther than it ever has, chairs empty and pushed in like they're waiting for people who will never return. I can't go seek out Drew—I'm not sure what to say to him. I'm not close to Adrian, and I don't know where Kasey is.

I hardly eat—just pushing food around my plate until I can't stand the sight of this room anymore.

By the afternoon, I'm growing worried. I'm facedown on

the parlor couch, waiting for the Voice to come to life and instruct us for whatever is next.

Nothing.

There's only silence.

Hours pass like this. I drift through the house like a ghost, pretending I have somewhere to be. I pace the halls. I sit in the library and stare at books without opening a single one.

Adrian passes me at one point, but until dinner, he's the only person I see. Not that I'm actively looking.

Kasey finds me while I'm sitting on the balcony, watching the sun go down. Oranges and reds bleed together in perfect harmony.

I wish I could touch it.

"It's crazy to me that something beautiful can still exist," she says, plopping down next to me.

"Nothing feels real anymore."

She hums. "Have you noticed anything different today?"

I lean my head back against the house's exterior, eyes still stuck on the sunset. "Yeah. The silence. It's so, so quiet."

"I think the Voice is doing it on purpose. Trying to drive us nuts."

I scoff. "I went nuts a long time ago."

She laughs, and it's freeing. It makes the corners of my mouth twitch. I forgot how good it feels to make someone laugh. To not worry about what I'm saying, or what they're saying. I forgot what it's like to not be watching your back every second to make sure you don't do the wrong thing.

"What happened last night?" she asks. "With Josh?"

I stiffen. "He gave me a warning."

I expect her to ask more questions, but she just holds up a hand to stop me before I can offer more. "None of my business." She exhales through her nose. "But are you okay?"

Weirdly, I appreciate that out of her. Though a small piece of me wishes she had pressed for information. It's not necessarily something I want to have on blast, but maybe we could have talked through it together. "Surprisingly, yes."

She closes her eyes briefly, like she needs a moment to pretend she's alone. "I think Adrian is our next best option."

I wasn't ready to talk strategy. "Why do you think that?"

She hesitates. "I've been watching him. You. Everyone. And he's jumpy. The humor... I think he's hiding behind it like a mask."

Kasey quirks an eyebrow at me. "And... if I'm being honest... I know you're not going to vote for Drew. Which means it's either Adrian or me. And I'd prefer it not to be me."

I appreciate her honesty. There's no way I could vote Drew out—not unless something terrible happened. Not unless he shows that he deserves it.

Chills rake my spine. And what if he does? At some point, I need to start playing this game for *me*, not for an us that doesn't really exist.

"What if Adrian's safe tonight?" I ask, knowing that we have to prepare for that. There's always a chance he could win whatever game we play, and makes it through tonight without being voted for.

She shakes her head and mumbles so low that I almost don't catch her words. "He won't be."

FORTY-NINE

The Voice finally calls on us after dinner, demanding our presence in the game room.

Speakers crackle. "Good evening."

No one moves a muscle, waiting for the Voice to continue.

"Today, there will be no game and no activity. Tonight, we will simply vote."

So simple. Kasey exhales from across the table, making eye contact with me. I nod at her, ready to do what I have to. For a brief moment, I feel regret that it's her I'm checking in with and not Drew. I have to shake it off, though. This is not a time for second-guessing myself.

"And by tonight," the Voice continues. "I do mean *now*. You may discuss."

As the intercom clicks off, no one opens their mouth to speak. We just look back and forth between each other, waiting for someone else to make the first move. None of us are safe. That means all of us are up for the vote.

I should have told Drew how Kasey and I are voting, but I didn't want to. Now, there's no space to hide behind; there are no loud teammates to take the fall. If I try to talk to Drew,

Adrian will hear me. And there's just… too much I need to say to him right now. There's no time.

A plan forms in my head. Without thinking, I go ahead with it, no regrets. "Adrian, I have to vote for you tonight. I hope you understand."

I can see Drew's shocked look on his face from the corner of my eye. Keeping my eyes on Adrian, I try not to let it get to my head too much.

Adrian looks at Kasey, astonished. Throwing his arm toward her, he gasps. "What about her?"

Before I can respond, Kasey cuts in. "Winter and I have something in common. We're voting together tonight."

He looks back and forth between the two of us before finally landing on Drew. Drew winces involuntarily.

"You too?" Adrian's voice is quiet.

After a few seconds of pause, Drew nods hesitantly.

I blow out a relieved breath. He's with us. We have the majority. I'm safe again. I'll live another day.

And so will Drew.

"I can't change your minds?" Adrian asks, head on a swivel as he looks the three of us in the face, completely defeated.

Shaking my head, I go ahead and write his name on my chalkboard, just to get it over with. No reason to wait for the Voice when my mind is already decided.

"I've been trying to become a better person," Adrian starts. He doesn't pick up his chalkboard yet. "I used to be someone I'm not proud of. But recently, I've been doing good. So when I ended up here, it felt like karma. Like maybe those bad things were finally catching up to me."

I wipe a tear from my eye, trying to avoid the emotional weight his words place on my heart. Whatever his story of redemption is, I'm part of the reason it's being ruined. I'll never forgive myself for that.

I'll never be able to forgive myself for a lot of things.

He's crying too. "What I'm trying to say is, it's okay. All I've ever wanted was to become an actor—to take on Broadway. If this is as far as I make it in this life, I'll be alright. Maybe I can try again in the next one."

We're all sobbing now as he finishes, choking on his last words.

"Houseguests, the time for talking is over. Vote."

"Adrian," Kasey cries. "If it wasn't you, it was going to be me."

"Adrian," Drew mumbles. His eyes are far away somewhere, not looking at the rest of us.

"Adrian." I finish the vote, hands shaking, my heart broken into a million pieces. He didn't even vote. There was no point, no need. It wouldn't have mattered.

"Adrian, you have been banished from this game. Stay behind. I will see the rest of you in the morning."

Adrian's face drains of color as reality sets in. He looks at us—at me, at Drew, at Kasey—searching for something underneath a river of tears.

"Go," he urges, not wanting to take time for goodbyes.

I walk out slowly, filled with regret, unsure how I could take much more of this.

Just one more night, I remind myself. *Get Kasey out tomorrow, and maybe you and Drew will survive. Together.*

I walk the halls without looking around, every step I take way too loud in my ears. I shouldn't go looking for Drew—I've been avoiding him all day—but still, the thought comes to mind.

And then I turn the corner to go up the stairs, and somehow, he's there. Sitting, waiting for me, posture slumped.

My chest tightens as my hands clench into fists. I don't mean to be on the defense already, but I'm scared he's going to point out something in me that I don't want to look at too closely.

"Winter," he breathes. He's always so gentle, even

though I know all of this is hitting him the hardest. The urge to protect him at all costs rises so violently to the surface. He doesn't deserve to go through this again. "Can we talk?"

"Yes. No. I've been avoiding you," I say too quickly, unable to stop the words on their way out of my mouth.

He quirks a smile. "I know. I'm not stupid. I just assumed you had a reason."

"I needed space," I choke. "But I can't keep doing that."

He takes a step forward, eyes searching my own. "Why not?"

"Because I need you." I'm crying again, his face blurry through my tears. "But I hate that."

He reaches for me, pulling me in, enveloping me in warmth and safety. "You don't have to hate it, Winnie."

"I'm so tired." I'm full-on blubbering now, and my snot is getting all over his white t-shirt. "It feels so reckless. To care about you when all I should be caring about is myself and my survival."

He hums, and I can feel his jaw open like he's about to respond, but I cut him off. "But I don't want to survive anymore. I don't want to win. I'm a villain, and I deserve to die."

"Don't say that about yourself," he whispers. "Besides, there are no winners."

"I want it to be you," I admit. "I can't do it anymore."

He grabs hold of me, ushering me into the closet down the hall. I collapse against him, unable to stop the tears from pouring out of the deepest parts of me. I can't keep pretending that this situation doesn't have any effect on me. It's *ruining* me. I'm not strong enough for this.

"Winnie." He cups my face. "You're not alone in this. You don't have to be."

His thumb brushes the edge of my jaw, and I force the tears to stop, just for a second. I lean into him without meaning to, like my body chose before my brain could think otherwise.

"I see you. Right now. Right here."

Something fractures inside me.

All the fear that's been suffocating me, the guilt that's been eating me alive. The names I've written down and subjected to death. I push it all to the side, only wanting to focus on this present moment.

I look up at Drew—at my friend. The person who has been by my side from the very beginning. I shouldn't have let myself get attached, and yet, here I am.

Incredibly attached.

I grab the front of his shirt, pulling him in just a bit.

His breath stutters. "Winter…"

And then our mouths meet.

It's soft, unsure. And everything I need right now. There's desperation in the way he kisses me, like I might be his lifeline in all of this.

In this dark, small closet, it's just us. There's no worrying about tomorrow, or about the rest of our lives. Right now, there's only Drew and Winter.

As we kiss, I'm afraid that if I push him too hard, this moment might vanish into thin air. So for now, I'll memorize this feeling.

The warmth in my heart and the sound of his surprised breath when our lips met for the first time.

The way he's gripping me tightly, yet gently.

The small glimpses I get when he pulls back, just a bit, to check in with me and make sure this is still okay.

The way my head empties and silences as we kiss.

When we part, chests heaving, foreheads resting together, I feel wrecked and steadied all at once.

And for one stolen moment, the world around us completely disappears.

Still, tomorrow will come.

And I know I'm not ready for everything it will bring.

DAY EIGHT

FIFTY

I spend the night in Olsen's old bed, Drew across the room from me.

I don't dream tonight.

Or maybe I did, but my brain didn't let anything stick. I wake up feeling like I was never asleep at all, like I've just been drifting between time and space for hours.

I sit up slowly, rubbing my eyes, half-expecting to hear voices echoing down the hall. But silence presses down on me, heavy and final. There are only three of us now.

Three.

It sits wrong in my head. I didn't expect to make it this far. But for some reason, the Voice wants me alive.

And I still need to figure out why. Before it's too late.

I grab new clothes from my room and head downstairs. I catch sight of myself in a mirror as I walk: pale, red-eyed, bleak. There are dark circles under my eyes from crying, and I'm not sure they'll ever go away.

Drew helped my tears stop, though. For a moment.

My stomach twists.

I don't know what we are. I don't know what last night means in a place like this, where we are forced to fight for our lives day in and day out. I certainly don't know what will happen after this living nightmare is over.

If we make it out alive together, that is.

Heading toward the kitchen, I brace myself for whatever today may bring.

Kasey is already eating.

She's sitting at the table with a mug cupped between her hands, posture relaxed, steam seeping into the surrounding air. When she looks up and sees me, something flickers briefly across her face—relief, maybe.

"Morning," she says.

"Morning," I reply, voice hoarse.

We sit in silence for a moment, my spoon clinking against my cereal bowl. I pour some coffee even though I don't really want it—I'm only a coffee drinker if there's an immense amount of sugar. My university might offer free black coffee at every turn, but the taste of it has ruined plain coffee for me.

I shudder. College me doesn't exist anymore. How could I go back to that life after this?

If the Voice even lets you go, my inner fear taunts. *You might be the last one standing, but how do you know you'll get to leave here after all?*

Brushing that off, I look at Kasey. "How'd you sleep?"

She lets out a humorless laugh. "How do you think?"

I wince, apologetic. "Right. Same."

Another pause stretches between us. I wonder where Drew is—he wasn't in bed when I left.

I can't believe all of this ends soon. I've been living in a fever dream, neither here nor there. Maybe if someone pinches me hard enough, I'll wake up.

"I was thinking last night," Kasey says carefully. "About what the Voice said."

I wait for her to continue. "And?"

"There are only three of us," she pauses. "Which means this should be it. The last two can't vote against each other—it would just be a tie. There are no numbers to hide behind, no majority."

She makes a good point. How could only one person be left standing? Unless…

"Will the Voice make one of us sacrifice ourselves?"

She blinks. "It's possible."

A chill runs down my spine. I grip my coffee mug harder, refusing to take a sip. "It's a cruel thing. All of this."

She watches me closely. "One of us has to be the person on the inside."

"What are you implying?" I ask, voice tense.

"I think it's Drew."

Those four words slam into my brain like a head-on collision. I should have been expecting this—for her to make a case against Drew so that she's not the one to die tonight. Still, hearing her say it out loud is a punch to the gut.

"What could possibly make you think that?" I ask incredulously.

"He's very good at making people feel safe," she sighs. "My gut is telling me its not you, and I can promise you it's definitely not me."

I hold up a hand, stopping her. "Hang on, what if *I* think it's you?"

"Do you?" she challenges. I want to fight her on it, prove her wrong, but I can't. Josh was my prime suspect from day one, and I was obviously incorrect. My posture relaxes. No, I do not think it's Kasey. There's no reason for it to be her. "That's what I thought. You've suspected him, too."

"I don't want to," I mumble, looking down. Finally, my resolve returns. "He's been with me from day one. He's protected me and been by my side."

She looks toward the door, then back at me. "And hasn't that struck you as convenient? His story, his trauma? The way his panic comes and goes?"

The word *convenient* slices straight through me, ripping my heart to pieces.

"No," I say, but my voice wavers nonetheless. "He cares about me. He would never betray me."

"I'm sure he does care about you." She lays a hand on mine. "But that doesn't mean he isn't also playing both sides."

My chest feels tight. I can't get a full breath in. He would never...

"You haven't made a single enemy," she says. "Even Josh gave you a heads up in his last moments. And if you were the person responsible for all of this, who would *you* stick close to?"

I shake my head, grinding my teeth. All I want is for her to stop, but my brain beckons her to keep going. "Don't."

"The person everyone likes," she says anyway, ignoring me. "The person no one is looking at as suspicious."

My thoughts betray me then—Drew's gentle voice, the way he knows exactly what to say.

I push my chair back abruptly. "You're wrong."

She stands too, stepping closer. "What did he say to you last night?"

My heart slams against my ribs. "Nothing."

"Winter."

I swallow. "He said that I'm not alone." *And that there are no winners*, I don't add.

She nods. "How did that make you feel?"

"Like I was safe," I whisper, admitting part of what I really don't want to. There's a possibility there that, if I touch it, my whole world might come crashing down.

"Winter." Her voice softens, just a bit. "What if that's the point?"

The room feels like it's tilting. If I stand here for one more second, I'm going to be sick.

"You're asking me to believe that everything—" I choke. "*Everything* he's done and said has been manipulation. I would *know* if it was. I've been here before, Kasey. I'm not doing that again."

She looks at me apprehensively. This is what we've bonded over—our ability to be taken advantage of. Which means she knows how easy it can be to let someone slip a veil over themselves and only let us see what they want us to see.

I stomp my foot like a child. "I would know!"

She lays a hand on my forearm, kind and gentle. "I'm asking you to consider this as a possibility."

Tears burn at the corners of my eyes.

As she walks out of the room, she turns her head to offer me one more thing. "The person you trust the most is the person who can destroy you the worst. I hope I'm wrong. Truly, for your sake most of all, I do."

She shakes her head, hair swishing around her jawline. "But if I'm not, and we don't vote him out tonight… he wins. One of us dies, the Voice wins, and this was all for nothing."

My hands start to shake, so I shove them in my pockets.

"I need air," I whisper.

I shove past her before she can stop me.

FIFTY-ONE

Drew is in the game room, just sitting at the table, staring at the wall.

But when he sees me, his face lights up—then falls when he takes in my expression.

"Hey," he says, getting up. "What's wrong?"

Everything. Nothing.

I breeze past, taking a seat at the table, slumping. I cross my arms in front of me on the table, putting my face down into the cool dark.

Drew sits back down next to me, laying a hand on my back, rubbing it softly.

The action makes me want to cry and choke him at the same time.

"Kasey and I talked," I mumble under my arms, defeated. "She thinks you're the person working with the Voice."

He hums. "Oh."

The silence between us is deafening.

Drew exhales slowly, removing his hand. I'm cold without it, and I'm mad that I feel that way.

"I think you should vote for me tonight, Winnie."

I snap my head up. Nothing within me was prepared to hear him say that.

"Drew." I'm taken aback, completely at a loss for words. "What?"

"She's smart. She's been on the outskirts this whole time, watching."

"Why aren't you denying it?" I plead.

He looks down at me, eyes impossibly soft. "Would it matter if I did?"

I bite my lip. The truth is, I don't know if it would. I told him last night I don't want to win this anymore, but if I'm being honest… I do. A fire burns in my veins, free and unyielding. I want to get out of here and tell this story.

"Winter," he pulls my chair closer. "Look at me."

My heart breaks open.

"I want you to live. I want you to get out of here. I've bided my time—the earth has had me long enough. I'm ready."

Tears spill over. "Don't say that."

"There are no winners, Winnie." He clears his throat. "But if there could be one, I'd want it to be you. You're in good hands with Kasey."

"I don't know if I have the strength to write your name down."

He reaches out, brushing his thumb over my knuckles, one by one. "You do. You were meant to be the last one standing."

———

"Houseguests," the Voice interrupts my fog. "Gather in the game room."

I make my way there from the office, where I sat all afternoon, planning to write Drew a letter.

Words wouldn't come.

I couldn't make anything make sense on paper. I wanted

to tell him that he's smart and perfect and exactly what I wanted in someone to trust. That it's meant so much to me to have him by my side in all of this. That, no matter how tonight ends, I hope we find each other again.

If the deaths are fake, I will stop at nothing to search for him when I'm out of this.

If they're real…

The next life, then. But I don't want to think about that.

The chalkboard feels heavy in my hands. Drew and Kasey sit on either side of me in solidarity.

Drew squeezes my hand. "I don't regret it, Winnie. Any of it."

The Voice buzzes overhead again. "Houseguests, this will be the final vote. Choose wisely."

Kasey was right. This is it.

"Drew," Kasey says, voice calm. "I'm voting for you."

He nods. "I know."

I stare at him. "You're really just accepting this?"

He meets my eyes, searching them for something. "If you think, even for a second, that there's a chance she's right… You have to do this."

My hands tremble.

"And you? Who are you voting for?" I ask.

He smiles at me. "Kasey, obviously. I could never write your name down." His shoulder makes contact with my own, and it feels so *normal*. I almost hate him for it.

Almost.

As they lean down to write their respective names on their boards, I hesitate. Can I do this? I'm not sure I can.

Drew leans over, whispering in my ear after he turns his chalkboard facedown. "You don't have to carry this guilt with you after this. Let me carry it for you. It can die with me."

Something inside me wants to scream at him.

And it's at that moment that I know what I have to do.

My chalk squeaks against the black paint as I painstakingly write down those few letters.

Once my chalkboard is facedown as well, the Voice instructs us to read them aloud, starting with Drew.

"Kasey," he leans on his hand, a light in his eyes. "Obviously."

"Drew," she cuts in, even though I should have been next. "I'm sorry."

I straighten my spine, fingers cold and unfeeling as I turn my board around. "Kasey," I choke, words barely audible. "I couldn't do it."

Drew's jaw is on the floor, and Kasey looks just as shocked. But something else too—knowing?

"Kasey," the Voice says. "You have received the most votes and are now banished. Drew and Winter, I will have more instructions for you in the morning. Goodnight."

The speakers click off one last time.

I can't breathe. Turning to Kasey, I reach over and hug her, murmuring into her hair. "I'm so sorry. I couldn't do it."

Hysterically, I keep repeating those two phrases into her ear. Eventually, she pulls away from me, a sad smile on her lips.

"I hope you're right," she whispers. Nodding at Drew, he grabs my hand, pulling me from Kasey and the game room.

The door closes with a soft *clink*.

FIFTY-TWO

Two sets of footsteps echo down the hall.

Mine.

Drew's.

I keep expecting the Voice to come back over the speakers, or come out from a hidden panel in the walls.

But nothing happens.

We just walk. We live.

For now.

When we reach the stairs, I stop. Drew pauses immediately.

"You okay?"

I nod, then shake my head, face downcast. "I don't know. I don't think so."

He steps closer, wrapping his arms around me, his chest pressed against my back in solidarity. The contact sends a shiver through me. It's not fear—it's relief.

"She was wrong," I say. Drew stiffens. "She was wrong about you. I shouldn't have listened to her. I almost—" My throat closes. "I almost wrote your name down."

He turns me around, my head now buried in his chest. "But you didn't."

"But I doubted you," I admit. "For a second."

He searches my eyes earnestly. "Winter, you're allowed to doubt. Come on, in a place like this? Doubt is how we survive."

"I hate that I let it get that far."

He cups my face gently. "You trusted me when it mattered. That's what you need to hold on to."

I lean into his touch, pressing my forehead against his when he offers it to me. His heartbeat is steady and grounding, reminding me that we are still here and alive.

"It's just us," I breathe.

Us.

The word feels dangerous and foreign to my tongue.

Drew exhales a shaky laugh. "We might actually make it out of here."

The possibility hits me like a bolt of lightning.

"We could," I whisper.

For the first time since we were brought here, the future opens back up to me. The door that is freedom and safety opens, ready for me to grab hold and walk through.

We go to my room this time, feeling like we are safer together than apart. Sitting on my bed, we face Tatum's, my head resting on his shoulder.

There's too much to process. Was Kasey the person with all the information? I guess we'll find out in the morning.

"What if we get to leave tomorrow?"

He turns his head slightly, his cheek resting against my hair. "Then we'll run off into the sunset together."

"Sunset?" I laugh. "I'm not waiting around here all day for the sunset, Drew."

He chuckles, his dimples making an appearance. "Do you really think they'll let us both go?" He threads his fingers through mine.

My jaw tightens, just for a moment, as I consider the possibility of it. No, I really don't think so. A sacrifice might be the least of our worries. But I can't tell Drew that. "I think that whatever happens, we'll do it together."

I choose to believe that's the best answer I can give him. It *has* to be the answer.

Shifting so that I'm facing him fully, knees tucked under me, I ask, "What's the first thing you'll do?"

"When we're out of here?" he asks.

"Yes."

"Change my outfit."

I giggle. "I'm so tired of white shirts and jeans!"

"And I'll sleep. In my own bed."

I throw my head back. "That sounds *so* nice."

"What about you?"

I think about it for a moment. "Write."

He lifts an eyebrow. "Immediately?"

"Before everything starts to blur together. Before I forget things." I pause. "Before someone else tries to tell this story for us. I have to get to it first."

His eyes light up. "You're going to do an incredible job."

I shrug, suddenly shy. "This could be the biggest story I'll ever get the opportunity to write about. It could make my career."

"You're going to change things," he says with complete certainty.

I study his hazel eyes. "You believe in me."

"I do." He grins. "I always have."

Something warm envelopes my chest.

"I can see it now," I begin. "Going back to campus. Sitting in classrooms and being bored during classes."

He laughs, voice rising. "I miss being bored."

"And I want good coffee again!"

He shakes his head. "I'll take you to a coffee shop first thing. Buy you whatever you want."

My voice catches in my throat.

He blushes, realizing what he said. "If you wanted to, of course."

"I do. Yes. I'd love that."

His easy smile comes back again, and I'm relieved.

He grabs my hand, a thumb brushing across my knuckles, like he's savoring the feel of my skin. "What would your story say about us?"

My stomach flips. "That we found each other in the worst place possible. But together, we made it through."

"When this is over… we could visit each other. I could come see your campus. You can try my favorite coffee shop."

I smile. "I'll drag you to the one that kept me alive my first week of classes. It's a library too, with window seats looking out at the mountains."

"I'll sit across from you and pretend to study," he says. "But I won't be able to take my eyes off you."

I roll my eyes. "Creep."

He laughs. "You like it."

"I do," I admit softly.

The admission hangs between us, fragile and real. There are still so many unknowns, but I know for certain I have him.

He kisses me then—not rushed or desperate. It's like he's savoring the fact that we're still here, together. That I chose him, and that he chose me.

When we pull back, he rests his hand over his heart. "Thank you."

I tilt my head. "For what?"

"For trusting me."

Emotion swells in my chest, overwhelming and tender. "Of course."

We lean against the wall again, the lights still on. Neither of us wants to sleep yet, but tomorrow's fate beckons us closer.

"Winter?" he says after a while.

"Hm?" I mumble, half-asleep.

"If tomorrow really is the end… if we get out of here

alive. I want you to know, I wouldn't have traded this. Not for anything."

"Me too," I whisper, squeezing his hand.

Outside, the wind whistles against the sides of the house.

And for the first time, I let myself believe that I might know the feeling of peace again.

Tomorrow, we'll leave. We'll win.

Together.

I fall asleep holding onto that hope, unaware of how fragile it really is.

DAY NINE

FIFTY-THREE

My body knows something is wrong the second I wake up.

There's no sound that alerts me to danger, nor is there a crackle of the intercom as I come to.

No, it's the absence. The silence.

And the fact that my bed is empty.

Drew's arm was heavy around my waist when we fell asleep, his breathing slow and even. We should be here together, still holding on tight to the idea that we might be safe.

But instead, I'm cold. Alone.

I want to believe that he's just downstairs making breakfast—maybe bringing some up to me so we can eat together.

But somehow, my heart knows that's not the case. And my intuition has brought me this far—I'd be a fool to forsake it now.

I throw my bedcovers off my tired body, pulling on my tennis shoes in haste. The side of the mattress where he was sleeping is cold. My heart stutters violently, like it was slammed into a wall.

"Where is he?" I ask myself, voice already shaking.

Dizziness washes over me as I stand up too fast. I reach for my closed bedroom door, ready to tear this place apart, when I step on something.

A crumpled piece of paper.

My chest tightens as panic overtakes my emotions.

I don't touch it at first—I *can't*. My eyes are glued to the spot below me, mind scrambling for any idea of what it could say. Is it from Drew? It's just a note saying he left for food, I try to convince myself. Or maybe a love confession, a morning joke? I mean, really, it could be anything…

My hands are shaking when I finally reach for it.

The paper is thick in my fingers.

HOUSEGUESTS,
THE GAME IS NOT OVER YET.
THERE CAN ONLY BE ONE LEFT STANDING.
BY 10 A.M., ONE OF YOU MUST ENTER THE GAME ROOM.
YOU WILL NOT BE LEAVING ALIVE.
YOUR SACRIFICE WILL ENSURE THE SAFETY OF THE OTHER.
THE CLOCK IS TICKING. SEE YOU SOON.

I crumple it in disbelief, just like Drew probably did when he read it, my eyes filled with unshed tears.

He didn't wake me. He didn't tell me. He didn't say goodbye.

My stomach drops.

He's already gone. I just know it.

I fly down the stairs, needing to make sure, running to the game room with everything I have left in me.

The door is shut tight. I don't bother checking the rest of the house or calling out for him to show himself. He's in there, dead. Gone.

I scream, pulling on the handle, willing it to open and give me back my friend. My breathing comes out in broken sobs, and eventually, I can't comprehend the words coming out of my mouth.

Sinking forward onto the floor, I beat my hands against the wood until they're raw and bruised. I scream his name, the sound ripping my chest open again and again.

We were supposed to win *together*. We should have made it out of this *together*.

He didn't even bother to tell me goodbye.

I suck in an intake of cold air, hiccuping as I will my sobs to stop.

I didn't even get to tell him my real name.

———

My body falls asleep in that position, somehow. Leaning with my forehead against the door, my knees tucked into my chest. My eyes are dry—I have no more tears left to spend.

And my heart hurts.

I lurch to my feet after an unknown amount of time, grabbing the letter like it might change if I read it again. Maybe I was wrong—maybe the Voice meant something else.

But the truth is set, and my fate was sealed with black pen ink.

One of us had to sacrifice ourselves.

And Drew already did.

"Where is he?" I shout at the ceiling. "What did you do to him? What do you want with me?"

I start heaving, hands on my knees as I catch my breath.

There has to be something here. Something I'm missing. Why hasn't the Voice come to get me yet? I just want to leave.

I press my palms to my eyes until I see stars.

Breathe. *Think*, Winter.

As I walk toward the parlor, my legs feel like they don't

belong to me. One wrong step, and I might fold, subject to collapsing and dying on this cold ground.

I'm the only one left.

That thought pings something within me.

I won.

I lift my head slowly. The house looks unchanged. No person is waiting to escort me out. No torture but the grief I'm living in.

Crossing the hall as quickly as I can, I try to wrench the front door open.

Still locked.

Huffing, I look around. I can *feel* the cameras still watching me.

Fine, if that's how we're going to play.

Quickly, I run to each room, looking for a clue or something I might have missed. I check the couch cushions, behind pictures hanging on the wall, and under tables. I turn the house upside down, ruining everything I can see. There are no notes, no hidden panels sliding open as a way out, and no last instructions waiting for me.

The only thing changed is that my portrait in the parlor is the only one not marked out with a red 'x'.

"What am I supposed to do now?" I yell, waving my hands in the air.

No one answers.

Winning was supposed to feel like freedom. Instead, it feels like the beginning of another game—something else I don't recognize and don't know how to make sense of. And I didn't ask for it. I don't *want* it.

But as I walk upstairs, ready to rip apart the netting covering the balcony and jump like my life depends on it, something shifts.

It's not the intercom system turning on. It's not footsteps echoing down the hallway.

It's subtle, but it catches my attention all the same.

The lights flicker off for a few seconds, and I pause, waiting.

"Congratulations, Winter."

And then the front door clicks, the lock flipped open.

FIFTY-FOUR

A man steps through the front door. I freeze, like prey trying to remain unseen by a predator.

"Winter."

His voice is smooth, just like his appearance. There's not a single wrinkle on his tan-colored khaki pants, and his light blue button-up shirt is freshly pressed.

Sunlight streams in from behind him. From outside. From the direction of freedom.

I want it so badly.

I take a step back. "Who are you?"

He smiles, smug and assured. "I'm who you all have been calling 'The Voice'." He quotes those two words with his fingers, like it was just some stupid nickname kids made up. "But you can call me Charlie."

I squint my eyes at him. "Okay." He's younger than I would have thought—maybe mid-30s. He doesn't look completely crazy or insane. And on the bright side, he's very clearly *not* Mr. Pearson. I should feel relieved, but... "I'm confused."

A black headset hangs around his neck, and I hear faint

words coming from it. He smiles at me, ignoring it, teeth white and too perfect. "You won."

Charlie takes a step toward me, arms outstretched, but I move back again. My eyes dart between him and the open door beckoning me forward. His curly hair bounces as he laughs at my reaction.

"What do you want from me?" I take up a fighting stance, readying my feet to run toward the exit as soon as I get the chance. If he's come to kill me, I won't go down without a fight.

He notices my eyes bouncing around, and he takes a step to the left, blocking my way to the door. "This is it. You're done. There's nothing else we need from you."

"I don't understand." Slowly, after he doesn't say anything else, I put my fists down. "You're not here to kill me?"

Charlie sighs, like he's frustrated I'm not catching on quicker. "No. No, nothing like that. I suppose you wouldn't understand, but I couldn't help but hope..." Resigned, he straightens again. He motions with his hand for me to follow him. "Come with me."

He leaves, walking outside. The fresh air swings toward me, filling my chest with renewed hope. I take tentative steps toward the threshold of the door, as if I might be electrocuted if I walk out.

The sun is blinding today.

Gravel sounds underneath my footsteps as I walk toward Charlie, making sure to keep enough space between him and me that he can't grab me easily. I could run off, but I don't know exactly where I am and where the closest piece of civilization might be. More than that, I don't know what else is out there.

There's a black SUV parked in front of the mansion, the engine still on and running.

I can't see inside the windows.

Before Charlie can say anything, I choose to cut him off.

Maybe if I catch him off guard, I can get some answers. "You kidnapped us. Tortured us. Kept us in the dark and threatened our *lives*." Emotions get the better of me as I think of Olsen, of Tatum, and of Drew. And all the other people I've failed over the course of my life. "You killed them."

The last three words are but a whisper, and he dares to smile.

"Of course," he says. "That's how the show works."

FIFTY-FIVE

An incessant buzzing sounds in my ears, drowning out anything else he might be saying. His lips are still moving, but I can't hear him.

"What?" That one word is all I can muster, all I can force myself to say as my brain spins around in circles.

He tilts his head at me, green eyes surveying my body. "You're very pretty. That's probably one reason America loved you so much."

My chest isn't moving, isn't breathing. I might die right here on the spot. Part of me wishes I would. "America?"

He takes a step backward, knocking on the car's window. At the sound, doors open, and people flood out.

Or should I say, television crew? Boom sticks, huge cameras that must weigh a ton, and the sound of walkie-talkies overwhelm my personal space.

"She'll need to be touched up a bit," a lady with graying hair says. "Before the results show."

"Well then, we need to go, people! We have a schedule to keep!"

I shake my head slowly. I'm in a nightmare, surely. "What is going on?"

Charlie huffs, frustrated. "You should be *very* proud of yourself, Winter. You won a new and upcoming reality TV show. We're taking you to our studio so we can film the results show and get through your final speech as the winner. Is that tracking?" He looks at the man next to him, who is changing the batteries in something. "Man, I thought she was smarter than this."

I set my jaw, pushing off the lady touching my hair. She grunts, hands back on my head immediately. "You're lying."

He reaches up and touches his headset, clicking a button. The small voices coming from it stop. "I'm not."

I look around at the people now filming and watching me, but in real life.

Real life. This is real, somehow. This is… this is my life.

My ears are ringing again. I wonder if Charlie would mind if I threw up on his shoes.

"You killed them," I say, voice pitching. I'm trying so badly to fight the tears that want to show themselves, but I'm losing my grip. "For a show?"

Charlie laughs, throwing his head back, looking around at his crew. "They're not really dead, Winter. We're not monsters."

No. That can't… that can't be true. Even though it was the ending I was hoping for, it doesn't make *sense*. Not after everything I've gone through. *None of this makes sense,* I want to shout.

Before I can say anything else, I'm ushered into the car, squeezed in the back between two people I don't know. My body shakes controllably as the car pulls away. I whip my head back, watching the house I've been stuck in for nine days slowly disappear in the distance.

As if it never existed at all.

———

I'm in a chair, staring myself in the face, the LED lights surrounding the mirror too bright for my eyes.

"More eyeliner," the lady—Margaret—directs. "Her eyes need to pop. They're looking a little red."

"Because I've been crying," I mumble, but she's too distracted to hear me. It wouldn't matter if she heard me anyway—she's made it clear she doesn't care about me.

Charlie sits in the corner, staring at his phone, laughing to himself at something none of us can see.

The studio set is small, and the walls are painted a bright blue color that isn't doing the space any favors. There's a big black curtain separating me from what I'm assuming is the stage.

"How many people?" I ask Margaret, voice unsure. "Watching?"

She hums. "Millions."

My stomach twists. "How did I get here?" The question is more for me than it is for her, but I still want her to answer it.

Margaret tsks, clicking her tongue against her cheek. "I'm not allowed to say."

I gulp as they paint my cheeks with color that complements me perfectly.

I want to be sick. Closing my eyes, I think about the positives. I was right. The deaths weren't real. My friends are alive.

Nausea builds in my throat. I was right, and it doesn't matter.

Because I'm numb and hurting all the same.

Hands grab my shoulders, shocking me back to reality. I flinch, trying to get out of the chair.

Charlie stands behind me, holding me firm. "It's time."

"Time for what?" I ask, panicking. I'm not ready, I'm not ready—

"To go out," he responds. "They're all waiting for you."

"Who?" I ask, even though I know the answer.

"America. The live audience." He pauses, taking in the pained expression on my face. "Your friends."

I breathe in quickly. My friends are here?

They lead me down a hallway. I'm in a new outfit now, and my feet trip over the heels they have me in. It's not that I've never worn heels before, but my legs aren't connected to my brain right now.

"You're doing great," another woman murmurs.

I don't answer. There's nothing left to say. I've given up hope that someone might rescue me from my circumstances or be on my side. I'm on my own.

My slick palms find the satin fabric of my skirt. Wiping them does nothing to curb the nerves eating me up inside.

Noise grows louder as we reach an opening on the other side of the curtain. Music gushes from speakers as applause sounds at just the right times.

There's a crowd out there. Reacting to… something.

My heart starts to race again. This is not how this was supposed to go. Am I going to have to talk? To watch… things? I try to back up, but firm bodies behind me propel me forward.

Bright light spills through the cracks. Everything is so over-whelming. My head hurts. I can't take it anymore.

I turn to leave, ready to push through the crowd behind me, but firm hands stop me. They push me toward the entrance and onto the stage.

This is what winning looks like, I realize. This was always what was meant to happen. And I can't do anything about it.

Charlie leans in. "Just walk forward. We'll take care of the rest."

Against my better judgment, I nod, taking one step forward. My body is on autopilot, and my brain is still three steps behind.

I can't do anything but walk.

FIFTY-SIX

Stage lights press down on me like a hot, unrelenting sun. I can't help but squint. My body obeys my brain's command to keep walking forward without me realizing I'm moving.

Applause erupts from my left.

It's thunderous and perfectly timed. Somewhere, music swells in the background, but I don't catch the tune.

I can only blink, trying my best to orient myself to this… *thing*.

To my right, a massive screen flickers on, my name flashing across it in bold letters. In front of me, a green velvet couch, angled toward the audience like a live display.

The people sitting on it are dead.

They're supposed to be, anyway. But here they are, alive and in person, cleaned up as if our time together in that house didn't happen at all.

My knees nearly buckle, but I catch myself. I can't show weakness right now. Not in front of… all these people.

My grief-ridden heart doesn't know what to do with itself.

I let my eyes breeze over their faces, knowing that if I look too closely at them, I'll break. I make sure not to look too hard to see if Drew is in attendance.

Somehow, I just know that he is. I can feel his eyes on me.

I look away, toward a white chair in front of the couch, next to where Charlie sits in a twin seat.

The crowd starts to cheer as the cameras pan around the room. Cautiously, I take my seat, crossing one leg over the other. I change legs, shifting my body over and over again in an attempt to feel comfortable in this awful space.

"WIN-TER. WIN-TER. WIN-TER."

The rhythmic sound of my name echoes across the room as the crowd stands and applauds me. For what? I don't know. Surviving? Winning, in their eyes? Not being dead?

Maybe it's for being stupid enough to fall for it all.

I pick at my fingers as Charlie turns toward the crowd.

His voice booms through the speakers. "AMERICA! MAKE SOME NOISE FOR YOUR WINNER!"

I flinch without meaning to, his tone commanding like he was as the Voice.

The audience screams, still on their feet, now clapping along to the beat of the music. It makes my head pound repeatedly. It takes everything within me not to shut my eyes tight and try to block out the sound.

Charlie laughs, looking back at me, a microphone suddenly thrust into my hand by some stagehand. I grip it like a lifeline, making sure to keep it away from the sound of my labored breathing.

"Welcome to our very first results episode for the upcoming reality TV show, *Last One Standing*!" He laughs, the epitome of joy. "And what a first season it was, wasn't it, folks?"

The audience screams, chants, and yells. People throw their fists in the air in agreement, and I'm absolutely horrified. How could our pain bring these people so much happiness?

"Nine days. Fourteen contestants. And one unforgettable winner." He motions toward me, and the audience erupts again. "We stripped them of everything—their clothes, their routines, their idea of safety. And our contestants certainly came to play!"

A shiver runs down my spine. The stage lights are making me sweat, but I'm so, so cold.

The screen begins to change as footage starts to play.

Highlights. Behind the scenes. My every waking move videographed for the world to see.

Me, on day one, standing in the dark in the parlor. The way we all panicked as we ran around, trying to find a way out.

Me throwing up. I wince. The audience did *not* need to see that.

Then there's Drew, having a panic attack. Faith being our first vote. People's tears and doors slamming shut, and confusion over the games and what it all means.

Cyrus' escape shows on screen—he jumped from the balcony and fell to the ground, making a run for the trees before being tackled by a group of people in black clothing.

It's like I'm watching myself from someone else's body. The person they're showing on screen—the Winter they're highlighting—that's not *me*. It can't be.

The audience reacts perfectly—they laugh, they gasp, they cry.

I gasp as a scene of Stacey and Raven arguing in their bedroom flashes on screen. We assumed every room was being recorded, but…

There's a pit in my stomach as I realize I'm going to watch my kiss with Drew on screen.

In front of all these people.

Who have already seen it. They're going to watch it. *Again.* Maybe for the third, fourth, fifth time.

I shift in my seat, looking out of my peripheral vision to take in my friend's faces. I'm assuming Faith has known the longest that this was all just a television show, because she doesn't look shocked at all. She just looks… like a statue.

Drew, on the other hand…

He's disgusted.

I take a deep breath, grateful I'm not the only one struggling to comprehend this. I pause as I look at the rest of them, looking over their features, realizing Olsen and Reese are missing.

Dread pools in my gut. I hope they're okay.

I do a double-take. Josh isn't here, either.

Searching my brain for an ounce of me that cares, I can't find any. Good.

The audience starts to cheer, a few people whistling, and I look back at the screen to see what I missed.

It's Drew and me, sitting in the closet. You can't hear us, but I know what we're talking about.

Our pasts.

I'm going to be sick.

"The romance America couldn't stop talking about!" Charlie shouts. Again, the crowd erupts. He motions for the cameras with his hands to point toward the couch.

An in-house camera cuts to Drew. He looks tense, his mouth smiling, but his hazel eyes are dead to the world around him. When he glances at me, it's nervous and quick, like he didn't mean to.

A quick video of Drew's thumb brushing my jaw as we looked at each other dances across my eyes, and my throat tightens. This wasn't content for a TV show to me—it was life and death. It was real for me.

And I think it was real for him, too.

But now, it's been reduced to viral videos and snippets taken out of context. Scenes meant purely for the enjoyment of other people.

Disgusting.

The footage keeps rolling, now focusing more on me and my journey as people keep getting voted out.

Challenges, games, secrets, behind-the-scenes of others'

days that I wouldn't have known about, and our reactions during votes. Reese's meltdown and Stacey trying to kill Josh.

Then, the screen fades to black as a phrase lights up the screen:

THE FINAL NIGHT

FIFTY-SEVEN

My pulse spikes as the clips roll.

Charlie turns toward me when it's done—and toward the couch—and says, "Houseguests, you all played an incredible game. But as we knew from the beginning, there could only be one winner."

The word 'winner' hits me like a slap across the face. I don't look at my friend's reactions—I can't make myself. I focus on Charlie and on the unbelievable words coming out of his mouth.

"Every day, America got to vote for who they wanted to stick around. Now, to make this as real as possible for our contestants—" Charlie looks at us with a wink. "We could only do our best, letting the true vote still rest in their hands. But we knew we would need some extra help keeping the houseguests on track. That, and I had someone more than eager to play the part of informant to our very first group."

He stands, hand extended toward the couch. "Will our mole please reveal themselves to the audience?"

Nausea overtakes my stomach as the crowd silences. There's no music playing, no cheering in the background.

Only anxious anticipation. My vision grows black as I wait. If I don't slow down my breathing, I might make a spectacle of myself and pass out right here, right now. In front of everyone.

The group on the couch shifts, looking around, waiting for whoever betrayed us to make themselves known.

As if in slow motion, Kasey stands, her denim dress perfectly pressed.

She smiles brightly, not a care in the world, waving toward the crowd as if she's a Queen saying hello to her subjects.

The live audience screams, both in surprise and excitement, while Kasey makes her way toward Charlie.

"My daughter, everyone. Kasey Windhart!"

I nearly fall out of my chair. Daughter?

Charlie must be older than I thought.

Kasey perches on the arm of Charlie's chair, her eyes bright and *happy*. Side by side, there's a resemblance there for sure. I can't help but wonder, was all of it a lie? Or was her story about a controlling boss real?

I might never know. And honestly, after everything that she did, I don't care to.

My fists clench as I look at her, the microphone in my palm subject to my anger. She lied to me. She used us. She weaseled her way into my good graces at the last minute and nearly convinced me to vote Drew out before her.

I force my eyes away, squeezing them tight to avoid my incoming tears from showing themselves. Not here, not now.

Maybe never.

"With that behind us, let's move on to the exciting part, shall we?" Charlie asks the crowd. They clap, shouting. "Alright, alright, I hear ya."

"Winter," he turns to me. His tan skin gleams under the studio lights. "When your friends were being eliminated, what was going through your head?"

I stare at him.

Then, at the microphone.

And back to him.

"Uh," my voice comes out paper-thin. I clear my throat, and the sound echoes across the speakers. "I thought... I thought it was my fault."

A low murmur ripples through the crowd—as if they are empathizing or trying to sound understanding.

"I'm sure you did. And Winter, America is just *dying* to know—they've been tweeting about it all week." He winks at the cameras, and the crowd laughs. He's charming them for sure. "Was Drew part of your strategy? Or did things get a little... complicated?"

My spine stiffens. Do I have to talk? Is he going to punish me if I don't? "Next question, please."

Charlie laughs like we just shared an inside joke. "Right. Don't want to give away *all* your secrets. Especially with a certain someone," he peeks over at Drew, "In attendance. I understand that." There he goes with that stupid wink again. If he winks at me one more time—

"And Winter, one last question. What does the winner of *Last One Standing* want to say to the people who voted for you? The ones who didn't miss a single episode?"

I breathe in deeply, filled with rage and absolutely appalled that this is what this has come to. Nothing in me could have ever expected *this* to come from those torturous nine days. My brain has too many thoughts at once, and not enough time to sort through them all.

Charlie says this is the first season. I don't know how they'd pull off a second season now that people *know* the deaths are fake, but I can't let this continue. This is unfair, cruel, and gross. Maybe I'll make it through this, but others won't. There will be lives lost because of these people.

I can't let powerful people keep taking advantage of those

who aren't. I let it happen with Reagan—I can't let it happen again.

Facing the camera, I school my face, making sure to tuck away any emotion I might be feeling. If I cry, they'll claim it was the trauma of the experience getting to me. If I'm angry, they won't listen.

I have to be perfect. Practiced. Skilled.

Digging deep down within me to find all the resolve I can muster, I begin. "America." They cut me off by cheering, of course. I could throw up on stage right now, and they'd run up wanting pictures. Right now, to them, I can do no wrong. "You didn't just watch us, of course. You participated in the hardships we were experiencing."

The live audience stills as a hush falls across the room.

"Every vote, every social media post, every five-star rating. You gave the TV show crew and Charlie feedback, telling them that what they were doing to us was *okay*. In fact, it was better than okay to you all, wasn't it? Because you were having *fun*."

Charlie opens his mouth, but I don't let him speak. I need to hurry through the rest of this before they cut me off.

"You watched us grieve people who didn't really die. We were kidnapped, forced to share secrets that no one should have had to reveal. Our trauma entertained you. You *loved* us. You loved *me*."

People start to shift in their seats. I can see Tatum smiling from the couch, one hand on her stomach, her other arm intertwined with Faith's. I keep my eyes from landing on Drew.

"And I know that at some point, it was hard to watch. I'm sure it was. But still, you chose not to turn it off. You chose to give them what they wanted."

"Alright—" Charlie tries to interrupt.

"This didn't happen without you," I say, looking at the crowd now. "And that's not a compliment."

Pausing one more time, I look back at Charlie and Kasey. "If I were you, I would ask yourself how much of your soul you're willing to trade for entertainment. Because for me, the answer would be none."

Silence envelopes the room as my microphone gets turned off and the stage lights turn dark.

FIFTY-EIGHT

I'm instructed that I won't be allowed to speak again. I fight the urge to bite the finger currently being waved in my face.

"We understand," one of the stagehands says as he takes my microphone. "You have a lot to come to terms with. It's probably best if you don't say anything right now."

It's probably best if you find another job, I think, grumbling internally. My arms are crossed, the perfect picture of resentment.

Charlie comes over and claps me on the shoulder, trying his best to look unruffled. "Don't worry, Winter. Once you hear what you've won, you'll change your mind."

I fight the urge to turn my head and bite *his* hand. Instead, I nod and scream as loud as I can on the inside. Still, it's not enough. I don't know how I'll ever get rid of this simmering rage inside of me.

When we come back after a brief commercial break, Charlie gestures to the screen again, and it lights up immediately. He acts as if nothing happened.

This time, the screen shows footage I don't recognize.

It's more behind-the-scenes, but different—hidden cameras in secret tunnels beneath the house.

We watch Faith's elimination, her crying and alone in the game room after we all left. Then, a trapdoor pops open from the floor, and two men jump out.

They grab her, a hand over her mouth, and pull her down toward the tunnel.

Cameras pick up footage from there, walking her down a long concrete hall where they finally exit into the woods.

Faith fights the whole time, struggling against her captors, kicking and trying to scream.

But the men are too strong.

A black SUV awaits far from the house, and she's pushed in.

She looks so small and alone as the car drives toward a big farmhouse.

"Welcome," Charlie says on-screen to a frightened Faith. "We have lots to discuss."

The crowd laughs again, but it's quieter now. More… aware of what's going on. And maybe, just maybe, how we were all feeling. It's like they're seeing these circumstances through a different lens—one that isn't so rose-colored.

Similar clips play for all the eliminations. I watch my friends—who should have been as good as dead—get escorted away similarly, confused and angry.

Olsen's is a bit different. The camera work for his disappearance is shoddy and shaky. Someone runs in from the front door to grab him, whisking him away from the house. The next clip is him in a hospital bed, hooked up to a variety of machines.

"Our dear Olsen is alive, folks!" Charlie exclaims, interrupting the video stream. "Many of you were worried about him. But we have a special video straight from the source that will hopefully ease some of those feelings."

A brief clip of Olsen plays. He holds up his thumb to the camera.

He's skin and bones, but he has a little bit more color than when I saw him last. I'm hit with the overwhelming urge to find and visit him *right now*.

I could do that, I realize. When this is over, he's the first person I'll go see. Because he's alive.

My eyes find the couch again. They're all alive.

"Every elimination was carefully planned, executed, and monitored. Eliminated houseguests were taken to a remote farmhouse to stay for the remainder of the recording of this show. They were well-fed and clothed. No one was ever in any true danger."

A memory flashes across my mind: Stacey lunging at Josh with a knife in her hand. That's why they made us eliminate so many more people that day.

They didn't want to risk bad ratings. Or chance having an actual death on their hands.

But then… What really happened to Reese?

Part of me regrets stopping Stacey. Maybe that could have cut this whole thing short. Maybe it could have ended this show once and for all, before it had even truly begun.

Nausea curls around my stomach. I grip my chair's armrest, unsure what else to do with my hands.

The hands that want to choke Charlie.

"Winter." Charlie addresses me curtly. "You endured it all. You persevered in the face of pressure, guilt, and fear. And America—well, they watched every second."

He turns back toward the audience, a stupid grin on his face. "And they loved you!"

Applause roars.

I want to plug my ears to the sound. I'm over it—over him, over the lights, over the attention. If I'm never in a live show ever again, it will be all too soon.

Two stagehands dressed in black bring out a huge rectangular object.

A check, I realize. One of those comically large ones that people get in commercials and television shows.

I gulp. *A television show. Like this one. The one you're in. You're in a television show.*

"Winter, for being the last one standing, I present to you…" Charlie walks over to me, arms open wide. "Prize money of one million dollars!"

The crowd absolutely loses it.

I'm thrust to my feet, the check forced into my hands, as camera flashes blink around my vision. My brain tells me to smile, but there's a disconnect between my mind and the rest of my body right now.

My ears ring louder.

This is what winning looks like.

I don't want it.

I try to give the check back, but it's shoved back into my hands as people take more pictures.

My mouth opens, but nothing comes out. Am I losing blood? I think I'm going into shock…

Cameras cut to the front row, and that's when I see them.

My mom. My dad. My little sister.

FIFTY-NINE

They're standing, beaming in the bright stage lights, tears running down their faces.

Waving at me.

My heart wrenches.

"No," I whisper in disbelief. They couldn't *know*. Right?

My family is ushered toward the stage—toward *me*—but I'm frozen to the spot.

The big check disappears from my hands as my mom grabs me, hugging me tighter than she ever has. This moment of contact doesn't bring me relief. If anything, it makes me feel even more unsafe than I already did.

My dad beams over her shoulder like it's the proudest moment of his life. He's never looked at me like that, not once. I don't know what to do with that information. There's too much to process right now, too much for my brain to handle at one time.

Releasing me, my mom motions toward my sister, who stands there with tears streaming down her face, a hand pressed over her mouth.

My brow furrows as I lean down to give her a big hug. This moment, with her in my arms, feels right. She's shaking, gasping for air because of the harshness of her sobs. I grip her even tighter.

"They didn't tell me," Delilah cries into my hair. "They didn't tell me it was fake. That you weren't going to die."

Anger intertwines itself with my soul. I try to reassure her, to say *anything* to comfort my thirteen-year-old sister, but nothing comes out before she's pulled away from my body. I almost reach back out for her, longing to pull her close again, but I refrain. I don't want to give anyone any ammunition against me right now.

Not when there are still so many unanswered questions.

My mom clutches my shoulders. Her makeup is way too thick, and the blue of her dress washes her out in the bright studio light. "You were incredible. Everyone adores you."

My hands tremble at my sides.

"You—" My voice cracks. "You knew?"

My dad nods eagerly. More than that—*happy*. "We signed you up!"

My world tilts, freezes, collapses within itself. Those words don't connect with my understanding of all of this. Not that I had much understanding to begin with.

"What?"

"We didn't know they picked you until you showed up on our TV," Mom says quickly. "Imagine our surprise! We weren't allowed to tell you beforehand, of course. For the drama!" She emphasizes that last word, looking toward the crowd and Charlie for approval of what she's saying.

Her eyes are bright and alive, soaking up every moment of this fame.

I pull back from them. "How could you let them do this to me? To her?" I gesture toward Delilah, unable to help myself. "After everything I've gone through the last few years?"

My dad scoffs, shaking off my feelings as he usually does. "We used your new name, Winter. Sure, we gave the casting directors some... background information. But the world really only knows what you told everyone in the house."

For a moment, I forget everything. That I'm on stage, that cameras are watching my every move. "Which is *everything*," I grind out.

My sister reaches over and squeezes my hand. She's had a horrible time the last year, too—moving states, making new friends, learning a whole new identity that shouldn't have been her burden to bear. It's all my fault.

And now she has to shoulder this, too.

Suddenly, Drew is beside me.

I don't realize it at first. I'm staring at my parents—really, at complete strangers. But a warm body comes to stand at my left in solidarity, and I naturally relax without meaning to.

Turning my head slowly, I see him. He's really here. Alive. With me. His body is so close I could reach out and hug him.

And I want to, I realize. I really, really want to. My shoulders drop, and my jaw unhinges a bit. Not by much, but enough.

His face is pale, his expression unreadable, as if he's bracing himself for impact. He's not looking at me, not really. White knuckles are clenched at his sides. But he's here.

A realization drops into my brain like a boulder. Does he think I was using him?

Regardless of how he feels right now, he reaches out and takes my other hand. I'm grateful for its steady feel, for the warmth it brings to my skin and my heart. No matter how he feels about me right now, about the show, and about us, he's still here for me.

Once again, everything disappears. My parents, my sister's grief, and the world still watching my every move.

His palm is sweaty in mine, but I don't mind. He's *here*. I keep reminding myself of that. Maybe if I focus on that fact, I'll make it through this okay.

Charlie says something from behind us that makes the

audience laugh again, but all I can focus on are hazel eyes and the feeling of safety blooming once again in my heart.

"I couldn't have gotten through this without you," I whisper, hoping he'll hear me. It wasn't my intention to speak, but the words came out before I could stop them. I don't know what else I could possibly say to him, but this feels like an okay start.

There's so much, I realize. So much we need to debrief and go over. Every one of our possibilities for how this would end was wrong. We're in uncharted territory.

He just squeezes my hand.

My heart wrenches at his silence.

Behind us, stats flash across the screen. Graphs, engagement metrics, posts, viral reels, and memes made of our most horrifying moments. More than I could possibly count. More than I want to remember for a lifetime.

Drew flinches, just slightly.

That's when it hits me, a slow feeling of revelation.

Our late-night talks, our moments alone. To some degree, it was all staged. The Voice—Charlie—made sure to keep us both in as long as possible because America *wanted* us to stay in. They liked our romance. Or, trauma bond. Whatever it was. And that popularity kept us alive and afloat. It kept us together.

We were pushed together. Staged. Everything—staged.

I look at him again, thinking of the way my heart broke when I thought he had sacrificed himself for me and was dead without saying goodbye. The way he kissed me. The night we shared our past secrets and fears.

The hope we had when we thought we'd make it out together.

We did, I realize. But it looks a lot different from what we thought it would.

I let go of his hand, unable to stand the feel of it in mine any longer.

I'm not sure those hopes and dreams will be coming true.

Someone places a hand on my back, gentle but pushing, as the show ends and Charlie starts closing remarks. My family is taken back to the front row. Drew and the rest of the group are ushered off stage, just in front of me.

I step forward quickly, desperately needing off this stage right this minute. I need to go with them—I need to know how they feel. I want to shout at them that they should hate me, even though I desperately don't want them to.

Because I know that whatever comes next will change everything.

My inner narcissist scoffs. *As if everything hasn't already.*

DAY ?

SIXTY

Normal life no longer exists.

How could it? I'm not whole. My days are not gentle, and neither are the people around me. My weeks do not make any sense, and they do not bring me comfort or the feeling of regularity.

My parents suggested I take the rest of the semester off, but they only wanted me to do that so I could do "media tours" and other random interviews. Not only do I have zero interest in doing that, but I also knew that if I didn't go back now, I never would.

And I couldn't bear the thought of staying in their house and living with the people who subjected me to the worst kind of horror.

Do people stare at me across campus? Yes. Am I getting random messages every day in my school email, mailbox, and slipped under my dorm room door? Also yes.

But it'll die down. That's what I try to convince myself of every day I'm here. Eventually, I'll no longer be the shiny new toy everyone wants to play with. I'll be shoved in a drawer, forgotten, broken beyond repair.

It couldn't come any sooner, especially now as the semester draws to a close.

My classes are coming to an end—I can *see* the finish line. Not even cheap coffee in styrofoam cups could deter me from hitting "submit" on my last assignments. The homework has been a small reprieve in all of this. Mind-numbing work is my best friend right now.

Even a few of my professors watched the TV show, because *of course* they did. Once people realized there was someone from *their* university on it… I became a highly talked-about staple. People bet on how long I would last, and scrutinized my every word and action.

Especially because I was kidnapped right under the university's nose.

There were no repercussions for that. Not even a slap on the wrist to the security guards or the Resident Assistants that sit in the dorm lobby. Charlie and his team did an outstanding job—contacting people ahead of time to make the process as smooth as possible.

They all had to sign NDAs, of course. But once the show was on, they were all more than happy to tell the tale about how they helped.

One of my study peers was in on it, even. She's the one who drugged my ice cream the night I was taken. Charlie gave her everything she'd need.

I'll never forgive myself for allowing that to happen. For not recognizing the signs of something being in my system, and for not calling for help.

But if that happened, then I wouldn't be where I am today. One million dollars richer, and one million times more popular.

Just what I wanted.

I scoff under my breath as I return to my room. Throwing my bag down, I strip off my rain jacket and cold clothes.

We're stuck in a bad rainstorm today—somewhere between rain and icy sleet.

The two twin beds occupying the space are newly pushed together, creating a mega bed. My roommate was instructed to move into a different room a couple of weeks after I moved back in. There was nothing wrong with her—I really liked Sarah. But she was taking pictures of me at all times, submitting them to magazines for a paycheck. Again, no repercussions. Just a 'You're a celebrity now. You'll need to get used to it.'

I couldn't do it anymore.

It's been gray and hazy outside all day. My phone pings as I sit down on my powder blue bedspread, and I open my texts.

I sigh. Another message from a random number about the show.

> i cried when Drew died!!! & when u cried!!!
> UGH u were amazing!! i hope if i ever get cast,
> im as smart as u!!!!

I throw my body backwards, hands on my face. How do these people keep getting my phone number? And what is it with their obsession with the horrors we went through?

Dozens of texts lay unopened and unanswered within my messaging app. Mostly from my mom, who sends me what she calls "opportunities" every day.

"This is how you become a reporter, Winter!" she exclaimed on our most recent phone call. "This is how you get connections!"

"I don't want connections," I snapped. "I want to finish school."

She threw a fit until I eventually hung up on her, reminding her that she and dad will not be seeing *any* of the prize money. Even with her constant reminders that I wouldn't have won if *they* hadn't signed me up in the first place, I've held firm to that promise. I'm nineteen—I get to choose what happens with that money.

I have better things to spend it on, anyway.

Now that the semester is over and finals have finished, I have time to breathe again.

But time to breathe also means time to think.

Time to think about how none of the other players have answered my direct messages. Or found me, reached out to me in any way. There haven't been any headlines about any of them, which means they're not doing interviews either.

I haven't heard anything from Drew. From Tatum. I even called the hospital, where Olsen was staying after bribing Charlie for that information, and they said he didn't want to see me.

Which is fine. I paid off his medical bills, anyway.

The next morning, as everyone else starts packing up their belongings and cars, I wander to the cafeteria. Gone are the days of my sitting with my friends at a round table, discussing anything and everything. Now, I take my meal to go back to my dorm room.

And eat alone.

It feels stupid to admit that Reese's cooking in the house was ten times better than what the college provides us. Thinking of him makes my stomach pinch—I wish I knew what happened to him, and why he wasn't at the final show.

But my research efforts have proved to be worthless.

My mom has called me six times already today. I groan between bites of chicken, blocking her number. For fun, I block my dad's number too. Why not? I don't need it. I don't need *them*. They've brought me nothing but hardship and regret these last few months.

Then, I text my sister. She's not supposed to have a phone,

but I bought her a secret one with my prize money. Every time my mom calls incessantly and I choose not to answer, I text Delilah to make sure she's okay.

Delilah responds to my text with a picture, something from art class today. I smile, saving the photo and making it my new phone screensaver. It's a stick-figure drawing of the two of us under a rainbow.

I look out my window toward the bleak weather. I'd kill to see a rainbow right now.

Wincing, I mentally take back my words. *I would not kill*, I chant, over and over. *I am not there. They do not have me. No one died.*

No one died.

No one died.

No one died.

Finishing my meal and throwing it away, I wander the halls for a few minutes. This is the part of being back that feels the most natural. Right now, there's a busyness in the halls as everyone packs up their rooms and belongings. It reminds me that I'm somewhere else, and that there are no cameras here watching my every move.

But that's also hard for me to wrap my head around, because I don't know who I am without Charlie and his team watching.

My feet take me to my mailbox. It's a Thursday, and the last day before everyone else moves out for break. I'm staying —I got special permission. It's possible I used my 'celebrity status' to my advantage, but what do they care?

I haven't checked my mailbox in a few days, and today's the last day I'll get mail this semester. I want to empty it before the break. That thought fills me with relief. I've had to change my mailbox number seven times already because people keep sending me random stuff.

Again, how they keep getting this information, I have no

idea. My best guess is that people are watching me and selling that information to the public.

There's a green paper slip in the box, stating there's a package waiting for me in the mailroom. I go to the front desk and hand them the slip, wondering what the package could be.

She brings back a yellow manila envelope, thick and flat. There's no return address, and my name and address are typed cleanly on a white label.

WINTER CARLISLE

My stomach tightens. I want to throw it away immediately, but something deep inside me is curious to know what my mystery package could be. On the off chance it's from Drew or Tatum, and they just don't want me to have their address…

I clutch it tightly all the way back to my dorm room.

When I enter my room, I lock the door behind me. I rarely do that during the day—I don't like being locked in—but for some reason, it felt necessary.

As I open the envelope, I see there's a black laminated binder inside.

Pulling it out, I survey the binder before opening it. There's no logo or branding. On the spine, a few simple words read:

WINTER CARLISLE—CONFIDENTIAL

SIXTY-ONE

My fingers hesitate.

But I can't wait long. Patience has never been my strong suit. I pull open the binder, not sure what to expect—

The first page stops my breath.

My picture. The one from the picture frames in the house, the one I posted on social media. My parents chose this one on purpose, telling me that they thought it would be a friendly touch for me. They sent it in to show Charlie and whoever else what I looked like.

The next page has basic information about me written on it.

SUBJECT: WINTER CARLISLE
AGE: 19
MAJOR: JOURNALISM
LOCATION: UTAH
IMMEDIATE THOUGHTS: RELATIVELY
ATTRACTIVE, INTERESTING STORY, SECRETS
WOULD MAKE FOR GOOD TV

My breath catches as I turn the page.

Notes overflow the white space, with bullet points in the center of the page.

- EX-BOYFRIEND WITHIN THE AGE RANGE OF THE SHOW CASTING. COULD CAST BOTH
- UNCOVERED A PUBLIC SCANDAL
- HAD TO CHANGE HER NAME—IN THE WITNESS PROTECTION PROGRAM
- PARENTS SOUND SURE SHE WOULD BE LIKED BY MANY AND ARE VERY EAGER
- AT SCHOOL, AND WOULD NOT BE MISSED FOR 2 WEEKS' TIME

As I continue to flip pages and read, I realize it's all there.

The teacher scandal I uncovered, the guilt and truth that blew my life apart. Even our old address and details about my recent name change.

Secrets that no one outside of my immediate family and a few others should know; it's all here in black and white in front of me.

Highlighted, annotated, and taken note of.

A sticky note falls onto my lap.

POTENTIAL:

REDEMPTION ARC POSSIBILITY OR CHANCE SOMEONE KNOWS ABOUT HER = DRAMA

(COULD GO VIRAL?)

SINGLE (POSSIBLE SHOWMANCE?)

REACHED OUT TO EX-BOYFRIEND, HE SAID YES TO PLAYING

I close the binder, only a few pages in, but I'm not sure I can take it anymore.

My spine straightens on its own as my brain makes up its mind before my heart does. I have to keep reading. Whoever sent me this… it was for a reason. And I won't waste that. They *want* me to know the truth. The whole truth.

I turn the page with shaking hands.

NICK UNDERWOOD.
RESPONSIBLE FOR THE DEATH OF A FOOTBALL OPPONENT AS A TEEN

RAVEN SMITH.
KIDNAPPED AS A CHILD, ALMOST DIED OF STARVATION, BLACK SHEEP OF THE FAMILY, AND ESTRANGED

FAITH RIDNEY.
ON ACADEMIC SUSPENSION FOR SETTING FIRE TO A CHEMISTRY LAB

My eyes fly through the pages, taking in as much information as I can. It feels so wrong, and yet, somehow so right. This is exactly what I needed right now…

DREW PARKER

I slam the binder shut, chest heaving.
I can't. Right? I shouldn't.
But I have to.
Slowly, I inch the binder back open to where my finger holds my spot on his file. I lean back a bit, as if Drew's file will bite me if I get too close.

DREW PARKER

Lone school shooting survivor*

*Charlie's top pick

My room suddenly feels too small.

This wasn't just random casting.

It was careful curation.

They didn't choose us despite our trauma; they chose us *because* of it. I keep flipping through the pages, appalled. There are charts, color-coded graphs, probabilities, and even a page for bets to be placed on by the crew. Who will break first, who will get voted out on night one, among other things.

A section titled "Stressors to Use" catches my eye. Under it, sentences like isolation, sounds, and sleep disruption jump out at me from the page. I knew it was a planned TV show, but this just makes it feel so… real.

Pages blurry from my tears, I chuck the binder across the room. My hands are numb, and so is my heart. We weren't selected for good TV. We were selected to put on a show for those watching. They *wanted* to break us.

Charlie is just as much of a monster as I thought he was. And so is his daughter.

I wasn't just a winner—I was a freaking case study. I was something Charlie chose and collected. My secrets were treasures he hoarded. He's probably proud of getting someone like me on the show. His ego must be huge.

My parents are idiots.

I'm an idiot. Even though entering the game wasn't my doing… I can't help but hold on to the blame with tightly clenched fists.

———

I wake to someone shouting outside, louder than the rain pounding on the roof.

For a moment, I have to remind myself where I am—safe, in my dorm room. Not in the house. Not in North Carolina.

A shiver rakes my body as something taps against my window.

I sit up, eyes straining to see in the dark.

Another tap.

I freeze.

The sound is sharp. Not rain, I don't think.

I move slowly, preparing myself for anything. This is the third room I've lived in this semester—I wouldn't be surprised if there's some sort of news reporter outside my window right now.

Pulling back my curtain just enough to look down, my heart begins to hammer in my chest.

He's standing there, looking up.

In the rain.

Soaked through, hoodie darkened, hair plastered to his forehead. He has one hand shoved into his hoodie pocket, and the other raised like he's about to throw something.

He does. *Clink.* The small rock hits my windowpane.

My breath leaves me all at once as he reaches for another.

Drew.

I open my window hurriedly, as if he might disappear if I wait one more second to let him know I see him.

Of all the ways he could have come back into my life—a text, a letter—

He chose this. To come to me. To *find* me.

This means… he was looking for me. He had to have been.

But why did it take him so long? I've been looking for him since… Well, since the results show. Since the end.

Rain keeps falling as I lean my head out my window, wet drops now plastering my hair and skin. He doesn't move, and neither do I. He just looks up at me like I'm all he can see.

I don't know what to say. I don't know what *he's* here to say.

But for the first time since before the house—before the stage and the secrets and the heartache—

Something real is waiting for me.

And I won't let him slip through my fingers again.

SIXTY-TWO

One second I'm leaning out the window, rain soaking my hair and the sleeves of my crewneck, and the next I'm tearing down the hallway. I fly down the stairs two at a time, my heart slamming into my ribs so hard they might crack. I didn't grab shoes or my rain jacket.

I don't slow down until I reach the front door.

Yanking it open, I will my body and breath to slow as I leave the building, butterflies fluttering around my stomach.

I'm *nervous*. But I don't know why he's here, or what he wants. It could just be to cuss me out—to tell me off and then leave once and for all.

But for now, he's right there. Standing, looking, perceiving, noticing.

Watching.

Getting rained on. For me.

In a moment of weakness, I throw away all sense of self-restraint. Consequences mean nothing to me right now. Drew barely has time to look up before I'm colliding with him, my arms wrapping around his middle as if he's a ghost that might disappear. His clothes are soaked through, and the wet fabric is cold against my face.

But his arms wrap around me instantly—tight, certain—like he's afraid that if he loosens his grip, I might disappear, too.

He smells like rain and something I can't place. But the sound of him exhaling into my hair nearly takes my legs out from under me.

For a second, neither of us speaks.

We stand there, holding each other like we're the only two people left on this planet.

He's solid. Real. Here.

He's actually *here*.

My hands fist the back of his hoodie, fingers curling tightly around the fabric like he's my anchor. Before I can stop it, a broken sob leaves my mouth. I bury my face in his chest, trying to refrain from crying, but I can't. Something within me has shattered, and I can't pick up the pieces right now.

One of his hands slides up to cradle the back of my head, his thumb moving back and forth against my skull.

"I've got you," he says quietly. "I'm here, Winnie."

The words undo me.

My knees give out, but he catches me. Just like he's always done. He braces us both, chin resting against the top of my head, rain falling relentlessly around us.

When I finally pull back, I'm certain my eyes are red-rimmed and shot. Despite that, he holds my gaze, looking into my very soul.

Drew searches my face like he's making sure I'm okay.

Like I'm… still me.

I swallow. Am I still me? Does he even *know* me?

"You're shivering," I say, not wanting to search for the answers to my internal questions.

He quirks a small smile. "You too."

I realize then that I am. My hands, my shoulders. My entire body is quivering, but my brain isn't registering it at all.

"It's raining," I say, as if that isn't obvious. Good one, Winter.

He leans in to whisper in my ear. "We both know that's not it."

I scrunch my nose as he pulls back to watch my reaction. My hand playfully hits his arm, and I remove myself from his embrace. But without his body, it's so, so cold outside.

My heart is cold without his next to mine.

Before I can invite him inside, his expression furrows. "What's your real name?"

My heart drops. What?

"What?" I say out loud this time, unsure if I heard him correctly.

He hesitates, taking a step backward, like he might turn around and leave. Then, quietly, he repeats himself. "What's your real name?"

My world tilts. When I thought he died, one of my biggest regrets was that I wasn't completely honest with him about who I am. But now… I don't know if I can do it.

I don't want Drew to *know* that version of me outside this game. When it's not life or death between us, who are we, really? Can we ever come back from that?

My head spins. Will he only ever see me as the person with the backstory worth enough to win a TV show?

For a split second, I'm back in the house, hiding in the closet with him. He's safe—I've always known that. No matter what we were *in there*, we can be so much more now. Out here in the craziness of real life. But that can only happen if I'm honest with him.

My mouth opens, but nothing comes out.

Raindrops chill my skin. Every instinct I have screams that I shouldn't tell him—that I shouldn't let anyone else know anything about me *before*. That I should run away and disappear and change my name *again*.

To not give anyone anything that they can then take for themselves.

But he shifts his weight, and that's when I notice it.

A backpack behind him in the wet grass.

He grabs it slowly when my eyes land on it, like I'm a wild animal he doesn't want to bolt, and unzips it.

There, in his hands, is a black object that I'm now all too familiar with.

A binder.

SIXTY-THREE

I turn around and throw up in the grass. Ever since the house, nausea has been an unwelcome friend of mine. I don't know if it's the leftover anxiety still riddling my body, or something else that messed me up entirely. Either way, I haven't been enjoying it.

Drew doesn't need to say anything about the contents of the binder. I just know.

He holds it up, rain dotting the cover, and probably getting the pages wet. My stomach is so sick it hurts.

"I got it in the mail a few days ago," he says. "I'm assuming by your reaction you got one too?"

I just nod. There's bile in my throat. Words don't exist for me right now.

"I didn't open it at first. I couldn't. I thought that, if I didn't look, maybe I could forget all about it. About the house, the show."

His wounded eyes meet mine. "You. But I needed to know. And then, I saw your profile."

He takes a step closer. "What's your real name, Winnie?"

Something inside me breaks, wholly and completely.

And it feels devastatingly slow.

My throat tightens, and I let out the sob I've been holding back. My hand finds my mouth, but it does nothing to keep the sound from leaving my chest.

Tears spill over as I shake my head. "I was going to tell you," I say, voice fracturing. "Before you died. I thought you were dead."

He runs back over to me, wrapping me in his arms as I fall to my knees. I cry into his shirt, into his chest, and he holds me steady.

I pull away from him, ready to stop running.

From my past. From my trauma.

From him.

I take a deep breath. Then, I tell him the name I haven't said out loud all year. The one I practiced not responding to, the one I shed like a snake sheds its skin. This is the name of a girl who lived in a different house and had a different life.

And she doesn't exist anymore. To me, and the world that remembers her, she's dead.

"Danielle," I whisper. It tastes strange in my mouth. "Danielle Winnie Darling."

I watch the moment the pieces click together in his brain.

"That's why Josh called you 'Darling'," he whispers.

I nod. "That, and he just likes to stir up trouble."

He hugs me, and relief floods my body. "You let me call you 'Winnie'."

I put a hand on his cheek. "You mean something to me. I wanted so badly to tell you everything. But I knew we were being watched. And I'm so grateful—so grateful—that I didn't say it in there. The world can't know. Mr. Pearson, he could find me. And I'm not Danielle anymore anyway—she died last December. I could only give you pieces of myself."

He pauses. "Thank you."

I tilt my head, taken aback. "For what?"

"For trusting me."

I give him a small smile, relieved. "I always have."

———

The rain lets up eventually, but we go back up to my room, anyway. I grab the biggest, warmest clothes I can find for him to change into.

We sit in silence for a while, letting my room's heating unit soak into our bones.

Then, I pull out my binder.

The binder.

"I knew you'd have one too," he whispers in disbelief. He flips through a few pages, then closes it when getting to his own profile.

"They knew everything," I say. It brings a shiver to my body, chills erupting all over my skin.

He nods. We trade discoveries and thoughts in low voices, puzzling together the truth like our lives depend on it once more. We talk about how they tracked us, why they chose us, the bets and odds placed against us. And just not him and me —*all* of us. It feels… normal again. Like it hasn't been months since we've seen each other, but days.

"They never cared about us. They only cared about the entertainment they'd be able to deliver to viewers and their ratings." Anger burns in my chest, another feeling I'm once again accustomed to and familiar with. I haven't been this angry since Reagan took her life.

Drew's jaw tightens. "They underestimated us."

I look at him. "Yeah?"

He meets my eyes, something fierce burning within them. "Yeah."

I pick at my fingers. "My mom wants me to go on tour. Do some interviews, put my name out there as a celebrity. Tell people about it."

He grabs my hands, stopping my fingers. "You should."

I gasp, looking at him like he grew antlers. "What?"

"Charlie thinks he won," he explains. "He thinks this

season is done just because the cameras are off and you got a check."

I lean forward, understanding. "What are you thinking?"

He breathes, slow and rhythmic. "Expose them. Tell your story. *Our* story. Expose the binders, the casting process. Tell the world about the manipulation. Make it impossible for Charlie and his team to hide—"

"And for them to make a second season," I interrupt. Possibilities run rampant in my mind as Drew's eyes light up.

"You won't just ruin the show."

A slow smile spreads across my face. "I'll ruin the people who created it."

His hands squeeze mine, a team once again. The rain keeps falling outside, but I don't mind. I'm done letting my life rest in other people's hands.

Today, I take control of what was always meant to be mine.

EPILOGUE

ONE YEAR LATER

The camera light clicks on, but I don't flinch.

A year ago, that sound would have sent my pulse soaring. But my thoughts don't scatter—they stay settled and clear. I'm ready. I've prepared for this for the last year. Nothing here can hurt me; I will not let it.

I fold my hands neatly in my lap—spine straight, breathing even—and look the reporter sitting across from me in the eye.

I'm calm.

Composed.

Eager, even.

The reporter gives me a practiced smile, one I know first-hand. "Whenever you're ready."

I nod once. She'll never know this, but I've been ready for a while. I've been waiting for the right time, for the right opportunity. And whether she meant to or not, she gave that to me.

She looks into the camera, now in show mode. "Good evening, America! I'm your host, Kelly Laughlin. Today, we have a very special guest with us. Please welcome the winner of the hit TV show *Last One Standing*—Winter Carlisle!"

A clap track sounds from somewhere in the room. There's no live audience today. There's just me, my agenda, and a dozen cameras.

And Drew. He gives me a thumbs up from behind Kelly, off-stage, dressed to the nines in a polo and blazer.

I stifle the real smile that threatens to bloom across my face.

"Winter," Kelly begins. "I'm so glad you finally decided to do this interview. Our team must have been hounding you relentlessly!"

I fake a laugh. "That's right, Kelly."

She laughs with me, all for show. Abruptly, she cuts her giggles off. "Now, I'd love to get into the interview, if you don't mind." I wave my hand, motioning that she should go ahead, keeping a smile plastered. "First, I see that we have Drew here today. We'd love it if you have updates about any of the other players to share with us."

I let out a slow breath. I was ready for this question. Putting on a calm smile, I relax. "Absolutely. It's been a crazy year for some more than others. Nick became a Little League football coach and is raising money for mental health resources for athletes. Adrian is in the midst of auditioning for Broadway. Olsen is recovering well."

Pausing, I breeze past the rest of the boys. Josh was arrested for taking advantage of minors, even though it happened years prior. Reese is also in prison. Because of the show, he was caught in a years-long lie and was arrested for the murder of his mother. That's the real reason why he suddenly disappeared from the house.

Cyrus' story isn't mine to tell. He's gone off-grid. I'm not sure we'll hear from him again. "Raven became a bestselling author, as you probably know. And Tatum gave birth to a perfect baby girl." *She named her Dani,* I think warmly. "Faith moved across seas to become a nurse for the United States Army."

My internal mood shifts, but the smile stuck on my face does not. *Cady took her life,* I think, mourning. She was at the results show, but then went quiet shortly after that. I don't know if it was Reese's arrest, the trauma from the games, or both. But something was too much for her, and none of us could do anything for her.

I push my thoughts of her aside. She's why I'm doing this. *They* are why I'm doing this.

I can't stop now. Not when I'm so, so close. Closer than I've been all year.

"Wow, that's incredible." Kelly looks at the camera as if it's a person. Surprisingly, she doesn't press for more information on those I didn't mention. "To switch tunes a bit, we all know you were given one million dollars for winning *Last One Standing.* I'm curious—what have you done with the prize money? Life changing, I'm sure!"

I don't take a second to think before I answer. "Drew is going to graduate from medical school debt-free. Tatum's birth and labor costs have been covered. Olsen's hospital bills are paid in full, and I made sizable donations to Nick's fundraiser and to an organization raising money to find a cure for Leukemia."

I paid for Cady's funeral.

"Wow!" Kelly says again. I think I caught her off guard just a bit, by the way she's rapidly blinking. Still, she regains her composure easily. "Don't tell me you haven't spent any of it on yourself? I know I would!" She winks at the camera.

I laugh at her reaction, as if I'm just here for a good time. "I haven't. And why would I? I didn't win through my abilities alone. The show was not something I was expecting, but I am certainly not one to put money to waste."

Kelly nods, looking down at her notecard in her lap. Once she's checked over her notes again, she leans forward, like we're old friends swapping secrets. "Winter, I have one question for you that I am just *burning* to know the answer to."

She quirks an eyebrow at the camera, as if letting them in on our moment, then turns to face me once more. "Why did you agree to this interview? You've been off the grid for a year now, and as far as I know, you haven't accepted anyone else's offers. Why this? Why us? Why *now*?"

Finally. A slow smile spreads across my face. This one's real, unpracticed.

"The second season of *Last One Standing* was just announced," I begin. "This time, the producers are taking it outside of America, so that the people chosen for season two are just as shocked as we were. We thought the deaths, the threats, the isolation, were real. And so will they."

Kelly doesn't say anything, but I know I have her attention.

I tell Kelly about the kidnapping and being drugged. Losing days of memories. I recount the story of how the games worked, and how fear became a feeling we grew accustomed to. My brain moves on autopilot, telling her about the votes and the goodbyes. How, every night, we were forced to decide who deserved to die more than anyone else.

Most of all, I explain to her that our survival didn't feel like success—it felt like a mistake we'd never recover from.

Finally, I tell her about the binders. About our families, how many people were involved in our kidnappings and circumstances than we ever could have imagined. Illegal things became excused simply because they were for someone else's entertainment.

When Drew and I realized everyone got binder, after Faith reached out to us about her own, we tracked everyone down. One by one, we met with as many as we could. Hearing their stories, getting to know them outside of the games…

Asking their permission to blow the whole thing up.

"They chose us because we had traumatic, 'good for TV' backstories," I quote with my fingers. "They wanted our secrets to fuel those watching."

Then I pause. "And we didn't agree to any of it."

I keep going as Kelly's hands still. My eyes are watching my body from somewhere outside of it, recounting how the TV producers had plans for each of us before we ever set foot inside that house.

Even though some won't care, I tell them about how real our fear was of dying. How overwhelming the grief was that we held onto.

And how none of it stopped being real just because everything was staged.

"Trauma doesn't disappear when the cameras turn off," I say. "Neither does responsibility."

Kelly's smile disappears. "We didn't know…"

I cut her off. "Now you do. Now *America* does. The cast of season one does not approve of the show being approved for season two. And hopefully, that will mean something. It *should*. Because if it doesn't, then lives will continue to be lost."

Stunned, she thanks me. Our interview timer has run out just in time, as I planned for it to. The cameras click off.

Around the corner of the stage curtain, Drew hugs me tightly. Here in his arms, it's safe.

What I said doesn't feel like enough, but I hope it is. It has to be. He reassures me I did great out there, that I was meant for this. Still, an unsettling feeling curdles in my gut. I only had one shot, and I hope I didn't waste it.

The interview airs three days later. Kelly and her team pride themselves on taking live interviews and not changing a thing once it airs, which is why I chose them. I chose correctly—my words in the final product are my own.

I almost don't watch the interview back, but I have to. I owe it to my friends to make sure everything I said was correct, thoughtful, and *real*.

By the end of the week, the interview is everywhere. The world has been begging to hear from me for months, and I finally gave them that opportunity. It's another reason why I chose to just do one interview and call it good—when you say the same things repeatedly, they lose their spark.

It clearly worked. People are taking clips of what I said and sharing them. More than that, they're arguing about them.

People pause the footage to screenshot my facial expressions or dissect my tone. Hashtags trend and influencers start a movement. Comment sections explode. My former house-guests—my friends—speak up on their own. The ones that can, anyway.

Crew members from *Last One Standing* start to leak messages and plans from seasons one and two. Screenshots surface, and overwhelming scandals awaken.

International sponsors pull out one by one.

Networks start dropping the show like flies.

Statements are released. Charlie does his best to do damage control, but it's not enough. People are calling for his head, angered at how he could do this to impressionable young adults.

His apology means absolutely nothing.

Finally, on a Wednesday afternoon, while Drew and I are sitting on the couch in his apartment, I get a call.

"It's canceled," Stacey squeals from the other end of the line. Her profile in our binders said she was chosen for one reason—to be a scapegoat and create more drama. She's had a hard time coming to terms with the fact that it could have been anyone in her shoes. "Winter, you did it!"

I slump, wide-eyed. Drew looks at me, mouthing, 'What is it?'

Bidding Stacey goodbye, I head straight for social media.

There it is, all over my explorer pages and friends' stories.

The show is canceled.

Not postponed. Not rebranding.

Canceled. Completely.

More than that, it looks like Charlie has disappeared from public view, along with Kasey. People are speculating where he went and what he's going to do next.

"You did it," Drew breathes. He grabs my face, pulling me in for a quick kiss. "It's over, Danielle."

My real name on his tongue causes butterflies to erupt in my stomach. I pull back a bit to look at him, hardly able to believe that this is real life.

"*We* did it," I respond, breathless.

He wraps me up in his arms, and we stay there for a while as messages pour into my phone. Eventually, I turn it off, content to sit in silence with Drew. Grateful and at peace doesn't even begin to cover it.

It took a year to get here. Therapy sessions, meetings, getting through the nights I woke up shaking and confused. Some of my wounds didn't close completely, but they're scarred over.

And those scars prove I made it through. If nothing else, I survived. And I survived because of the people who had my back through it all.

Drew puts a hand on my jaw, pulling my lips closer to his. There's overwhelming pride in his eyes. He still doesn't understand that I couldn't have done it without him, but I'll happily spend the rest of our lives reminding him of that.

Later, as we walk out of his apartment and onto a busy sidewalk, cameras wait across the street to take our picture. The world longs to get a glimpse of the people who made it out alive.

Together.

I ignore the photographers and place my hand in Drew's.

They tried to tear us down in the name of other people's enjoyment.

But they failed.

Because the truth—and their own character—was louder than that.

I wasn't the only one left standing in the end.

Together, we're stronger. We're better.

We're not alone.

ACKNOWLEDGMENTS

Hello, my friend! If you're someone who's been around since *The Mountain's Crown*, I'm grateful you're back. If you're new to me and my books, welcome! I'm so glad you're here.

Acknowledgements are so hard for me to put together, because how could I possibly wrap up my 'thanks' for those who helped me write this book in just a page or two? And yet, somehow, this is also my favorite part of a book.

My greatest thanks to my Savior, who I hope to glorify in all I do and with every word I write. If you don't know Jesus, find me. I will happily tell you of all the ways He's saved my life.

Hunter, my best friend. Thank you for watching the Traitors with me so I could find the inspiration for this book. Thanks for encouraging me to write this one next. Thanks for being my first preorder. I think I've made it a tradition now to say this but… Ice cream?

Since writing *The Dagger's Tide*, I've gained an amazing writing community that I trust and lean on wholeheartedly. Thanks to my online writing friends, who let me send them ideas and rough draft scenes and yap as much as I want. A special thanks to my Pen Pals. I'll love you guys forever!

Rachael and Paige: Thank you for adopting me as your own. I can't wait to read your books!

Sierra, Leslie, and Alex: Thank you for being as excited about my books and ideas as I am.

To my beta readers: You helped make this book better.

Thank you for your feedback and the time you spent reading the messy draft of *LAST ONE STANDING*!

My friends and family: Thank you for every text, social media comment, question you've asked, word you've read, and preorder. Thank you *especially* for showing up to my events. I love you!

To my arc readers: Your early reviews, comments, messages, shares, posts, and everything else under the sun are *everything* to me. Thank you for supporting me, and other indie authors in your life.

Also, shoutout indie authors. You make the world go round. Dream big. I'm rooting for you!

LAST ONE STANDING has been done since January 2026. I decided to spend some time querying it to agents, hoping to start the process of getting traditionally published. I received so many personalized messages from literary agents, and it really gave me hope for my writing career. In the end, this wasn't the right time for me. But I am *so* grateful for the time those agents took to read my pages, message me, and encourage me.

Finally, to you, my reader! This story is now out of my hands and in *yours*. Whether you're just now finding me, you've known me forever, or somewhere in between—you are welcome here.

Reading is both a safe space and home to my heart. I hope you find delight and rest in the words of these pages.

All my love,
Macayla Dawn

ABOUT THE AUTHOR

Macayla Dawn is a reader first and a writer second.

Growing up, she found herself drawn to worlds filled with demigods, fae, mystery and magic. The characters on those pages became more than just words in a book—they became friends. She is passionate about Jesus, grammar, fantasy, creativity, and ice cream.

In her free time, she loves to read (duh!), write, and explore different ways to express her creativity in all she does. She stays active through tennis, pickleball, working out, and walking with her husband and their dogs. She loves to soak up the sun and host gatherings of all sorts.

Originally from Southeast Kansas, she now lives her dream life in Indiana.

Be sure to follow her Instagram and TikTok: @authormacayladawn.

Photograph taken by Hunter Redmon.